Unable to prevent himself, Alexander leaned forward and captured Grace's soft mouth in a fierce, wholly possessive kiss. He would drive all thoughts of other men from her mind, he told himself, only to have his own thoughts scatter like leaves in an autumn wind as sweet pleasure spiraled to the pit of his stomach. A soft moan was captured in his throat as he lifted his hand to stroke the fine line of her jaw. The pleasure was almost unbearable, but even as he leaned forward to deepen the kiss, a sharp pang in his thigh had him pulling back with a gasp. Glancing down he discovered a black kitten hanging on to his thigh with its front paws. With a resigned sigh, he plucked the intruder from his ill-treated leg and allowed it to curl upon his arm.

"I believe Bryon is attempting to warn me that we have been gone long enough."

Clearly flustered, Grace rose to her feet, her eyes as brilliant as gems. "Oh."

Alexander also rose, deeply regretting that their moment alone was over. "Grace . . ."

It took a moment before she could force herself to meet his gaze. "Yes?"

"Happy Christmas, my dear."

from *Christmas Miracle,* by Debbie Raleigh

BOOK YOUR PLACE ON OUR WEBSITE AND MAKE THE READING CONNECTION!

We've created a customized website just for our very special readers, where you can get the inside scoop on everything that's going on with Zebra, Pinnacle and Kensington books.

When you come online, you'll have the exciting opportunity to:

- View covers of upcoming books
- Read sample chapters
- Learn about our future publishing schedule (listed by publication month *and author*)
- Find out when your favorite authors will be visiting a city near you
- Search for and order backlist books from our online catalog
- Check out author bios and background information
- Send e-mail to your favorite authors
- Meet the Kensington staff online
- Join us in weekly chats with authors, readers and other guests
- Get writing guidelines
- AND MUCH MORE!

**Visit our website at
http://www.zebrabooks.com**

CHRISTMAS EVE KITTENS

Cathleen Clare
Wilma Counts
Debbie Raleigh

ZEBRA BOOKS
Kensington Publishing Corp.
http://www.zebrabooks.com

ZEBRA BOOKS are published by

Kensington Publishing Corp.
850 Third Avenue
New York, NY 10022

All Kensington titles, imprints, and distributed lines are
available at special quantity discounts for bulk purchases
for sales promotion, premiums, fund-raising, educational or
institutional use.

Special book excerpts or customized printings can also be created to fit specific needs. For details, write or phone the office
of the Kensington Special Sales Manager: Kensington Publishing Corp., 850 Third Avenue, New York, NY 10022. Attn.
Special Sales Department. Phone: 1-800-221-2647.

Zebra and the Z logo Reg. U.S. Pat. & TM Off.

First Printing: October 2001
10 9 8 7 6 5 4 3 2 1

Printed in the United States of America

Contents

CHRISTMAS CATTITUDE

Cathleen Clare

One

Absently stroking Fluffy's soft, soothing fur, Stephanie gazed out of the carriage window at the bleak December scenery passing by so slowly. The trip from Kent to Yorkshire had been long and most uncomfortable in the old Blythe traveling coach, but it was nearing its end. In about an hour, before dark, according to the innkeeper at the luncheon stop they'd made, they would reach their destination, the Horse and Hound Inn, owned by Stephanie's aunt and her husband. Already Stephanie missed her home. Even in the drab winter one could find greenness in Kent. There was seemingly nothing to cheer one in these desolate Yorkshire moors. What green could be glimpsed was swallowed up in a gray, murky haze. But Stephanie was not a gloomy young lady, and she was determined to make the best of the unfortunate situation.

When her father died, the entailed estate went to a distant nephew, a man of coarse and thoughtless tendencies, whose one desire was to remove his relatives from his sphere of endless parties with others of his ilk. Only the dower house and a small quarterly stipend was left to Stephanie's mother. Lady Blythe and her daughter soon realized that remaining there in the unwholesome atmosphere was definitely not to their liking. Their allowance did not amount to enough to allow them to set up their own establishment in a different location. After many letters to and from Lady Blythe's numerous relatives, only the missive to her younger sister had borne fruit. So Stephanie and her mother accepted the invitation to reside at the Horse and Hound Inn indefinitely. Lady Blythe had wept numerous tears over the fact that they must live in such a place, but it had to be better than the environment of Blythe Manor.

Stephanie turned from the window and glanced surreptitiously at her mother's pinned-lip profile. The poor, thin lady must be even more uncomfortable than she. With the handsome, curved build of a finely formed young woman, she could withstand the hard seat and the chill much better than the elder lady. Her heart went out to her mother. Perhaps it might have been a bit more pleasant had they waited till spring, but Lady Blythe had been determined to remove her daughter from "the cursed atmosphere of that disgusting rake."

Her mother tilted her head, as if she could feel her daughter's perusal. "Don't worry about me, Stephanie. I shall be all right, although I do admit my feet are growing frigid. The foot warmer has long become cold."

"Perhaps mine has held more heat." Stephanie reached down to move the soapstone object.

Lady Blythe waved away the offer. "You keep it, my dear. I insist. I shall be fine."

"But . . ."

"No. We must keep your pretty feet in condition to dance." She passed a limp hand across her forehead. "Though I don't know why. Where can you find a likely young man in this desert? Oh, Stephanie, that is what I hate the worst about this dilemma. You should have a Season in London—routs, balls, and trips to the opera, and what have we here? A ghastly inn in who-knows-where! Your father wasn't in his right mind when he wrote that will. Oh, no, he wasn't!"

Stephanie knew to avoid that subject. She moved the cat, Fluffy, from her lap to her mother's. "She is very warm. We could even have her lie on your feet."

"My goodness, no! She would freeze down there." Lady

Blythe smiled with guilt. "We do spoil this beast, don't we?"

"Indeed, we do, but isn't she precious?"

Lady Blythe stroked the feline, drawing forth audible purrs. "Yes, she is, and she's also in the family way."

"What?"

"I can tell. We'll soon have kittens."

"No, Mama. She's simply grown a bit hefty from inactivity."

Her mother laughed, gently fondling Fluffy's abdomen. "Not in this particular region."

"Oh, dear." Stephanie frowned helplessly. "It is outside of enough to ask Aunt Caroline and Uncle George to take Fluffy in, but kittens?"

"Such things happen." Lady Blythe's eyes sparkled merrily. "Oh, what a trick on that innkeeper it will be!"

Stephanie looked at Rose, her mother's lady's maid, seated across from them. "What do you think?"

The servant smiled enigmatically. "I believe your mother is right."

Stephanie sighed. "What shall we do, Mama? How shall we find homes for them?"

"I am certain Caroline knows many people who will provide good homes. Besides, kittens are so adorable." Lady Blythe hugged Fluffy. "We will not tell Caroline and that innkeeper at first. . . . We'll give them time to see how wonderful Fluffy is. I'm looking forward to these babes—almost as much as I would for a grandchild! Alas, I shall probably never be blessed with that joy."

Her daughter flushed. "Really, Mama. Must we return to this subject?"

"It is true! Certainly there are members of the nobility who have country homes in Yorkshire, but I doubt we would ever see them. Also . . ." She daintily lifted a perfumed handkerchief to her nose. "Also, we must face the facts. Your Aunt Caroline cast herself quite beyond the pale when she wed that *innkeeper.* As a result, no person of quality will notice us."

"Her husband has a name, you know," Stephanie murmured.

"Pshaw! Who cares?"

"He is *my* uncle and *your* brother-in-law."

Lady Blythe rolled her eyes. "Don't remind me. It was the saddest day in the world when Caroline ran off with that man. None of us could imagine how she met him, but then, Caroline always did like to go riding alone. To escape her groom was a game to her. She probably met him then."

"I wonder why Uncle George was in Kent?"

"Looking for young ladies to kidnap, no doubt."

"Oh, Mama, please do not speak ill of our relatives," Stephanie begged. "They have offered us a home. We must treat them with the utmost kindness and courtesy."

"That man?" Her mother snorted. "Mark my words. He'll hear all sides of my tongue before we've been there twenty-four hours!"

"You mustn't!"

Lady Blythe smirked. "He's probably waiting for it."

"Then surprise him. Don't do it. You are a lady. Demonstrate to him how a lady conducts herself."

Her mother merely looked out the window and smiled to herself, gently stroking the cat.

Abandoning her pleas, Stephanie, too, gazed out at the sameness of the landscape. A snowflake drifted down and was soon followed by another. She loved the snow, but she hoped it wouldn't begin in earnest until they reached their destination. If the road was heavily covered, it would be very easy to become lost on the moors. She drew her cloak more snugly around her shoulders.

"Ah, civilization," Lady Blythe announced.

Stephanie glanced ahead and saw a farmhouse and outbuildings, soon followed by other farms. A village lay ahead. "I hope this is our stopping place."

Her mother looked rather grim. "I imagine it is. Oh, dear, in such a short time I shall no longer be regarded and respected as a lady of the *ton.*"

"Fustian!" cried her daughter. "You are Lady Blythe, the

widow of a baronet and the daughter of an earl! People will always look up to you."

"Not that man."

Stephanie gritted her teeth and said no more as the carriage entered the cobbled street. The sign of the Horse and Hound Inn rose prominently at the edge of town. The coachman wheeled through the iron gates, sparks flying from shod hooves. In an instant, a hostler rushed out to catch the bridle of the leader. He was closely followed by a cheery, waving couple, Aunt Caroline and Uncle George.

Stephanie briefly perused them. Aunt Caroline was a round, motherly sort of woman, with the same facial features, silvery hair, and pretty blue eyes as Lady Blythe. Uncle George was massive, with a full growth of brown beard and merry brown eyes. Neither wore the first stare of fashion, but in this setting it didn't seem to matter. Instinctively, Stephanie liked them. All would be well, unless her mother stirred up trouble.

Uncle George let down the carriage steps and opened the door, extending his hand toward Lady Blythe. "Welcome, Dor'thy! And here's little Stephanie. . . . Well, she ain't so little now, is she?" He nodded to Rose, but the ghost of a frown flitted across his face. "You too, miss."

"She isn't a 'miss,' " Lady Blythe corrected tightly, passing the cat to her daughter. "She's my maid, Rose. And *I* am Lady Blythe."

"Yes, ma'am." Eyes twinkling, he handed her down, whereupon she was enveloped in her sister's embrace.

"Miss Stephanie." He lifted Stephanie to the ground with a big bear hug that nearly squashed Fluffy. "Not 'Steffy,' for short? Had a boy named Stephen, called him Steffy. Our only child. Died when he was three."

"I'm sorry," Stephanie said kindly, "but you may call me whatever you wish."

"Then Steffy it'll be! Got a cat, I see."

"Yes, sir. I hope she can live here, too. She has very good manners."

"Wouldn't separate a gel from 'er cat!" He laughed.

She had a sudden fear of Fluffy living in the stable. "She's an inside cat, sir. She has a special box where she . . . uh . . . tends to her needs. I keep it very clean. You will not notice any uh . . . er . . . odor."

He shrugged. "Do with her what you will. And no more of this 'sir' business with me! I'm your Uncle George."

"Thank you, Uncle George."

He waved a hand and turned to assist Rose. "Well, Miss Rose, will you be staying with us awhile?"

Rose sent a pleading glance toward Stephanie.

"Rose is Mama's maid, Uncle George. Mama cannot do without her."

"I see." He patted Rose's shoulder. "Ready to learn the toils of an inn maid, too? Everybody works at the Horse and Hound."

Lady Blythe overheard. "Just what do you mean by that, George?"

"I mean what I say, Dor'thy. We ain't rich. We work, an' we work hard. That's why the Horse and Hound's the finest inn around."

"Well, I'm not going to be an innkeeper!" her ladyship said spitefully.

"No." He smiled mirthfully. "That's my title."

"I won't be some sort of tavern wench, either!"

Aunt Caroline quickly tucked her sister's arm through her own. "No matter now. Let us go inside. It is too cold to be conversing out here."

"I am a lady, not a beast of burden!" Stephanie heard her mother state unequivocally as they trundled into the inn.

Oh, dear! It hadn't occurred to her that her aunt and uncle would expect labor from them all, but in a sense, it stood to reason. Uncle George and Aunt Caroline were in business. They were apparently working very hard. After all, Stephanie, her mother, Rose, and Fluffy weren't here on a visit. They were to be permanent residents. They must share in the duties and responsibilities.

She bit her lip. She didn't mind work. She had a good, strong back! Fluffy was a good mouser. Rose could certainly make beds and tidy rooms. But Lady Blythe? What could she do, or more truthfully, what *would* she do? Stephanie could only hope that she could do her work and her mother's share, too. That must please Uncle George! The tasks would be completed. It didn't matter who did them.

The common room of the Horse and Hound Inn was warm and fascinating, with its ages-old oak long burnished with polish, tobacco, and hardwood smoke. Brass candelabrum with rich, glowing patina blazed above round, scarred oak tables where several customers sat. In the huge fireplace, giant logs burned with welcome.

Aunt Caroline hurried them through the large gathering room, but not before several catcalls and wolf whistles greeted their entrance.

"Shut up!" shouted Uncle George. "This 'ere's my wife's family!"

"What disgusting behavior!" Lady Blythe thrust her nose in the air as if she were smelling a particularly noxious odor.

"Aw, they don't mean no harm," George muttered.

"None of us shall ever enter this room again," she proclaimed.

"You will if you don't want to use the back door," he countered.

"Let us hasten," begged Aunt Caroline.

The private salon she entered was entirely different from the heavy Tudor styling of the taproom. The top two-thirds of the walls were papered in blue-and-cream toile. The part below the chair rail was a deep blue. Matching toile curtains hung full length at the windows. The furniture was walnut with upholstered pieces in dull gold. A gold-and-blue Aubusson-style rug covered the floor.

"It's beautiful!" Stephanie cried spontaneously.

Lady Blythe lowered her nose. "Quite pleasant, Caroline."

" 'Tis my wife's handiwork," Uncle George bragged

fondly. "I wouldn't know where to start with something like this."

"Of course not," Lady Blythe sniffed.

Aunt Caroline flushed. "It isn't *all* my handiwork. My goodness, George, I only made the curtains and pillows."

"Well, you thought it all out! You told those workmen what to do."

"Yes, I suppose I did," she said shyly.

"Is this to be my dining and sitting room?" Lady Blythe asked abruptly. "If so, I wholly approve."

"This room is rented at a very high price—at least, unless prospects look dim, like tonight," George declared, "when we lower the price a bit. When it isn't being rented at all, you may use it."

"You tightfisted, money-hoarding, old curmudgeon!" Lady Blythe snapped. "I am not accustomed to being treated in such a common fashion. Tell me, where is your's and Caroline's salon?"

"Right this way." He bowed and showed them the door.

"No, George," Aunt Caroline complained. "I thought we would dine tonight in our nice room, to celebrate our relatives' arrival."

"Fustian! No point in getting it dirty." He leered. "Unless Dor'thy wants to clean it tomorrow."

Lady Blythe stiffened her shoulders and drew back her neck like an incensed goose.

"Oh, my," Aunt Caroline bemoaned. "I fear, Stephanie, that these two will forever be at swords' points."

Stephanie looked at her mother's snide, challenging expression and her uncle's twinkling eyes. "I vow I do believe they enjoy jousting with each other." She laughed.

The corners of Lady Blythe's mouth twitched. Uncle George broke forth into a wide smile.

"She's a fine partner," he said and led them toward the family sitting room.

Poor Aunt Caroline's decorating talent had not extended that far. The salon was clean, but shabby. Rends in the lace curtains were all too obvious, as were suspicious lumps in the upholstered furniture.

"Eventually we will redo all the rooms at the inn," Aunt Caroline explained. "But the customers come first."

"We'll eat in here," pronounced Uncle George, yanking a bellpull. "I'm more comfortable here, anyway."

"Why am I not surprised?" mused Lady Blythe. "Such a country oaf! This is probably better than what you grew up with."

"Indeed, it is." Uncle George settled down in what proved to be his favorite chair and lit his pipe.

Lady Blythe coughed.

Slipping away from the inevitable duel, Stephanie crossed the room to the rear window. It was dark now, so she couldn't see if Aunt Caroline had a garden, but she could discern the roof lines of numerous outbuildings. No doubt they were stables and carriage houses.

Aunt Caroline came up behind her. "About the work George mentioned . . ."

Stephanie turned. "Think nothing of it. I can do my share, and so can Rose, but Mama . . ."

"Yes, I know."

"I am willing to do her share, too," Stephanie said with determination.

"I have told George that Dorothy is of a different breed. I wondered if it would be too far beneath her to do the mending."

Stephanie's spirits rose. "Certainly. She is accustomed only to fancy work, but I think I can convince her to take on this chore. She will complain of handling fabric that strangers have used, of course, but in the end I hope to prevail."

"It will be clean before she ever sees it!" Caroline cried. "I insist on cleanliness at the Horse and Hound. There will never be a louse or flea in this establishment!"

"I am sure of it." Stephanie smiled. "Fluffy will assist, too. She is an outstanding mouser."

"Perhaps she can teach our old Sarum some new tricks," Aunt Caroline laughed.

"You have a cat?"

"Definitely. Every inn needs a cat, actually more than one! Sarum is getting old, though, and spends most of his time soaking up heat in front of the fire." She smiled fondly. "Once in a while his ancient bones and joints warm enough for him to engage in the chase. We've needed a new cat for some time, but just haven't gotten 'round to it."

Stephanie felt further relief. "Fluffy will help in all ways possible!"

Two maids entered to set the table and bring the dinner, taking Rose with them to the kitchen. Uncle George ate in total silence. Fluffy puttered about the room, sniffing openings in the woodwork, while Stephanie kept a sharp eye that she did not come too close to the table.

Aunt Caroline, unfortunately, brought up the subject of work. "You could help me a great deal, Dorothy, by doing the mending. Your stitchery was always exquisite."

Lady Blythe nodded congenially. "Embroidery, ribbon work . . . I shall be delighted."

"Mending sheets and pillowcases."

"Why, the seamstresses take care of that. Are they behind?"

Aunt Caroline smiled ruefully. "I don't have seamstresses. I do it all. Sometimes, if the burden is too heavy, I must ask one of the maids, but they are not very deft. Dorothy, you could help me to no end if you would take on that chore."

Stephanie crossed her fingers beneath the tablecloth. "It's merely placing a few stitches on *clean* cloth, Mama."

"Well, no . . ."

"It isn't physically demanding, either, like making beds," she cajoled.

Uncle George interrupted his meal long enough to snort.

"Mama, we must make our contribution," Stephanie urged. "It is only fair."

Lady Blythe's eyes filled with tears. "I suppose we must.

Oh, why did your father leave us in such a situation? Taking charity, no less. And from you, George! My life as a lady is gone forever, unless you, Stephanie . . . unless there is a wealthy, bachelor nobleman in the neighborhood. . . ." She looked hopefully at Caroline.

Her sister slowly shook her head. "I am sorry, Dorothy. There is no one like that, but there are some fine young farmers' sons, who will, one day, be well-to-do by country standards."

"Not even a widower squire?"

"Our local squire is a young man, with a wife and little children."

Lady Blythe burst into tears.

"Come, I will show you to your room," Aunt Caroline soothed and assisted Stephanie's mother to her feet.

"Stephanie . . ." the lady whined.

"Do allow her to finish her dinner," Aunt Caroline intervened. "She will be just fine."

"If George will not become vulgar."

"Oh, for heaven's sake!" Caroline forcibly pushed her sister from the room.

Stephanie ate in painful silence until Uncle George offered a comment. "I suppose it is a comedown. Grand lady, living in a mansion, and all. Hard for you, too. Servants, fancy food, rich clothes. Never knowin' anything else. It was hard for Caroline, I know, but we . . . we were in love." He blushed deeply and bobbed his head. "Still are, for that matter."

"That's wonderful," she breathed. "Thank you for telling me that."

"Poor old Dorothy may never get used to all this. Guess I'm too hard on her."

"Don't worry about her share of the toil," Stephanie said firmly. "I've a strong back, and I'm very willing. I think that operating an inn will be fascinating."

Uncle George glanced at her in disbelief.

"I do!" she insisted. "People coming along from everywhere, all with their own stories. You must take great pride in making them comfortable."

"I do, Steffy." He smiled broadly. "It ain't easy to satisfy everybody."

"I'm really looking forward to learning and helping."

"Maybe you'll like it so well that you'll run it yourself, when Caroline and I are too old." He chuckled. "Unless you take up farming!"

Although she would never let him, or her aunt, or definitely her mother know, Stephanie felt her spirits descend to her toes. She wanted a husband someday, but a farmer's son? She visualized dirty fingernails and a sweating brow. Oh, no! Surely a man like that would not be in her future.

The man she dreamed of did not have to be a nobleman, but he must be what society deemed a gentleman. He did not have to be wealthy, though it would be nice if he were well-to-do. And he must love her, above all else.

It did not seem probable that there were any men like that in this neighborhood. If not, well then, she might never marry. She would become the best lady innkeeper in all the land.

As if he read her thoughts, Uncle George embarked upon a training plan. "First'll be the kitchen. Food's important, and your aunt's an Incomparable when it comes to cookin'."

"This meal is delicious," Stephanie complimented.

"Is, indeed. Come now, let's have a quaff of ale to toast your success!"

"I've never had ale," she admitted.

"Time you did. How will you know if your vendors cheat you, if you don't know about the product?"

She nodded. "That's true."

Uncle George went to the taproom and returned with two foaming mugs. They moved to chairs beside the fire and sipped the bitter brew. Stephanie didn't care for it, but her uncle raved on and on about its full-bodied qualities. She supposed he was right in teaching her all about it. But if her mother saw her now . . . la, she'd have a conniption fit.

* * *

Uncle George was right. In the days following their arrival, Stephanie did work and learn. In fact, the next morning had not dawned when Aunt Caroline touched her shoulder. She blinked at the darkness. Was something wrong? Had her mother become ill? She sat up frantically, but her aunt's smile and laughing eyes told her that naught was amiss.

"For those who wish to learn innkeeping, it is time to arise." Aunt Caroline chuckled.

"So *early?*" Stephanie was immediately ashamed of her reaction. She'd sworn to be willing. By questioning the hour, she wasn't getting off to a very good start.

"I'm sorry, Aunt." She flushed and tried to look wide-awake. "My only excuse must be that I am not unwilling, just unaccustomed to rising so early. I am truly anxious to begin."

Aunt Caroline laughed outright. "Dear Stephanie, I know this is one of the least popular aspects of innkeeping. We'd all rather stay abed, but we do have several guests who may begin clamoring for their breakfasts. They're men, however, so their palates shouldn't be difficult."

"There is a difference?"

"Oh, yes. Men, mind I didn't say *gentlemen,* don't often concern themselves with food, as long as there is plenty of it. These fellows will be satisfied with great quantities of bacon, sausage, and eggs, along with large slabs of warm, buttered bread."

"Those choices sound delicious to me, too." Stephanie swung her legs over the side of the bed.

"Indeed? Then you don't have the normal appetite of a *lady.*"

"Oh?"

There was a tap at the door. One of the inn's maids entered, bearing a ewer of steaming water. "Good morning, my lady. My name is Meg."

"I'm not a *lady,*" Stephanie explained, then glanced at her aunt and burst into laughter. "Oh, dear, Meg, forgive me. I'm not laughing at you. It was something my aunt said earlier. However, my mother, I do assure you, *is* a lady and will expect to be addressed as such."

"Yes, miss." Meg bobbed a curtsy and left the room.

"A good gel." Aunt Caroline nodded approvingly. "Well, now, dear, tend to your morning ablutions and join me in the kitchen. There are back stairs that go right to its door. Simply go to the end of the hall and you will see them."

"Yes, ma'am. I'll hurry."

When her aunt had left the room, Fluffy crawled from beneath the covers and yawned mightily.

She paused to stroke the cat's fur. "Would you like to come with me to the kitchen? I'll wager we can find a saucer of milk and some bits and pieces of all the wonderful breakfast foods."

Fluffy yawned again and meowed loudly, as if in agreement.

"Very well. No doubt you'll meet old Sarum, the inn cat. Do you think you'll like him?"

The feline blinked slowly. If she could understand English, the elder tom would have been the least of her worries. Fluffy had always been the queen of cats at Blythe Manor, and she would expect to assume that rank and privilege here.

Smiling, Stephanie quickly completed her personal hygiene, dressed, and hastened downstairs, clutching Fluffy in her arms. Immediately, she was almost overcome by the mouthwatering aromas of freshly baking bread and smoky bacon. Breathing deeply, she looked around.

The huge barn of a room was not as large as the one at her former home. Pots, skillets, and utensils occupied nearly every free space of the whitewashed walls. Mixing and baking pans were stacked high in big dressers. Herbs hung overhead. While her kitchen experience was practically nonexistent, Stephanie couldn't imagine that anything could be lacking.

A corpulent, white-haired woman in a huge, sparkling clean apron was standing at one of the tables, slicing golden brown loaves of bread with an enormous knife. She turned and favored Stephanie with a scanty-toothed grin. "Ho! You must be Miss Stephanie. Your aunt's in the taproom. She'll be right back."

"Yes, I am Stephanie." She stepped forward, smiling.

"So that's the new cat. In the family way, I see. Well, we're low on cats right now." She stuck out her hand, man-fashioned. "I'm Betsy. Been here for more years than I can remember."

Stephanie shook the cook's hand. "I'm happy to meet you. And yes, this is Fluffy. She's a very good mouser."

"That's what I heard. Where's that ole Sarum cat?" She glanced around. "Must be in the cellar. I keep the door cracked so he can go down. Doesn't do it much nowadays. His rheumatism is as bad as mine. He's a good old cat though. He's just worn out."

"Age must be tiresome," Stephanie said sympathetically.

Betsy burst into a cackling laugh. "Now, what would you know of it? A pretty young miss like you. What you should be thinking of is getting a husband. We've got some fine, strapping lads in this neighborhood!"

Stephanie flushed and hurriedly changed the subject. "Did you make our delicious meal last night?"

"Mostly." She waddled to the fire where she turned bacon in an enormous skillet. "Got folks ready for their breakfast."

"Oh, can I help?" Stephanie volunteered, wishing for a few bites herself.

"Reckon so. How 'bout starting the toast? Anybody can make toast."

Stephanie couldn't. What did one do? Hold bread over the fire with a long fork? She glanced up at the wall for such an implement, then reached for it.

"No, not that!" Betsy cackled. "This kitchen might be old, but it ain't that out-of-date. We got us a toaster."

"A toaster?"

"Right there." The cook pointed with her toe.

"I see." Stephanie retrieved the long-handled, swiveling iron rack from the hearth.

"It's usually hung up there," Betsy said kindly, helping to cover Stephanie's ignorance. "I just got it down already."

"Yes." She stared at the implement. Apparently, one put bread between the slice-sized holders and stuck it into the fire. She did exactly that, propping the handle on the hearth.

"No!" Betsy squealed as flames shot up.

"Oh!" cried Stephanie, jerking the toaster out of the flames. It was too late. The bread was blackened and smoldering. The acrid odor of burned toast arose.

"What is this?" Aunt Caroline entered the kitchen, fanning her hand in front of her nose.

"Poor gel can't even make toast," Betsy explained sorrowfully.

"I've never done it." Tears filled Stephanie's eyes. "I've scarcely ever been in the kitchen, let along tried to make something."

"Of course not." Her aunt slipped her arm around her waist and squeezed. "No one expects you to know."

"That's right," Betsy soothed. "I shouldn't have set you to it."

"But I should have known better," Stephanie protested.

"Not necessarily. I wasn't exactly at home in the kitchen when I came here." Aunt Caroline exchanged looks with Betsy and both women broke into laughter. "We've our work cut out for us!"

David, Marquess of Donnington, looked anxiously from the carriage window at the sparse snow flurries beginning to dust the ground. The weather could become a worrisome matter. They still had to spend one more night on the road before reaching Donnington Hall. If the snow began in earnest, travel would be difficult. Given the rutty December condition of the thoroughfare, they might be forced to seek accommodation at whatever inn, decent or not, was nearby. David didn't particularly like that for himself; for his ward, he dreaded the very thought.

Surreptitiously, he glanced sideways through his long dark lashes at the little girl. For the past hour Eugenia had been sinking into the darkest pout he had ever seen. He wondered if they would reach their evening's destination without an explosion of the gravest proportion.

David sighed. He couldn't handle this newly orphaned child of his sister and brother-in-law. Once in a very great while, she smiled. Other than that, she showed no emotion, save spoiled displeasure. She seemed barely to tolerate his very presence. She drove away all the governesses he had hired and threatened to do the same with every staff member with whom she came in contact. He was hoping that the more relaxed Donnington people, and especially his old nurse, would have more success in gaining her favor than their stiffer London counterparts. Someone, surely someone, would know what to do with her.

As he perused her, he noticed that she was looking back at him in an impertinent way that made him want to smack her rosy cheeks.

"Why are you staring at me?" she asked sourly.

"I was wondering if you were warm enough, Eugenia," he queried, setting his jaw and gesturing toward an unused carriage robe on the opposite seat.

"No!" She ripped off her expensive fur muff and threw it down. "If you'd gotten me the cat I wanted, it could have lain on my hands and kept them warm!"

"Cat?" he asked with surprise. "I didn't know you wanted a cat."

"I told you! You ignored me as usual!"

He steadied himself to be patient. "Please, Eugenia, be fair. You know I do not ignore you or your requests. Haven't I always gotten you everything you wanted?"

"Then where is my cat?" she asked pertly.

"Perhaps you told someone else, only thinking that you told me," he suggested.

"What difference does it make? You didn't get me a cat," she whined.

No one could follow or comment on logic like that.

David picked up her muff from the floor and physically placed her hands in it. He certainly didn't want her to catch a chill. An ill Eugenia would definitely be a tyrant.

"I want a kitten," she went on. "A little, soft, cuddly kitten."

She would probably pull off its head, David visualized.

"Eugenia, baby animals are usually born in warm weather. You might have to wait until spring, or settle for a grown cat."

She mulled over his comment, seeming almost placated.

David took a long breath and exhaled slowly. Thank heavens! Was she satisfied, at last?

"A *human* baby would be nice, too," she announced. "I'd like you to be married, Uncle David. Then there would be *real* babies. You must marry right away!"

He smiled painfully. "It isn't that simple, Eugenia."

"Why not? Mama always talked about all the women fluttering around you. Just marry one of them."

"I don't want to," he said flatly. "I haven't yet met anyone I want to marry."

"I suppose you have to marry to have babies, don't you?"

"Yes!"

"Where do babies come from, Uncle David?"

This talkative Eugenia was worse than the pouting one. He tried to distract her by pointing out the window. "Look at the snow, Eugenia."

As he looked out, too, he surprised even himself. In the length of time he'd been engaged in conversation, it had begun snowing so hard that he didn't know how the coachman could see the road. Suddenly mixing with particles of ice, the snow began battering against the windows with a rattle that would wake the dead. Eugenia screamed.

"It's all right, my dear." David slipped an arm around her as the coach wheeled to a sliding halt.

The hatch opened. "M'lord, I can't see!" the coachman shouted down.

David saw blood on his servant's face. "Cover the horses and come inside. They're trained to stand, aren't they?"

"Yes, m'lord, but Dennis and I can crawl underneath the coach."

"Inside, Charles. That is an order," he said firmly.

"Yes, m'lord!"

His ward wrinkled her nose. "Rough servants in here with us?"

"Observe the weather, Eugenia. I won't have them lying in the road."

A gust of wind flung ice against the coach. Eugenia whimpered and turned her head against his coat. "I don't like this! Make it stop!"

"We will be all right," David soothed. "We have the finest team, the sturdiest coach, and the best servants in all the land. And soon the ice will cease."

"I'm afraid!"

"You're with me, my dear. I'll keep you safe." He looked up at the leaden skies and disliked what he saw. The ice might abate, but the snow would come. From the appearance of those dark, bulging clouds, it would be a heavy storm. They would have to seek refuge as soon as possible.

His coachman and footman climbed inside, bringing with them a blast of frigid air and a strong odor of horses, leather, and tobacco. Their faces were nicked by the ice, and they were shivering and snuffling loudly.

"Bless you, m'lord, for lettin' us come inside," Charles pronounced with feeling, wiping his nose on his sleeve.

"Yes, sir," echoed the footman, Dennis. "It is warm in here."

"It's cold." Eugenia turned her head away from the folds of her uncle's greatcoat to gape at them. "And you stink."

"Eugenia!" David gasped, feeling heat rise to his cheeks.

The footman looked furious, but the coachman's expression didn't change.

"I must apologize for my niece," David told them.

"She's doubtless right," Charles said.

Dennis seemed as if he would like to reply, but he glanced at the elder servant and maintained his silence.

"Phew!" Eugenia held her nose and hid her face again.

David knew his unfortunate trait of blushing displayed to his servants how absolutely mortified he was. Also, they'd doubtless heard of Eugenia's difficult personality from the other servants. They probably thought he should box the girl's ears and was too weak, where she was concerned, to do so. Eugenia! Whatever was he to do with her?

"We can go outside, m'lord," the coachman offered quietly.

"That will not be necessary. You will remain here, where it is warmer, until the ice storm passes. Then we will have to find lodging as soon as possible."

"I believe I remember a small inn at the next village. It shouldn't be too far," he suggested. "We've never stopped there, but from the road, it looks neat and decent."

"We'll hope they have room for us," David muttered. "With weather like this, there may be others ahead of us who are stranded."

"Oh, they'll have room," answered Dennis, flexing his fists.

The marquess narrowed his eyes. "There will be no trouble, my man."

"No, sir!" The footman grinned with guilt. "I only meant that you being a marquess . . . They will recognize the honor and privilege due you."

David smiled. "You know, Dennis, sometimes I think you would make a better peer than I."

"Oh, no, sir!" The footman's eyes twinkled mischievously.

"M'lord means you're arrogant, like a good many of the nobs I've seen," Charles spat. "It's a warning, you dolt, to mind your ways."

The marquess did not comment, looking instead out the window. He made it a practice not to interfere in servants' minor tiffs. Moreover, Dennis did sometimes act a bit high in the instep.

The ice had stopped, perhaps for good, and snow had taken its place. They would give it a few more minutes to make sure; then the coachman and footman would have to return to the elements. They would have to move swiftly enough to get through the snow before it became too deep, but slowly enough to be safe.

Charles glanced out. "The road looks slick, m'lord."

He nodded grimly.

"Dangerous," he said in an undertone. "If we see a farmhouse, should we stop there?"

David visualized the cramped cottages of most English tenants and their large families. Even if the inn were crowded, it would be far preferable. Eugenia might be most terrible in a small, private situation, probably bedded down with other children. At an inn, money spoke loudly. He'd probably be able to have someone turned out of their room, in favor of his ward.

"I'd rather try to reach the inn," he told Charles. "However, if you see a farmhouse, we will consider the conditions before deciding."

Again, the coachman studied the road, more thoroughly this time. "With your permission, m'lord, I think we'll go ahead and try it."

"Very well." He nodded sharply.

Charles drew himself up. "Lord Donnington, 'tis a fine team, a good coach, and . . . and I'm as good a driver as the next 'un."

"*Better* than most," the marquess emphasized. "If anyone can get us through, Charles, it will be you."

"Thankee, sir." He opened the carriage door and stepped into the driving snow.

"Lord Donnington," Dennis acknowledged and followed Charles.

When the carriage door closed behind them, Eugenia peeked out from his coat. "Uncle David, he said the road was slick. He said it would be *dangerous.*"

"You have big ears, my dear."

"Well, it is a very small space," she said in adult tones.

"Yes. Perhaps Charles shouldn't have said that. We knew it anyway, didn't we?"

"Yes, but I'm scared!" she wrenched out. "I'm afraid we'll turn over. We couldn't walk to the village, could we?"

"I'm sorry, child," he soothed, "but it's too far and too cold. It would be slower. I'm afraid you'd freeze to death before we reached shelter."

"But the servants are out there. Won't they freeze?"

"The servants are not gently bred young ladies."

The coach moved forward with a small skid. Eugenia screamed. "We're going in the ditch!"

"No, we are not," David assured her. "See? All is well now. Charles has straightened us out."

Although he and the footman must be miserable in the driving snow, the coachman sacrificed greater speed for more security. He tried a very slow trot, but when the coach began to fishtail, he pulled to a walk. That was the best they could do, but they were at least moving.

Lights glowed a short distance away. When they drew nearer, David could see a small barn and a mean farmhouse, smoke curling from its crumbling chimney. Charles halted and opened the hatch.

"What d'ya think, m'lord?"

He didn't like it. With that chimney, the place was a firetrap. The cottage was so small, they'd all be falling over themselves. The occupants were probably very poor and might not have enough food. It would be warm, but Eugenia would probably throw multiple temper tantrums. He shook his head.

"It isn't suitable," he answered, "but maybe it's a sign that the village is close by."

"Yes, sir." The hatch closed.

David was sorry for his servants. His decision caused them to remain out in the bitter weather for a longer period. If they found an inn, he vowed he'd turn his head if they wished to become roaring drunk that night.

Eugenia leaned forward out of his greatcoat to look at the farm. "You are right, Uncle. That isn't a nice place."

"My dear, you know we might not find a place as nice as you wish, but you will be safe. With me."

She shivered, with fear or from the cold, David couldn't answer. "I hope we find a place soon. Please, Uncle David, if we find a nice place, let us not leave until the snow is gone."

That could be spring. He couldn't promise that. "We will stay until it is very, *very* safe to travel."

"Promise?" she whined.

"I promise that I will never, ever take you to a place, or put you in a position, that is dangerous."

"I will remember." She tucked herself into his greatcoat and snuggled against him.

David slipped his arm around her and held her tenderly. Eugenia had never drawn so close to him. Why couldn't she always be this way? A child could be so warm and cuddly. It made him think about a wife and children of his own. Would he never find a lady who would suit? He had been looking seriously for a year or more.

They passed several more farmsteads, but all were very small, though some were in better condition. The hatch opened.

"M'lord, there are cottages, but I feel we're nearing the village," Charles voiced.

"Keep on," David agreed.

The coachman urged the team to a slow trot as they reached a low rise. The coach skidded badly, throwing David against the wall. Screaming, Eugenia leaped from his coat.

"It's all right," he soothed, arm aching. "Charles has it straightened out now."

"I'm so scared!" Eugenia began to weep again.

David lifted her into his lap as the carriage wobbled atop the grade. "There's the village, my dear! See?"

"It looks all ghostly!" she wailed.

"That's because of the snow. People will be friendly." He hoped his words were true.

"Tell me when we're there." She dived back into his coat.

David drew a deep breath of relief. They had survived what could have become a very grave predicament. Now, if Eugenia would only behave . . . Maybe she would be so happy to be safe from the storm that she'd act like a proper young lady and not give trouble to anyone. Somehow, though, he doubted it.

Two

Stephanie peered out the window at the bludgeoning storm. Their last two customers, two strapping farmers' sons, whom she felt were mightily interested in her, had quickly drained their mugs and fled for home when the ice had started. Though it was only late afternoon, there were no overnighters. Still Uncle George was going about, lighting all the oil lamps to chase away the darkness of the blizzard.

"Never know when a stranded traveler might come our way," he remarked.

"Then you don't want me to lock up?" she asked, turning.

"No, not yet." Aunt Caroline deftly began to wipe off the tabletops and chair seats.

"Aye," agreed Uncle George. "It's happened before, and they're usually so grateful that they leave big tips."

"To say nothing about it being our Christian duty," his wife answered dryly. "I'd take in anyone, money or not, at a time like this."

He chuckled. "That's why you'll never be rich, Caro."

"Fiddlesticks! I knew I'd never be rich when I married you, George."

Smiling, Stephanie turned back to the window. Having transformed the trees into crystal silhouettes, the ice had ceased falling, and snow was blanketing the courtyard. The footsteps of the farm lads had already been obliterated, leaving nothing but pristine snow. It was beautiful, but it was treacherous. She remembered the minor slippages they had experienced on the way to the inn. That weather had been nothing like this.

Aunt Caroline joined her, fondly rubbing the small of her back. "Oh, dear, it is getting bad. I think I'll send the girls home before it becomes any worse."

"Good idea," nodded her husband. "No point paying them, if there ain't customers to serve."

"And Betsy may go to her room. Her rheumatism is acting up terribly. We three can handle whatever might occur. Oh, Stephanie, you've only been here two weeks, but I don't know what we ever did without you!"

"That's right," Uncle George seconded.

"Is there anything I can do now?" Stephanie asked her, pleased.

"Why, yes, dear. You can go ahead and sweep the floor," her aunt called over her shoulder, walking toward the door to the service area.

Obediently, Stephanie fetched the broom and began the task. Uncle George strolled behind the bar to draw himself a mug of ale. Footfalls sounded on the stairs.

"Stephanie, what are you doing?" Lady Blythe demanded imperiously.

"Hullo, Mother." She paused, leaning on the handle. "I'm sweeping, of course."

"But this is the taproom!"

"There is no one here," she said firmly, "and someone has to do it."

The lady switched her attention to her brother-in-law. "Just look at you, George! Drinking up your profits?"

"Oh, Dor'thy, it's only a glass of ale. Haven't had a drop since lunch."

She threw up her arms in aggravation. "Must I suffer so? My nerves are shattered! My head is bursting! This storm has driven me and poor Rose out of our wits! Why, when the ice beat against the windows, Rose crawled under the bed, and so did Fluffy!"

"Fluffy? So spineless?" Stephanie couldn't help teasing.

"Well, she is now out from under and is lying in front of the fire, licking dust motes from herself . . . er, Fluffy, that is. Rose is still beneath." She heaved a long, exaggerated sigh. "George, I require a drink to soothe my trembling body."

"Of course, Dor'thy." He grinned. "Shall I pour you a great mug of ale?"

She eyed him disparagingly. "A glass of sherry will be fine. Then you may light the fire in the salon. Stephanie and Caroline may join me for a chat."

"I must finish my sweeping first, Mama." She returned to her task.

Uncle George examined his bottles. "Have to go to the cellar for sherry, Dor'thy."

"Well, be about it!" she snapped and sank into the nearest chair. "My goodness, Stephanie, why doesn't one of the maids do that job?"

"Aunt Caroline has sent them home so they won't be snowbound with us. There are no patrons here, so we don't need the extra help."

"There's a blessing! Maybe it will continue snowing so that we can have Christmas in peace."

"I still have a bit of shopping to do." Stephanie worriedly glanced out of the window, then startled. "Oh, my! It's a carriage!"

"A carriage?" Lady Blythe rushed up beside her. "A fine one, too! I can scarcely see for all the snow and road dirt, but is that not a crest on the door?"

"I don't know." She nodded approval as two of Uncle George's hostlers darted from the stable and struggled through the storm to assist.

Her mother seized her elbow. "Come, we must disappear!"

"Why?" Stephanie cried.

"No doubt there are members of the *ton* in a carriage such as that. No one must see us like this!"

"But the storm . . . We must help them!" She jerked free, dropped her broom, and hurried toward the door.

"No, Stephanie! They will think you a tavern wench!"

Ignoring her, Stephanie pulled open the door to a soaked, muddied footman.

"M'lord Marquess of Donnington requires accommodations!" he shouted above the storm.

"Certainly!" She nodded assuringly. "We have room for all!"

As he dashed back to the coach, she turned to face her mother.

"I heard!" Lady Blythe was almost in a panic, darting aimlessly back and forth in front of the window, wringing her hands. "I have heard of him, Stephanie! He is a most eligible *and wealthy* bachelor. You *must* go to your room, for now."

"What is the to-do?" Aunt Caroline entered the room with George trailing.

"The Marquess of Donnington!" Lady Blythe babbled. "A wealthy bachelor! Oh, George, do light the fire in the salon."

"Yes, I suppose he'll want the salon."

"No, you dolt!" she screeched. "It will already be taken by my daughter and me, fellow travelers. We shall, of course, invite the marquess to join us. Stephanie, *go upstairs!*"

Uncle George eyed his sister-in-law with aggravation. "Fustian! The marquess'll pay me good money for that room and you, Dor'thy, wouldn't give me a brass farthing."

"I would. I would! It's an investment! Explain to him, Caroline, what this could mean!"

It was too late. The marquess strode into the inn, stamping snow from his elegant boots. "Thank God you were here. I don't think we could have gone on much farther."

Stephanie felt as if her heart had completely flipped over. Even in profile, Lord Donnington had to be the most handsome gentleman she had ever seen. His face was finely chiseled like a priceless Greek sculpture with a slender, aquiline nose, aristocratic, strongly cut jaw, and shapely cheekbones. From under his hat gleamed silky, dark hair.

Wondering how devastating his eyes would be, she took a deep, steadying breath.

"Welcome, m'lord." Uncle George bowed deeply while the ladies curtsied. "We are proud to be here to offer you custom. We're not the largest, but I think you'll find us to be the best of any inn, anywhere."

"Then I shall be doubly lucky." A slow smile exposed breathtaking dimples. "I will require rooms for myself, my servants, and my ward. Also a salon, if possible." He opened his many-caped greatcoat to reveal a quaking child.

"Oh, it's a little girl!" Lady Blythe expostulated.

"Poor poppet," crooned Aunt Caroline, gliding forward and extending her arms. "You must be very cold and frightened."

The child nodded, sniffling.

"Come to the fire and let's warm you."

The girl glanced up at her guardian.

"Go ahead, Eugenia." The marquess moved to shuck off his greatcoat. "I don't suppose I'd be triply lucky to find that my valet, Lady Eugenia's maid, and our baggage coach had stopped here."

"Sorry, m'lord." Uncle George hastened to assist him with the heavy garment. "You'll have the place to yourself, though. There's only my family and our old cook. I'm George Collinswood, and that's m'wife with the young lady. This's my sister-in-law, Lady Blythe, and her daughter, Miss Stephanie Blythe."

Stephanie curtsied and looked him full in the face. His eyes were deep blue and darkly framed by long, dark lashes. He smiled, displaying those heart-stopping dimples that somehow seemed familiar.

She was struck speechless. *It's him,* she thought. He was the gentleman she'd always dreamed of. In dreams, she'd won him to her heart. But then, anything was possible in dreams. In real life? A marquess? Even if she were still Miss Blythe of Blythe Manor, he would be too high in the peerage for her. It would be like landing a whale on a thread of gauze.

"Well!" Uncle George broke the silence. "M'lord, I'm sure you'd like a glass of my finest brandy."

"Very much," he intoned in his beautifully cultured accent.

Aunt Caroline straightened. "I'd hazard a guess that young Lady Eugenia would like me to make her a mug of warm chocolate."

The child's lips curved into a tiny smile.

"Come, missy, while I prepare your drink, Stephanie will take you to your room and make you cozy."

"I'll do that," Lady Blythe chimed in, strolling forth to take the child's hand. "Stephanie, you help George, and do show Lord Donnington to the salon."

Little Lady Eugenia hesitated.

"Do come with me, dear," Stephanie's mother cajoled. "I promise you that I adore children. And you may meet Fluffy, my daughter's cat."

"A cat?" the girl piped up. "I want a cat!"

"Maybe Stephanie will give you a kitten when the time comes. It won't be long."

"Kittens!" Uncle George thundered, forgetting his company. "I thought that cat was getting fat from catching mice! I swear I will drown . . . Oh. Excuse me, m'lord."

"You will do nothing," his wife ordered.

"Stephanie! Show Lord Donnington to the salon!" Lady Blythe reminded sharply and dragged Lady Eugenia up the stairs.

Stephanie blinked. She knew Uncle George would not drown the kittens. He was all bark and no bite. But she hoped he hadn't overset the marquess's ward. She must explain.

"This way, my lord." She crossed the room and started down the hall without a backward glance at him, for fear she'd freeze into a trance. Opening the door, she drew a breath of relief. Uncle George had lit the fire. Thank heavens Lord Donnington would not witness her crawling all over the hearth, trying to perform a chore at which she was definitely not adept.

She looked over her shoulder to make sure he had followed. "Do make yourself at home, sir. Perhaps you would like a tidbit before dinner?"

"That would be pleasant." He chose a chair beside the fire. "I suppose I am discommoding your family from the use of this room?"

"Think nothing of it. And think nothing of my Uncle George's threat about the kittens. He will not follow through."

"Mere gruffness?" He grinned.

"Yes, my lord." Her knees turned to water. Swaying slightly, she quickly slipped through the door, as her uncle entered with his lordship's brandy.

Stephanie entered the kitchen to discover Aunt Caroline placing the chocolate on a tray along with a plate of macaroons. Her aunt was frowning.

"Your mama shouldn't have sent you off alone with the gentleman, nobleman may he be."

"I didn't fear him," she said quietly. "He is kind and decent. He is a gentleman."

"You don't know that. He could be a rake of the first degree. Stephanie, remember that you have basically no experience whatsoever with men."

"Don't ask me how I know, but I do." She patted her aunt's arm. "I'm more concerned about Mama and his ward. I've an idea that she is completely helpless around children."

"I'll put it to rights. Dear, will you help me with dinner? Betsy is finally asleep, and I hate to awaken her."

"Of course." Stephanie waved her from the room and began preparing a platter of thinly sliced ham, smoked hard sausage, cheeses, and sippets. This should please the marquess, she thought.

She was passing through the common room when Lord Donnington's footman and coachman stamped in with what appeared to be the last of the luggage.

"Girl!" the footman called, "pull us a mite o' ale!"

"Momentarily," she replied.

"Momentarily." He mocked her upper-class accent. "Why are you aping your betters? You're just a tavern wench."

She lifted her chin, taking a deep breath to control a flash of anger. "We will serve you shortly. Just now, I'm taking this plate to Lord Donnington."

The name served to remind the servant of his master. He moved off to the fireplace, chafing his hands. "Hurry up, then. We're cold and hungry, too."

She nodded briskly and fled. Aunt Caroline was right. Some men could be offensive. She would stay away from that footman. He was trouble.

With another deep breath, she entered the salon. "Uncle George, Lord Donnington's servants wish service. Will you attend them?"

Studying her face, the marquess narrowed his eyes. "Was Dennis, my footman, a problem, Miss Blythe?"

Avoiding his gaze, she lowered the tray to the table and straightened some of the sippets.

"He is sometimes rather cheeky with the opposite sex," he explained. "I will speak to him."

"That is not necessary, my lord. Besides, I do not wish to be thought a tattler." She curtsied and started toward the door.

"Under the circumstances . . ." His voice interrupted her flight. "Your uncle has told me of the circumstances faced by you and your mother. I will not stand by to see ladies importuned by my servants. Therefore, I do intend to speak with them."

"What about ordinary women, my lord?" Overwrought by her nervousness, she whirled to face him, the words bursting from her mouth as if she had no control of them. "Do they deserve the rough side of a man's tongue, just because they are female?"

The marquess was clearly taken aback.

So was Stephanie. She held her hands to her burning face. "My lord, I am so sorry! I have never been so . . . so impertinent!"

"Nevertheless," he said slowly, "you are correct. Thank you for pointing me straight."

"But I shouldn't have . . ." She miserably bowed her head.

"I simply have never thought about it," he marveled, shaking his head, "and I have always considered myself to be fair and thoughtful of others, regardless of their station in life."

"I'm sure you are." She inched desperately toward the door.

"But I wasn't. You have taught me a lesson, Miss Blythe."

She wondered if he was being candid or teasing. There was no smile on his face, nor sparkle in his eyes. With relief, she closed her hand on the brass doorknob.

"You will excuse me, Lord Donnington? I have much work to do." She darted out the door before he had a chance to reply. In the hall, she leaned briefly against the wall. My goodness, how her tongue had run away with her! If her mother ever got wind of it, she might as well start off walking down the lonely road, snow or no snow. Now, she would be forever mortified to face the marquess. Ah, well, nothing could come of her hopeless attraction. He would always remain in her dreams.

She pushed away from the wall and strode toward the kitchen to assist Aunt Caroline with the meal.

Aunt Caroline knelt to place jacketed potatoes in the hot ashes of the fireplace. "Times like this, I'd love to have one of those new Rumford stoves. I do so want to serve a spectacular meal to Lord Donnington."

"I believe you'll have more than one chance." Stephanie looked out the kitchen window. "It's still snowing fiercely."

"Yes. In all my years, I've never seen such a storm as this. We're truly snowbound." She straightened, rubbing her lower back. "For heaven's sake! I suppose I'll end up with back trouble like Betsy."

"Then I'll take care of you." She heaved the round of roast beef from the spit to the carving board and began to cut juicy, pink slices.

"Pshaw! You'll have a husband and family to care for by then."

"Maybe we'll be apprentice innkeepers right here. Do you know, Aunt Caroline, that I really like to cook? It's so satisfying to create something utterly delicious, especially like your secret seasoning for this beef." She forked the slices into a hot mixture of beef and chicken broth with crushed garlic cloves, which added a most delightful flavor to the roast. "I wonder what a touch of onion would do?"

"Don't experiment on the marquess!" her aunt begged laughingly. "We'll try it on ourselves first. It sounds interesting."

Stephanie smiled, wiping her hands on a towel made of flour sacking. "If the marquess has gone upstairs to freshen, I'll set the table. I suppose Lady Eugenia will be joining him?"

"I imagine so." Her aunt frowned. "There is something about that child . . ."

"Oh?"

She lifted a disapproving eyebrow. "Something thoroughly obnoxious."

"Really!"

"Yes. Soon after we had her settled, she became quite whiny and plaintive. There was a sharp edge to her voice, and she wrinkled her little nose in a most disgusting fashion."

"Maybe fright and weariness caught up with her," Stephanie suggested.

"Maybe." Aunt Caroline shrugged. "She was fine with Fluffy, though. The dear cat rubbed against her so soothingly."

"Good. Probably all she needs is a restful night's sleep."

"I hope so. I left her with Dorothy and Rose. They were trying to tell her fairy stories. Perhaps that will cheer her."

"Yes." Stephanie left the kitchen for the salon and startled to see her mother seated comfortably by the fire. "Mama! What are you doing here? The marquess is renting this room."

Lady Blythe smiled smugly. "I know that. We are to be his guests, my dear. Even George!"

"What?" she cried.

"Lord Donnington has invited us to dine with him. Isn't that nice?"

"No! Mama, how can I dine with him and serve him, as well?"

"Well . . . I'm not sure." She tilted her head, frowning. "But it is imperative that you do so. Perhaps Caroline and George will abandon their places at the table and do it."

Stephanie shook her head in wonderment.

"Don't be obstinate!" Lady Blythe cried. "Time is running out! You must freshen and change into something pretty. Aren't you attracted to Lord Donnington?"

"It doesn't really matter." Suddenly she felt exhausted. Never in her days of hard work had her youthful spirits given out. Today they were beginning to.

There was an invisible swirl of emotions swinging heavily in the air. Nothing had ever affected her like this—not the move, the chores, nor the descent in social class. It was because of the marquess, of course. He had wreaked havoc within her and within her mother, as well. Was this his way of making up for his earlier, demeaning comment?

"Stephanie," Lady Blythe said firmly, "I will not allow you to let this opportunity slip away. Who knows when, or if, a gentleman like this will pass our way again! You must attempt to steal his heart. Your marriage to a wealthy man is our only road out of here. This way of life was Caroline's choice, not mine nor yours. So why should we have to live it, too?"

A stifling wave of guilt swept over her. She couldn't do as her mother wished. Aunt Caroline and Uncle George needed her help. In addition to the marquess, his ward, and Lady Blythe, there were Rose, the stablemen, Betsy, and his lordship's servants to feed.

She flung a pretty lace cloth over the table and set down the plates, one for the marquess, one for Lady Eugenia, and one for her mother. Lady Blythe watched silently as she placed the napkins, goblets, and silverware on the table. Stephanie could hardly glance at her.

"Mother," she said quietly as she finished, "I will think about what you've said, but tonight . . . Tonight is impossible."

David was surprised to find only Lady Blythe in the salon, and the table set merely for three. Maybe only the Blythes had accepted his invitation and no one had thought that Eugenia would dine with the adults. In fact, he wished that she had stayed in her room, eating from a tray and feeding tidbits to the cat, as she surely would do. But when he entered the child's room, he found her dressed for dinner and Lady Blythe's maid looking totally frazzled. He hadn't had the nerve to ask the servant to stay with the girl.

Eugenia must have thrown a temper tantrum. The few clothes they had brought in the personal coach were strewn about the floor. The coverlet had been jerked from the bed and lay in a tangled heap. The ewer and bowl had been broken to smithereens, and water spilled all over. Someone would have quite a mess to clean up.

He thought about Miss Blythe's comment about servants. Unnecessary extra work wasn't fair, either. But what could he do? Frankly, Eugenia was a brat, and no one could control her. That was the awful fact.

With an apologetic look at Lady Blythe's maid, he had taken Eugenia off her hands. The child had insisted on bringing Fluffy. The marquess didn't like the idea of a cat in the dining room, but he didn't want to start another fracas. So here he was with cat and brat, and hoping for the best. And damn, if Miss Blythe smiled and chatted, it would probably be worth the strain.

Lady Blythe must have seen him scanning the table settings. "It is only you, Lady Eugenia, and myself tonight, my lord. The others send their regrets. It seems they are rather shorthanded at present."

"I see." She looked so unhappy that he added, "I know I shall enjoy your company very much."

"Thank you, my lord." She sighed. "My poor daughter! She was especially disappointed; however, she is such a responsible young lady that she *will* sacrifice her own happiness to help others. Oh, what a low to which we have descended!"

"What low?" Eugenia asked, tossing her head.

"To be without money, dear child, and forced to accept charity in such a place as this!"

"Not as bad as losing your parents," she retorted.

David gasped.

"Dear Lady Eugenia, I *have* lost my parents," she wailed.

Eugenia wrinkled her nose. "But you're so old it doesn't much matter."

"Eugenia!" the marquess admonished in horror.

Lady Blythe raised a hand. "It is all right, my lord. Of course the gel mourns her parents. Hopefully, she will look upon you soon as another papa, but she desperately needs a mama, too. All little girls need mothers, especially at her age."

"All I need is a cat," his ward stated, "and I want this one. Uncle David, will you buy her for me?"

"Fluffy is not for sale." Miss Blythe entered the room, bearing a tray. "You may have one of her kittens, though. It should not be long to wait."

"There," said David, relieved, "a kitten will be better, my dear. It would grow up, knowing only you as its caretaker."

His ward stuck out her lip.

David recognized the symptoms. Now would come the tantrum. And his horrible embarrassment at his own ineffectual guardian skills.

Miss Blythe, also, must have had an inkling of what was to come. She set down her tray and squatted in front of

Eugenia, stroking Fluffy's back. "Just think, Lady Eugenia. You will be able to choose your own baby and name it what you wish."

"If Uncle David bought Fluffy, I'd have all the kittens," the child noted with practicality.

"You may have them all, anyway. I'm sure your uncle wouldn't mind." She flashed an upward glance at David, her speaking green eyes begging for help. "But you can't have Fluffy. I would miss her so."

"I don't care! I want Fluffy!" Eugenia flounced across the room and plopped down on a settee, holding the cat tightly and pressing her cheek against its head. Fluffy began to knead Eugenia's lap with her front legs as if to soothe the girl.

David was grateful that the outburst amounted to nothing more than that. He extended a hand to Miss Blythe and assisted her to her feet. "I'm sorry. I . . . I . . ." He shrugged unhappily.

"The child wants discipline," Lady Blythe said emphatically. "She needs a mother."

"Perhaps." He forced a smile, unable to look away from the sympathetic green eyes of her daughter. The chit was a charmer. With those expressive eyes and that gold hair, she belonged in a London ballroom, certainly not here. Yet, unlike the ladies of the *ton,* she had a comfortable way about her that was totally without artifice.

"My lord"—Stephanie smiled beautifully—"I believe you would benefit by a glass of brandy. Although I do not think alcohol is a solution for problems, it might ease you enough to give you a good appetite for the delicious meal we have prepared."

"I wholeheartedly agree." His smile relaxed into a genuine one. "Perhaps you and Lady Blythe will join me?"

"Sherry would be quite welcome." Lady Blythe nodded.

"Thank you, my lord, but I cannot," Miss Blythe demurred.

"Yes, you will, Stephanie," her mother interceded. "You

must have a little rest. You have been run off your feet all day."

The two determined ladies stared at each other. The marquess could barely keep from chuckling. He wondered if they realized how much alike they were. Two strong, stubborn women. If they worked together, they would be formidable. He wished, however, that Lady Blythe would win this battle. Talking with a young lady over dinner would have been pleasant. But it was not to be, for Miss Blythe was edging toward the door.

"You will excuse me, my lord? Maybe another time."

"Of course," David said over Lady Blythe's protest, as the girl fled.

Her mother tried to hide her disappointment with a smile. "As I said, she does insist on helping."

"Kindness to others is a virtue," David remarked as he crossed the room to the sideboard to pour drinks from the selection of bottles the innkeeper had assembled there.

"Yes, but"—Lady Blythe suddenly moaned—"my Stephanie wasn't born for . . . for this!"

"It is unfortunate," he murmured, feeling as if she expected him to do something about it. But what? There was nothing reasonable. Besides, he had his hands full with a much younger lady. Gad, but he hoped Eugenia would mind her manners for the rest of the evening.

Lady Blythe gratefully accepted her glass of sherry. "Thank you, my lord. Do forgive me for bursting forth about my woes. My life is simply so frustrating."

"I understand, ma'am. To be uprooted so drastically would be quite a shock." He handed her a glass of sherry and sat down across from her. "You haven't been here long?"

"No. How I wish we'd been able to pass one more Christmas at Blythe Manor." She smiled wistfully. "We celebrated so sumptuously! Greenery, red bows, kissing balls . . . and the food, oh my. Christmas is such a special time of year. I wonder how Caroline and George celebrate here. Certainly nothing like that, of course."

Her words served to remind him how close it was to the holiday. Idly he wondered if he and Eugenia would also be spending Christmas at the inn. The snow showed no signs of abating. He was glad he'd placed some of Eugenia's gifts in his personal, better-sprung carriage for a safer ride. Eugenia, awakening on Christmas morning to find no gifts, would be an awful experience.

"I shopped before coming here," Lady Blythe went on, "not knowing what kind of merchandise would be available in the village."

"I brought some of Eugenia's things in our carriage. I'm beginning to think it was a good idea." He glanced pointedly at the window, though it was too dark to see out.

"Indeed." She looked up as her daughter entered the room, balancing a large tray.

David quickly arose. "Allow me to assist."

"No, my lord. I am fine." She set the tray on the edge of the table and began to remove the bowls and platters.

He could see how proud she was of her culinary efforts by the way she placed the food with a bit of a flourish. The offering did look delicious, though there was not a huge variety. It was probably difficult for the remote inn to obtain supplies in the winter. But what was there smelled delightful.

"One more tray," she said and hastened out.

"You will find that the meals here are excellent, my lord." Lady Blythe got to her feet. "I suppose there is nothing wrong with a young lady knowing something of food preparation, so that she may conduct her household more efficiently."

"Not at all." David seated her and Eugenia, nearly having to pry the cat from his ward's arms. "My dear, I'll put Fluffy in front of the fire. She can take a nap and be ready to play a bit more before bedtime. A mother-to-be needs her rest, you know."

Eugenia begrudgingly gave her up and happily did not utter a spiteful comment.

Miss Blythe returned with another fragrant tray of victuals, which she carefully arranged on the table. "Can I bring you anything else?" she inquired.

"It seems we have everything and more," David smiled, "and it looks wonderful. Are you sure you won't join us?"

"Yes, please, Stephanie," her mother stressed.

"Another time, thank you," she demurred sweetly and departed.

With Lady Blythe and David chatting casually, they began to eat the superb meal. Even though the choices were simple, he did not know when he had eaten tastier food. The beef alone would put his expensive London chef to shame. He noted that his ward ate heartily, too, when before, she had usually exhibited a very finicky appetite. But in addition, she was sharing tiny bites, for Fluffy had left the hearth and come up beside her. Fearing a tantrum, David pretended not to notice.

Unfortunately, Miss Blythe did. Gliding into the room to check on the diners, she spied Eugenia slipping a tidbit of beef to the cat. "No, Lady Eugenia! Do not feed Fluffy from the table!"

His ward startled. Her face suffused with anger. She stuck out her tongue at Miss Blythe and fed Fluffy another bite.

"I said *no*," the young lady repeated, green eyes snapping.

"Stephanie, surely . . ." Lady Blythe began.

"Mother, you know what this will cause. Why, you never even allowed Fluffy to enter the dining room!"

"Yes, I know what it will cause, and you should too," the lady warned.

David's cheeks warmed. Lady Blythe was not speaking of bad habits the cat might learn. She was referring to Eugenia's bad manners.

"Eugenia," he instructed, "if you are to play with Fluffy, you will have to obey the rules."

His ward defiantly dropped a piece of meat on the floor. Before the cat could respond, Miss Blythe pounced forward and swept her up in her arms. "I warned you, Lady Eugenia. Now Fluffy will go with me."

His ward screeched piercingly.

"Be still," Miss Blythe ordered. "Rules are to be followed. No matter what kind of tantrums you exhibit, you will not win me over. You will only exhaust yourself and receive a very sore throat for your efforts."

"You can't tell me what to do! You're just a servant!"

"Perhaps I am, but I'm also the cat's owner."

"My uncle is a marquess!"

"Oh, I am aware of that." Miss Blythe nodded sagely. "Still, the courts of England uphold legal ownership, no matter what the owner's social standing."

"Uncle David, are you going to let her treat me like this?" his ward shouted, pounding her fists on the table.

David set his jaw. He hadn't missed a word of the exchange. Miss Blythe had come up against a regular child-tyrant, and she was winning! Her determined strength gave him hope. Maybe his ward could be controlled.

"Yes, Eugenia, I believe I shall," he replied with a calm he didn't feel. "Miss Blythe is correct in this matter, you know."

Flustered, the little girl whirled on Lady Blythe. "You're her mother! Make her give Fluffy back!"

The lady winced. "Oh, no, child, I cannot."

"Uncle David!" she screamed.

Hearing a noise of movement, he glanced toward the door and saw the innkeeper and his wife and all the servants assembled there, huffing and puffing as if they had run to the scene as soon as they heard a raised voice. "I think it's time you left the table, Eugenia. You will sit quietly by the fire until I finish my meal. Gad, you have made a spectacle of us all."

Seeing all the adult eyes upon her, Eugenia crumpled. A tear slid down her face.

Everyone seemed frozen in place, until Miss Blythe set down her cat and stepped forward. She crouched beside Eugenia and put the child's head to her shoulder, slipping an arm around her. "It will be all right, Lady Eugenia. Growing up is hard. I did so myself, not very long ago."

"Can you make those people leave?" the little girl gurgled.

Listening acutely, David waved everyone away.

"They are gone now," Miss Blythe assured, wiping Eugenia's eyes with a napkin and holding it to her nose.

His ward blew loudly.

"Better now?" Miss Blythe asked.

The child nodded.

"Good! Now if all is better, I'm sure your uncle will relent and allow you to remain at the table to eat some of the wonderful dessert we have prepared." She looked up at him.

"Yes," he agreed, lost in those beautiful eyes.

"May Fluffy stay, please?" Eugenia begged.

"If you will not feed her."

"I promise."

"Very well." Miss Blythe rose. "If everyone is finished, I shall clear the table."

All nodded.

"The meal was above excellent," David told her. "But more than that, I appreciated your counsel."

She colored. "Oh, that was nothing."

"Nevertheless . . ." His gaze locked with hers. He realized he needn't say more. She understood.

"Uncle David, why are you looking at Miss Blythe like that?" Eugenia piped.

His cheeks burned. Miss Blythe flushed more deeply and quickly began to gather up the soiled plates and cutlery. He didn't know what to say to his ward.

Lady Blythe came to the rescue. "Child, your uncle simply lost the thread of the conversation."

"He looked funny."

The lady skipped over that. "Oh, Stephanie, tell us what is for dessert. I am so anxious. I do love my sweets!"

* * *

Stephanie sat up in bed and blinked at the murky daylight. It was morning, and she was still exhausted. She desperately wanted to roll over and sleep a bit later, but the chamber was growing quite chilly with only coals glowing in the fireplace. Leaving her warm cocoon, she dashed across the frigid floor, stoked the fire, and pulled back the curtains. It was still snowing! Surely no guest would get up early. There was nothing to do. Making a quick decision, she scurried back to bed and snuggled beneath the covers.

She was physically tired, not mentally. She had gotten enough sleep. Uncle George had sent her, her mother, and aunt up to bed while he remained downstairs with Lord Donnington and his servants. Along with caring for her mistress, Rose had tended to Lady Eugenia, too.

Fluffy leaped onto the bed and slipped beneath the covers, lying against her mistress's shoulder. "I hope you won't tire of Lady Eugenia," Stephanie murmured. "It seems that you are her only pleasure. Well, she did eat a good meal last night, though, so she must enjoy her food."

Fluffy began to purr loudly.

"Yes, you know you are special, don't you?"

Stephanie closed her eyes. Just a few minutes, perhaps half an hour, then she'd arise. She drifted into a light slumber.

When she awakened, she heard the inn's subtle morning noises. Hopping from bed, she performed her morning's ablutions and dressed. Since the two maids had gone home, her water was icy cold. That meant bringing hot water to the guests and stoking the fires, the girls' usual job. Rose would take care of her mother, but what of the marquess and his ward? Her pulse pounded in her throat. Hopefully Aunt Caroline or Uncle George had done it. She just *couldn't*. What if Lord Donnington was still in bed? Or in his dressing robe? Oh, my! Perhaps she should stay in her room a bit longer.

She took a little more time with her hair, brushing it until it shone and sweeping it up on her head into a simple knot. After she finished, she felt guilty. Uncle George and

Aunt Caroline needed her. She just couldn't stay in her room any longer. Desperately hoping that Lord Donnington had been served, she let herself out into the hall.

"Miss Stephanie!" Rose, stepping out of her mother's room, beckoned to her.

She obediently walked down the hall. "I cannot tarry long. I have already overslept."

"My lady is ill, Miss Stephanie."

Her heart seemed to fall to her toes. "Oh, no. What is wrong?"

"I don't think it's serious, miss. Just miserable. Lady Blythe has sniffles and a wretchedly sore throat." Rose whirled back into the room.

Stephanie numbly followed. She had wished that Rose and her mother would see to Lady Eugenia's care today. Because of this, it was certainly not to be. Well, Lord Donnington himself would have to mind his ward. After all, the staff of this inn was not here to be nursemaids. The little girl was his responsibility.

"My dear Stephanie," Lady Blythe croaked, extending a beautifully manicured hand, "I am such a nuisance."

"No, Mama, never that. You are merely a bit under the weather." She sat down on the edge of the bed and took her mother's hand in hers. She couldn't help but notice the difference in their grooming. Lady Blythe's nails were long and graceful, while hers were work-worn and chipped. No man would want to hold such a hand as hers.

"Good gracious, gel," her mother rasped, seeing it too. "Your hand! It is so rough and callused."

"Do not worry about that, Mama. Just concentrate on getting better. What do you wish for breakfast?"

"Nothing."

"You must eat something," Stephanie scolded, "to keep up your strength."

"A piece of toast and jelly, then. And a cup of hot tea with honey."

"Very well." Stephanie rose. "I shall be back as soon as possible."

"I'll come down to fetch the tray," Rose volunteered.

"We'll fix a plate for you, too."

"Thank you, Miss Stephanie." The lady's maid followed her from the room. "Miss, I doubt I'll be much help with the young lady today."

"I realize that. Mother is always so helpless when she is ill."

Rose hung her head. "I'm sorry."

"That's all right. We'll manage."

" 'Tis too bad your aunt sent those girls home."

She shrugged. "It seemed the thing to do at the time. How were we to know?"

"Yes, miss." Rose turned back to the sickroom.

Poor Lord Donnington, Stephanie thought, descending the stairs. He would have to take on his ward today. Fluffy could help to provide a distraction, but how long would that last? Children hopped from one thing to another so quickly. By evening, the marquess would be exhausted, and Eugenia would be totally out of control. She determined to hide Fluffy during meals. That, at least, would eliminate the potential of dining scenes. With his niece to watch, Lord Donnington's food would be his only pleasure. She would make sure that it was delicious.

As she passed through the taproom, she noted that the marquess's servants were already wolfing down their breakfast. Her guilty feeling increased. Oh, why had she gone back to bed? She quickened her step, half running through the hall to the kitchen. Uncle George and Aunt Caroline were sitting at the scarred oak table, while Betsy was at the hearth, frying bacon in a long-handled spider.

"I'm so sorry! I overslept," she admitted painfully.

Aunt Caroline narrowed her eyes. "I believe you should have stayed in bed. You still look tired, my dear."

"Goes at it too hard, when she ain't used to it," Uncle George remarked. "Don't want you to be a slave, Steffy."

Seeing that they were not angry, Stephanie relaxed. "I would have had to get up anyway. Mama is ill. That slowed me a little, too."

Aunt Caroline groaned. "How can we fetch a doctor?"

"It isn't necessary. She has sniffles and a sore throat. She only wants toast and jelly for her breakfast."

"I'll brew her one of my tisanes, too," Betsy offered. "I know it will help."

"I hope so." She frowned. "I'm sorry that Mama is ill, but I'm doubly sorry that she and Rose will not be available to aid with Lady Eugenia."

"I'll pitch in," Aunt Caroline stated. "Now that Betsy is feeling better, she can do most of the cooking. Eat your breakfast, Stephanie. I have finished mine. I'll go up to the little brat, wash her and dress her. When Lord Donnington comes downstairs, George can serve him while you do up his room."

She nodded. "Clean sheets?"

"Hell, no!" said George. "He's only slept on 'em one night! It'll just make more work."

"He is a marquess." Aunt Caroline smiled enigmatically. "If we please him, other members of the *ton* might stop here. You'd have a chance of becoming rich, George."

"Fustian."

"Clean sheets," Stephanie acknowledged and sat down at the table.

By the time she had finished eating, Lord Donnington was in the salon.

"Says he don't want a full buffet," George told Betsy. "Just a nice plateful. Kind of him. Thoughtful of others."

Stephanie smiled to herself, rising. Perhaps the marquess had taken her words to heart. "I shall do his room; then I'll be back, unless Aunt Caroline has delivered Lady Eugenia to the salon. If so, I'll do the child's room. Betsy, you'll see to Mama's and Rose's meals, please? Rose will be down for them."

"Don't you worry about your mama, missy. My tisane will make her fit in no time."

Stephanie hastened up the stairs and into the linen room, gathering up sheets and pillowcases. As she passed Lady Eugenia's chamber, she could hear squalls from within. Poor

Aunt Caroline! How much could everyone's nerves bear? Of course, Lord Donnington couldn't bathe or dress the girl, but he could certainly help entertain her. She would make sure he did!

Three

Days passed, but the snow did not end. One storm merely followed another. The hostlers continuously shoveled a path from the stable to the inn, where they ate their meals. Luckily, Uncle George had stockpiled a large supply of grain and hay for the animals, and Aunt Caroline had full larders for the people, with plenty of ingredients for extra special Christmas treats, for they were definitely snowbound. Since the storm had commenced, they had seen no other people or carriages. The long inclemency would probably be responsible for deaths from the cold and from starvation, but those at the Horse and Hound Inn would be safe.

Lady Blythe had recovered and was able to take a short turn in entertaining Lady Eugenia. She usually read to the child during what were supposed to be quiet times. Rose began to teach her to embroider and to sew simple things. At present, they were making a cat coat for Fluffy. Aunt Caroline introduced her to old Sarum. When Fluffy refused to sleep with her, choosing to remain with Stephanie, Lady Eugenia substituted old Sarum, carefully tucking him in with her every night. Uncle George put up with the child, every now and then, and taught her to pull a mug of ale from a keg. Stephanie prayed that Lord Donnington would not find out about that. The marquess or Stephanie played more actively with the little girl, engaging in hide-and-seek, spillikins, and find-the-treasure.

Eugenia's behavior continued to be problematic. When things did not go her way, she threw temper tantrums. If she wanted to do a particular thing, and the person who participated in it was not available, she would be horrid. Also, she insisted that Fluffy be with her at all times, except at night. Luckily, Fluffy was patient. Even when Lady Eugenia became overset, the cat would try to soothe her, tapping her leg with her paw or rubbing against her. The feline had an uncanny ability to settle the child. Stephanie wondered what they would have done without her pet. Old Sarum was not so gentle. When he became tired of the girl, he swatted her and went his own way.

She herself continued to be firm with the child. Usually Lady Eugenia minded her manners when she was with Stephanie. Now and then, she was forced to invoke discipline. She refused to allow the spoiled chit to get the best of her. The little girl was beginning to realize that.

Also with the passing days, Stephanie was becoming closer to Lord Donnington. Aware of her precarious heart, she tried to escape him, but within the close quarters of the Horse and Hound Inn, it was well nigh impossible. When they both were free of Lady Eugenia, he seemed to seek her out, trapping her into conversation that she was unable politely to avoid. She enjoyed talking with him, but she was still unaccustomed to his frightfully handsome face. Whenever he assailed her, she was unable to resist. One morning, with the aid of Aunt Caroline, he ensnared her into having breakfast with him. As she entered the kitchen and began to fill her plate with bacon and eggs, Aunt Caroline returned with a tray.

"Lord Donnington is having his breakfast, Stephanie. He has asked that you join him with yours. He wishes to speak with you."

Her heart tripled its beat. "I cannot do that! I am not dressed properly," she stammered.

"He has seen you in that kind of attire before," her aunt reminded. "Please do this, my dear. He was very serious."

"Oh, Aunt Caroline!" she cried, dismayed. "What can he possibly want? I *can't!*"

"I am depending on you," she said flatly. "I certainly don't wish to aggravate Lord Donnington."

"No, but . . ."

"Leave the door open, Stephanie, so the situation will not seem so intimate."

Stephanie gasped. "Isn't Lady Eugenia there?"

"No. Now, hurry along. Your breakfast will be cold. I shall serve the coffee and leave the pot on the sideboard." She swished out the door.

"Oh, heavens," Stephanie moaned. "Betsy, what shall I do?"

"You'll hurry to breakfast," the cook cackled. "I can't understand why a gel wouldn't want to break bread with a fine-looking man like him. And a titled one, at that!"

"That's just the trouble." Morosely, she picked up her plate and followed her Aunt Caroline, wondering what on earth the marquess would demand to talk with her about. Had she done something wrong, while watching his niece? What if he was going to give her a trimming? Her heart continued to pound ferociously.

When she stepped into the salon, Lord Donnington and her aunt were laughing. Well, at least he wasn't angry just then. He looked to be in a cheerful mood.

When he saw her, he rose. "Good morning, Miss Blythe. I am glad you accepted my invitation."

It was more like a summons, she thought, but she smiled and let him seat her at the table. "Good morning."

Aunt Caroline took her tray. "I'll be leaving you now. If there is anything you wish, just ring."

"If there's anything we wish, I'll fetch it," Stephanie murmured.

Lord Donnington grinned. "You look as if you are afraid of me. Haven't you learned by now that I do not bite?"

Flirting! She eyed him warily. "Your request was simply surprising, my lord."

"I'm weary of dining with only a child for company, so I asked Lady Blythe if she would invite Eugenia to breakfast with her. Make it seem special, you know. Also, there were some things I wanted to ask you."

"Very well." She took a dainty bite of eggs, visualizing what kind of meal her mother was experiencing.

"About Christmas," he began. "It's only a few days away."

"You would be better to ask my aunt. I have never spent Christmas here." She smiled wistfully, remembering the wonderful holidays at Blythe Manor. "I'm sure everything will be as nice as we can make it, especially for Lady Eugenia. Betsy, our cook, has already begun making sweet treats. As for greenery and festive decorations . . . I just don't know about that."

"I recall when I was a boy," he reminisced, "Christmas put stars in my eyes. Donnington Hall would be decked to the utmost with holly and fir. And certainly there was mistletoe in the kissing balls, which I did not appreciate until I was older! Everything smelled so fresh. I suppose it is that way now. Some of the guests might have arrived before the snow."

"You were having a house party?" Stephanie asked, enjoying hearing him talking about himself.

"We haven't missed a year. It is entirely composed of relatives. You must think that sounds dull, but I assure you that mine is a fun-loving family. Maybe the weather will clear, and we'll all be together for the New Year." He took a bite of bacon and chewed thoughtfully. "Every year, of course, there will be more or less of us. This year, I think there will be more, if everyone eventually arrives. It seems that we've had numerous weddings."

"I'm sorry you won't be there," Stephanie earnestly told him.

"Yes. Well . . ." Suddenly his eyes twinkled with mischief. "Miss Blythe, is there any way possible that we could find some evergreen?"

"There is some in Aunt Caroline's garden, if she would allow us to take it. We would have to cut very selectively. And we would have to shovel our way." She nibbled her toast. "It would be best if you asked her, my lord. Coming from you, she could not bear to refuse."

"All right," he said amiably. "I just want everything to be as nice as possible for Eugenia. It will be her first Christmas without her parents."

"I am so sorry. We'll certainly do everything we can to make it a special time." She bowed her head. There was nothing more to say.

"I would also like to speak with you about Eugenia, and I wish you to be very honest. Brutally so, if necessary."

Curious and somewhat alarmed, she lifted her gaze to meet his. "Yes, my lord."

His lips curved into a wry smile. "Eugenia is a difficult, obnoxious child, is she not?"

"Oh, I would not say that, my lord! She has some problems, yes, but . . ." She let her voice trail off, not knowing what to say.

He leaned forward. "I don't know how she was when her parents were living. The few times I was with her, she acted perfectly. But that is definitely not the case now. Miss Blythe, what am I going to do? You must have some knowledge in this regard."

"No!" Stephanie denied. "I know little about children."

"You know enough to realize that I am ineffectual in dealing with her."

She looked helplessly into his candid blue eyes. It was hard to admit that this beautiful man of her dreams had a fault, but he really didn't deal well with his ward. He was too easy with her. It was obvious that he gave her everything she wanted, even if it was a mere whim. He did not hold her to account for her misdeeds. He might try to correct her, but in the end, he merely pacified her. But she couldn't tell him that. It would be too terribly frank.

"Miss Blythe, as far as I know, you were the first to truly discipline her. Remember when you caught her feeding the cat during dinner? And I know you have disciplined her since. Tell me, do you have a particular method in mind?"

"Goodness, no!" she exclaimed. Her heart raced. Was he going to chide her for punishing the girl?

"Then what is it? She seems to behave herself better when you are nearby."

Stephanie relaxed a bit. Apparently he was not going to take exception to the way she handled his niece. In fact, he seemed to appreciate it.

"Lord Donnington, I have no theories on rearing a child. I am scarcely out of the schoolroom myself." She laughed.

He grinned. "No one would ever guess it, Miss Blythe. I find you a very mature and attractive young lady."

Attractive! Her heart leaped to her throat. He found her *attractive?* No, she couldn't allow herself to be taken in like that. She must remember that he was miles above her station in life.

"You seem surprised," he commented.

"I suppose one is often surprised to hear what others perceive in oneself," she managed.

"I daresay. What do you see in me, Miss Blythe?" His smile intensified.

"I see a kind gentleman," she said readily.

"Is that your first thought? Not my title?"

"I think first of your kindness." She felt her cheeks warming. "My lord, this turn of conversation is growing too personal."

He studied her closely. "Just one more question. How do you see me in conjunction with my niece?"

Oh, no! She barely controlled a wince. What could she say to him?

"Brutal truth, Miss Blythe," he reminded her.

Very well, that is what she would speak. She drew a deep breath. "You are far too easy with her, sir. She needs firmness and discipline. She has been allowed to go too long without taking responsibility for her own actions."

He sucked his upper lip. "I know. I just don't like admitting it to myself. What should I do?"

She shrugged lightly. "Lord Donnington, you must know

other, more experienced ladies who could advise you far better than I."

"She minds you better than anyone I have ever seen. Please tell me your method, Miss Blythe."

"I simply will not permit the little brat . . ." Stephanie flushed deeply. "Oh, my lord, I am sorry. I should not have called her that!"

"Well, she is a brat," he said slowly. "And I asked you to be frank with me. Please continue."

"I . . . I will not allow the Lady Eugenia to make mice feet out of me," she managed.

"And I do." It was a statement of fact. He knew it just as well as she did.

"But you don't have to!" she urged, feeling horribly sorry for him. "It won't be easy at first, because she thinks she has you wrapped around her little finger, but it will work. You must try, Lord Donnington! You cannot wish her to grow up like this."

He put his elbow on the table and lifted his hand to his forehead as if he had a severe headache. "How shall I start? Will you help me?"

"Of course, but it's actually simple. Do not give way to her, no matter how loud she shouts or how hard she beats her heels on the floor. Eventually, she will realize that she is wasting her time. But if you give in—just once—you'll be back at the beginning." She smiled ruefully. "At least, I *hope* that will work. It seems to be helping me deal with her. Also, I try to make the punishment fit the crime. If you can't come up with anything, you may send her to her room or stand her in the corner."

The marquess sighed. "I'm going to have to do something. I can't go on like this. But to listen to those screams . . ."

Stephanie nodded sympathetically. "It will be hard."

"But it must be done," he muttered.

"Yes." She rose. "You must excuse me now, my lord. I do have work to do."

He stood up. "Thank you, Miss Blythe. You have helped me immensely. Wish me luck?"

"Of course." She smiled.

He lifted her hand and kissed her fingers, lips light as a feather. "And remember, whether you wish to believe it or not, you are most attractive."

"Thank you, Lord Donnington." Trembling, she curtsied and hastened toward the door. "I shall return with a tray to clear the table."

But she would ask Aunt Caroline to do so. She couldn't bear to be with him that soon. He found her attractive! Now how could she keep from falling in love with him? Her poor heart was doomed.

David found himself a bit shaken after she left. There was something about Miss Blythe that defied the normal feelings he'd had about any woman. She *was* attractive. No, she was downright beautiful. If she were attired as a young lady of the *ton,* she would be perfection itself. But that which was most compelling was her inward beauty. She was a good, thoughtful young woman, a rarity in these days. She didn't even think about titles; she thought of kindness first. She would make a man a marvelous wife. He wondered if passion dwelled in her, too. If so, no man could ask for more.

He wandered to the window, clasped his hands behind his back, and gazed out, unseeing. Was Miss Blythe the *one* for him? He could very well picture her standing strongly by his side through thick or thin. He could easily visualize her as a mother, gentle and loving, but firm. And to imagine her snuggling in his arms was almost too much to contemplate. If only she weren't so shy with him, he could get to know her better.

He heard the door open and turned with a smile, only to see her Aunt Caroline, instead of Miss Blythe. The young lady was hiding from him again. He hoped his expression did not exhibit his disappointment.

"I am sorry to disturb you, Lord Donnington," she greeted, "but I thought you would be pleased to be rid of the dirty dishes."

"Whatever eases your day pleases me." He grinned.

She dropped a flirtatious curtsy. "Well, now, what if we all decided to take the day off? There would be no meals, my lord."

He lifted an eyebrow. "That would be worse than awful, ma'am. You must realize how much I enjoy your delicious repasts." He touched his flat stomach. "I shall be forced to lose weight when I leave here."

She laughed. "Not hardly."

He sobered. "Actually, I'm glad you came in. I have a favor to ask."

"Of course, my lord."

"I would like some of the greenery from your garden to decorate the inn for Christmas. Of course, I am willing to pay."

"Certainly you may have greenery, at no extra cost, but I don't know how we can get to it." She walked up beside him and looked out the window. "It's totally covered by snow."

"I'll dig my way to it," he stated.

She half gasped. "What? You, my lord? Dig? I won't have it!"

"Madam, this is not a service required of an inn. It is up to me to do it," he insisted. "It is personal."

"It is not. I *always* decorate the inn for Christmas. As a guest, you are entitled to have Christmas decorations," she pronounced. "My goodness, if my papa knew that I allowed a marquess to shovel my snow, he would spin in his grave! He was very arrogant about his title and that of others. I may have married beneath myself and reaped his everlasting abhorrence, but when I did it, I definitely knew right from wrong. For a marquess to shovel snow is wrong, and there's an end to it!"

"No, there is not," he stated in full lordly command. "Besides, I intend to cause my footman and coachman to assist."

"Then I will so order my stablemen," she said stubbornly, "and you, my lord, will not touch a shovel. If you do, there will be no greenery. I shall send Stephanie back and forth to report. She will tell me the truth. My niece is an honest gel."

Miss Blythe, passing the room with an basketload of crumpled laundry, paused.

Her aunt saw her. "Please come in, Stephanie."

The young lady set down her burden and entered, head tilted questioningly.

"My dear, Lord Donnington's servants and our stablemen are to dig a path to uncover some greenery. You will keep an eye on them. If Lord Donnington touches a shovel, you shall tattle to me. Understood?"

"Yes, ma'am." Her lovely eyes danced.

"Also, there are ribbons and bows and a crèche in the attic. They are in a trunk by the window that overlooks the stable. You and Lord Donnington may fetch them down."

Miss Blythe eyed him warily. What did she think? That he'd ravish her? Once and for all, he was going to get to the bottom of this. In the attic, he'd ask her directly why she always tried to avoid him.

"Why don't you do that now, while Lady Eugenia is happily occupied with Rose and Dorothy?" her aunt suggested.

"I have work . . ." the young lady began.

"I wish you to do this, my dear. We will manage what work needs to be done. We must ready ourselves for Christmas. It will be upon us in no time at all."

"Yes"—David took her elbow—"let us be about it."

"I could have done this," Miss Blythe protested as she led the way up the narrow, steep stairs. "It will be terribly dusty up here and probably full of cobwebs."

"Are you afraid of spiders, Miss Blythe?"

Her shudder was enough of an answer for him.

"Then you need me to protect you from the little monsters."

She glanced over her shoulder in midstep. "Are you making sport of me, my lord?"

"Certainly not! I know a number of men who are afraid of spiders." He watched the tantalizing movement of her hips as they continued to climb. Hmm, Miss Blythe was more attractive than ever he'd realized.

"But you aren't afraid of them," she called back.

"Not particularly, though I mash them whenever I see them."

They emerged into a large, but low-roofed space. David could stand up straight only in the middle, a major handicap for defending Miss Blythe against spiders. The attic was cluttered, but the trunk was in plain view.

"Miss Blythe"—he caught her arm as she started toward it—"why do you always try to avoid me?"

She lowered her gaze. "Do I? I wasn't aware of it."

"Don't fib. Tell me honestly."

She drew a deep breath. "I cannot say, my lord."

"Cannot or will not?" he gently persisted.

"Both," she whispered. "Please. Do not ask me more."

He acquiesced. He didn't want to press her, but she was driving him out of his wits. Here he was, free of Eugenia, and he wanted to get to know Miss Blythe better.

She walked quickly over to the trunk, started to open the lid, and screamed for all she was worth.

"What is it?" David rushed forth, banging his head on the low ceiling and knocking himself back a full stride.

"It's on me!" She wildly shook her hand. "It's still on me! *Oh God!*"

"A spider?" He bent and started forward.

She screamed again and flapped her dress, exposing delightful, shapely ankles.

"What is it, Stephanie?"

"It was a big brown spider. It jumped onto my hand, then my dress. It was awful, but it's gone now!" She began to cry.

David did the only thing he knew to do with a weeping woman. He took her in his arms. "It's all right, my dear."

"But it's still here somewhere!" she sobbed, clutching his coat and looking fearfully around.

"Did it bite you?"

"No."

He drew her to the center peak of the attic, where he could stand up straight instead of lolling over her shoulder. Withdrawing his handkerchief, he wiped her eyes and nose. "It probably ran under the trunk. Remember, it's afraid of you, too. You wait here, my dear. I'll fetch the Christmas things."

She nodded numbly and backed away from him. "Please hurry. I don't like this place."

"Do you want to leave now?" he asked kindly. "I can have one of my servants help me."

"No, I am here. I will help," she said, false bravery clear in her voice.

Miss Blythe—Stephanie—was terrified. It was strange to see one so capable and in control of herself brought down by a tiny creature. He wondered if there was anything else she feared.

"Are you afraid of snakes?" he asked to get her mind turned from spiders, as he strolled toward the trunk.

She screamed. "It's on me again!"

Whirling, he saw her standing frozen, her skirts lifted to her luscious thighs. Her face was white as foolscap. On her shin, crawling toward her knee, was a large spider.

"Don't move!" He leaped forward, again hitting his head. "Hell and damnation!"

"Oh, my lord," she said in a tremolo, her whole body shaking.

He bent over, his hands shaking at the sight of her lovely legs. Good heavens, she was beautiful. He could scarcely concentrate on his task.

She began to weep. "I am going to faint."

"Don't." The thought of the spider rushing up her dress made his manhood ache.

With a well-aimed hand, David flicked the arachnid onto the floor and stomped it with one shiny Hessian. "It's dead."

She wavered, almost going into a swoon. He caught her, holding her securely in his arms. "It cannot bother you now, Stephanie."

She turned her head into his chest and wept.

"You are safe," he crooned, giving her his handkerchief and stroking her back.

"I feel like a fool," she said in a muffled voice, gradually gaining control of herself. "I've never actually had one of them on me. I . . . I was ridiculous, wasn't I?"

"Not at all. Everyone has something they fear, Stephanie."

She looked up at him. "It is not proper that you call me by my first name."

He looked into her eyes and succumbed. "Perhaps not, but this isn't proper, either." He bent his head and brushed her lips with his. "Won't you call me David?"

"My mother would have a conniption fit," she breathed.

"In private, then," he begged.

She stared at him, eyes wide.

"I wish to know you better. Won't you spend more time with me? Or am I too repulsive to you?"

Her lips barely moved. "My lord, you are far from being repulsive. You are too . . ."

When she didn't finish her sentence, David lowered his lips again and kissed her more thoroughly. At first, she placed her hands on his chest as if to push him away. Then she slipped her arms around his neck. He deepened the kiss and she responded. Her mouth softly opened. He did not go further to probe her sweetness. He didn't want to frighten her. She'd had enough anyway, for she gently touched his cheek. He lifted his head and looked deeply into her eyes.

"I didn't want it to go this far," she murmured.

Before he could ask her what she meant, they both heard footsteps at the foot of the stairs. They moved apart. He wondered if he looked as guilty as she did.

"What's going on up there?" chirped Eugenia from below. "We heard screams."

"It's all right now!" David shouted down. "We were unpacking Christmas decorations. A spider got on Miss Blythe, and she's deathly afraid of them."

"I'm not! Can I come up and help?"

"Of course!" he replied. Eugenia asking permission? Any other time, she'd merely have popped onto the scene. Maybe the child was on her good behavior since the holiday was so nearby. Luckily she hadn't caught him kissing Stephanie. He didn't know what either lady would have done in a situation like that.

Lady Blythe, Rose, and Eugenia had heard the scream. As one, they dashed into the hall to listen. There was another.

"It must be Stephanie!" Lady Blythe cried.

Rose shook her head. "Miss Stephanie's never screamed in her life."

"But who else would it be?" Lady Blythe dashed to her daughter's room, but found no one within. "Where did it come from?"

"It couldn't be Miss Stephanie," Rose insisted.

"Well, it wasn't Caroline or that old cook," her mistress said flatly. "It was a young scream."

They dithered about, looking over the second floor railing and explored down both sides of the hall, including the servants' stairway.

"Where did it come from?" Lady Blythe repeated.

The scream echoed again.

"Upstairs!" Lady Eugenia shouted triumphantly.

They rushed to the steps and started up.

"Oh, what can be happening?" Lady Blythe panted. "Only the servants live here. Can those men have abducted my Stephanie? Oh, what will we do?"

"We'll save her!" To Eugenia, it was a wonderful game. It was like knights and damsels in distress. Only this time, she would be the heroine who rescued the lady. Everyone would drink toasts to her. Everyone would love her.

When they reached the upper floor, the halls were empty and silent.

"I know. The attic!" Eugenia held her finger to her mouth and stealthily crept toward the steep steps, which she had discovered during one of her secret explorations. "We shall take them unawares."

"How?" Lady Blythe croaked.

The little girl crept quietly up the stairs. She paused just as soon as she reached a height to see into the garret. Miss Stephanie was there; so was her uncle. They were kissing! Biting back a giggle, Eugenia softly backed down.

"What did you see?" Lady Blythe exclaimed.

"Miss Stephanie was there," she said smugly. "Uncle David was there. I don't think they wished rescue."

"What is going on?" Stephanie's mother demanded. "What was the screaming about?"

"I don't know, but I wouldn't go up there." The child couldn't hold back her giggles. "They were kissing!"

"Oh, my goodness!" Lady Blythe lifted her face heavenward. "Thank you, Lord!"

Eugenia curiously tilted her head. "For what?"

"Never you mind." Lady Blythe took her hand and tried to pull her toward the main stairs. "Let us go downstairs. Maybe the cook has prepared a new Christmas sweet we can sample."

Much as Eugenia liked her treats, she jerked away and went to the attic steps. "I'm going up."

"No!" pleaded the elder lady. "Let them alone!"

Refusing to listen, the little girl called, "What's going on up there?"

Stephanie ate luncheon in the kitchen with Betsy and Aunt Caroline, while Uncle George waited tables in the salon and taproom. She merely picked at her thinly sliced ham, beans, cheese, and warm bread. The kiss had shaken her so that she'd totally lost her appetite. She didn't know what to do. Lord Donnington—David—had broken through the frail wall she'd tried to build around her heart. Should she allow him to continue to batter her defenses? Or should she attempt to avoid him, a feat that had proved to be well nigh impossible.

Aunt Caroline pierced her reverie. "What is wrong, my dear?"

Stephanie snapped from her trance to find both her aunt and Betsy staring at her.

"You've scarcely touched your meal, and you look so pensive."

"I don't know what 'pensive' is," Betsy concluded, "but you look like you've got the weight o' the world on your own little shoulders."

She bit her lip. She would appreciate some advice, but she did not want her mother to know what had happened. Lady Blythe would do more than utter encouraging words; she'd set mortifying traps to ensnare Lord Donnington.

"Can you keep a secret?" she decided to say. "If Mama found out, it would be awful."

They nodded eagerly.

Stephanie sighed. "When we were in the attic . . . Lord Donnington kissed me."

"How wonderful!" Aunt Caroline cried, while Betsy applauded. "Oh, how wonderful!"

"Is it?" She clasped her hands together. "He could be toying with my affections."

Her aunt shook her head. "I don't believe Lord Donnington is that kind of man."

Hope sprang in her heart. "You don't? Honestly?"

"He doesn't seem like the type of man who would trifle."

"But he is so far above me. How could he think of me seriously?"

"Because you're so sweet and pretty!" Betsy claimed.

Aunt Caroline's eyes were thoughtful. "The marquess is very wealthy. He needn't marry for money. And Stephanie, you may be toiling in an inn, but you are a lady and you are the granddaughter of an earl. Wedding you would not be so far off for him."

"Then you think I should encourage him?" she breathed.

"If you would be happy with him."

Betsy cackled. "What more could a gel want? He's rich, handsome, 'n' has a title!"

"Most important to me is kindness and love," Stephanie mused.

"He certainly possesses kindness." Aunt Caroline smiled enigmatically. "It will be up to you to find out about his love."

"I'll see him back and forth, when the men are digging out the greenery, this afternoon."

"Be forth more than back," Betsy advised. "We can handle the work that needs doing 'round here."

"Change into a nicer gown," her aunt suggested. "Have you a fetching bonnet?"

"I won't wear a bonnet out there! He'd think I was crazy!" Stephanie was able to laugh. "Perhaps a scarf."

"No! You'd look like a waif!"

"Then I'll go bareheaded as I'd intended. I might change my dress, but he won't notice it under my coat." She stood, tossing them a saucy smile. "Remember, though, he kissed me in *this* dress!"

They laughed.

Stephanie took her plate into the scullery. As she scraped it into the scrap bowl for the hogs, she though of how her life had changed. First, she'd been waited upon by servants. Now, she'd actually become one. Could it be possible that she would be coddled and served again? A marchioness! Her mother would be ecstatic. But all the pampering, wealth, and title would mean nothing to her, unless she had the deep, unswerving love of the marquess. And that was why her mother must not know. If there came a decision, she would make it herself.

* * *

Stephanie spent a great deal of time outside in the frigid weather, but she helped in the kitchen as well. Betsy had prepared a dark, rich beef broth and was adding paper-thin slices of onion to it. The odor was mouthwatering.

"I vow you've outdone yourself," she complimented.

"It'll be tasty for the men when they come in from the cold," the cook stated. "Buttered toast squares floating on good soup. That'll take the chill off 'em."

"They will be delighted." She walked to the window, just as screams pierced the air. "What on earth?"

Eugenia, having insisted on helping, veered around the corner from the new path they were making and stopped, beginning to pound on the snow wall with her fists and to kick it with her toes.

"Oh, no." Stephanie reached for her coat.

"Little brat," Betsy muttered, hurrying to observe. "Needs a whoopin'."

"Lord Donnington would never allow that." She shrugged into the garment and began to button it.

"Wait! Look!" The cook clutched her arm. "Here he comes. See if he can handle it."

Eugenia, catching sight of her uncle, began drumming her toes against the snow wall. Within the blink of an eye, she went down hard on her bottom. Waving her arms, she screeched outrageously.

Betsy cackled.

Angrily, the little girl leaped up, slipped again, and fell. She rolled over, beating her fists and feet on the ground. The marquess stood helplessly watching, though he did seem to be speaking some words.

"I must go." She dashed from the door and down the path to the scene.

"Thank heavens," she thought she heard David say under his breath.

"They won't let me shovel!" Eugenia shrilled, when she saw her.

"It would be hard for you, and they are in a hurry,"

Stephanie explained. "Besides, it isn't really a proper occupation for a young, well-bred lady."

"No," said David flatly. "It's very cold out here. The men are freezing. We want to finish quickly."

"You're mean!" Eugenia wailed.

"Come along." Stephanie grabbed her flailing arm and jerked her to her feet. "You're coming inside."

"No!" the little girl screeched.

"My, what a set of lungs," she commented, "but they will get you nowhere."

"This behavior is outside of enough!" David warned severely. "No one will put up with it any longer, not even the servants."

"It's her! It's this tavern wench!" The child spit at Stephanie.

Before she could think, Stephanie caught better hold of the child and swatted her on the bottom with her hand. It couldn't have hurt. Eugenia was bundled quite thickly, and Stephanie hadn't struck very hard. But it served the purpose. The child stood still and silent, eyes large.

Immediately, Stephanie loosened her grasp and stared at the marquess. My goodness, what had she done? Had she truly spanked his ward? He would be angry. He would despise her.

David was standing very straight and looked actually arrogant. His cold gaze alighted on his niece. "You will apologize to Miss Blythe at once, Eugenia."

The little girl warily eyed him.

"Now!" he snapped.

She whirled. "I'm sorry, Miss Stephanie. I was rude and cruel."

Stephanie clasped her hands together to still their trembling. "Thank you, Eugenia. Shall we now forget that it ever happened?"

"I'd like that."

"Very well. And you will never disparage anyone again. Am I correct?"

She hung her head. "Yes, ma'am."

"Go into the kitchen," David commanded.

Eugenia ran toward the inn, fell once, picked herself up without complaint, and ran on.

"I'm sorry, my lord," Stephanie began.

"What happened to 'David'? We are in private."

Warmth flooded her cheeks. "David. I should not have taken it upon myself to strike your niece. I will never do so again. I . . . I don't know what happened. I just lost my temper, a thing one should never do when disciplining a child."

"If a tap on the derriere is what we have to do, then we shall do it. I certainly had my legs switched often enough when I was her age . . . and my backside, too."

She giggled. "That is hard to imagine. You are so kind and patient."

He grinned. "I wasn't always that way, not that I was as bad as Eugenia. My father would not have allowed it. Will you watch her a bit for me, Stephanie? It seems to be growing colder, and I want to finish this job."

"Of course I'll watch her." She smiled. "When you finish, we have a wonderful treat. Betsy is preparing the most delightful soup for everyone."

"We shall be there." He gave her a playful chuck under the chin. "You won't avoid me?"

"No," she said softly, lowering her gaze.

He squeezed her hand and turned back down the new path.

Stephanie's spirits soared. Eugenia would probably be well behaved for the rest of the day. They might have some fun together. After all, if she and David . . . That was thinking too far ahead. But could her dream really be coming true?

Christmas Eve! The salon was beautiful with its evergreen boughs, red bows, and crèche. There was even a rather lopsided kissing ball, made by Eugenia, but it did have a dried up piece of mistletoe that David had found mixed in with the ribbons. A table was stacked with gifts. It was a time for feasting and celebration, though there were still tasks for the workers at the inn. David wished he could cause everyone to sit back and enjoy the festivities, but it couldn't happen. This year, at least.

Stephanie, Lady Blythe, and her aunt and uncle did join him and Eugenia at dinner, however, making more of a party atmosphere. He wished Stephanie could sit closer to him, but proper seating demanded that Lady Blythe and her sister sit on his right and left. Stephanie and Eugenia faced each other in the middle, while George sat at the other end.

Eugenia was very excited, but her behavior was under control. She'd been good all day. He prayed she remained so.

"Won't you give the blessing, my lord?" Stephanie's aunt requested when everyone was seated.

"Wait a minute!" Eugenia cried, and then she leaped up and ran around the table to whisper to Stephanie.

His heart fell. Were they going to have to discipline the child on Christmas Eve? He decided to let this misde-meanor pass and hope for the best.

"Excuse us a moment," Stephanie said, rising and leaving the room with the child.

"What was that?" Lady Blythe disapproved in a high voice.

"The child is so excited, she may have made herself ill," returned Caroline.

"Didn't look ill," George remarked, staring hungrily at the big pink ham in front of David.

"Shall we continue?" asked Stephanie's mother.

"Let us give them a moment." David knew his statement was the final authority, though he disliked commanding them. But this was a special evening for Stephanie, too, and he did not want her to miss any of it. In fact, with luck he planned to make the entire holiday even more special.

The two young ladies returned. Stephanie bore a tray. Eugenia carried Fluffy and old Sarum, one cat in each arm.

"It's Christmas Eve for the cats, too," Eugenia said pertly.

In front of the fire, Stephanie set a bowl of milk and a saucer of minced meat for each cat. Eugenia carried the cats to the table and sat down. She grinned mischievously, as the adults looked askance at her.

"The cats want to be part of the blessing, Uncle David."

"Very well." He bowed his head and composed a prayer, ending with "God bless the cats."

"Good!" Eugenia carried the felines to their dinner by the hearth and returned to her seat.

"Now we can eat," George pronounced.

Conversation was bright as they filled their plates, but grew more desultory as the actual feasting began, until the innkeeper spoke up.

"The snow's stopped. Hasn't snowed all day."

"I thought that it seemed brighter," his wife remarked, "but I was so busy, I paid little heed."

David had noticed. There was still a huge amount of snow on the ground, but the storm that had locked them in seemed to have passed. It was a matter of time before the roads would be open.

"We'll be going to Donnington Hall," Eugenia mused. "What is it like, Uncle David?"

"Big," he told her.

Stephanie stared at her plate and laid down her fork.

"It must be very grand," Lady Blythe enthused. "I bought a guidebook before traveling north. It was listed as a home of architectural superiority, with outstanding gardens."

"Yes." David smiled. "We have many travelers stop to see it."

"How many rooms?" asked George.

"I truly don't know that anyone's counted." His wealth, his possessions, suddenly seemed embarrassing. He closely watched Stephanie. She was growing pale.

"I would like to see it sometime," Lady Blythe said.

"Of course, madam. You, and everyone here, will always be welcome. I hope you will come as often as possible."

Stephanie seemed to recover, lifting her chin. "Oh, you will probably forget all about us, my lord."

"No, Miss Blythe, I assure you I will not," he said earnestly.

"I won't," declared Eugenia. "I'll never forget you, because you're going to give me Fluffy for a Christmas present. You are, aren't you? You're going to surprise me!"

David's heart felt like a chunk of lead.

"We've been over this ground before, Lady Eugenia," Stephanie warned wearily.

"That is right," David seconded. "Miss Blythe has promised you one of Fluffy's kittens, or all of them if you wish. Now there's an end to it!"

"I want Fluffy!" his niece screamed.

Lady Blythe covered her ears with her hands. "Be still, child! It's Christmas Eve."

"Lady or not, needs a whoopin'," George muttered.

David rose. "You're going to your room. We have had enough of this."

"I want Fluffy!" she shrilled. "I want old Sarum! I want them both so they can have kittens!"

The marquess lifted her from her seat and dragged her toward the door. In a flurry of anger, she kicked him in the shin. As quickly as Stephanie had done, he tapped her bottom.

Eugenia burst into wild tears. "I want my mother! I want my papa! But they're dead!"

Stephanie rushed to his side. "Allow me to take her."

Before he could blink, Stephanie and Eugenia were out the door. David stared after them, then turned to the open-mouthed diners. "I do apologize. . . ."

Lady Blythe waved a hand of dismissal. "It's finally come out."

"My lord, did she ever cry for her parents?" Caroline asked.

"No, not to my knowledge. Everyone thought it was rather strange. . . ."

"She's kept it bottled up, then." Lady Blythe sighed. "Let us hope that this clears the air for all time and that Eugenia will begin to start a new and happy life, without tantrums and negative thinking."

"It will certainly be a start," her sister agreed.

Stephanie did not return to the salon for a very long time. When she did, she merely stood in the doorway. "All is well now. We talked for a long time, and she has begun to come to grips with her unresolved grief. She is sleeping. With Fluffy. I'm sure she will sleep through till tomorrow. She exhausted herself."

Stephanie, too, looked very weary, but David wished she would stay a bit. And that the others would retire, so he could talk with her in private. "May I fetch you a glass of wine, Miss Blythe?"

"No, thank you, Lord Donnington. Please excuse me. I must seek my own bed." She smiled weakly. "Good night."

The others responded with understanding.

"Wait!" David hurried across the room to her.

"Yes, my lord?" The green eyes were dull with supreme tiredness.

He didn't have the heart to detain her. And the question he wanted to ask couldn't be spoken with others looking on. He would have to wait until tomorrow.

"I wish to thank you," he substituted. "I imagine you handled the matter much better than I would have."

"Oh, I doubt that, my lord." She swayed a little.

"Shall I assist you upstairs?" he asked hopefully.

"I shall be fine."

"If you're certain." He watched her walk down the hall and up the stairway, before returning to her relatives. Hopefully, tomorrow would be the day. If he could see her alone, which was sometimes quite difficult.

* * *

Christmas Day dawned. Stephanie was awakened by frantic pounding on the door. Worried out of her wits, she leaped from the bed, flung on her dressing robe, and ran to answer the summons.

"Miss Stephanie! Miss Stephanie! Come look!" Eugenia shrieked, grabbing her hand and pulling her down the hall.

"What is it?"

"Kittens!" the little girl shouted. "When I awakened, there were kittens all over! I think there are six, Miss Stephanie!"

Lord Donnington, clad in his dressing robe, burst from his room into the hall. "What is it? What's happening?"

"I am not dressed!" Stephanie cried.

"It doesn't matter! Come! It's only Uncle David!" Eugenia shrilled.

"It does matter!" she protested. "It is the height of impropriety."

"So might be kissing in the attic!"

"You saw that?" Stephanie gasped.

"Oh, yes, and everyone knows. Come look on my bed."

She stumbled forward. Surely enough, Fluffy and six newborn kittens lay comfortably at the foot. The cat looked at her mistress and blinked her big eyes, almost smiling with pride.

"They seem to be doing fine," said Eugenia, "but there is one thing wrong. The kittens' eyes are all closed. Maybe they were born too soon."

"Kittens, and some other animals, are born with their eyes closed," David informed over her shoulder.

Stephanie startled. She looked first at him and then toward the door, praying no one would spy them. "I must dress!"

Fleeing down the empty hall, she dived into her chamber. Oh, how lucky she was! No one else had heard the consternation, thus there were no witnesses. There was only David, and he certainly wouldn't tattle. He'd be compromised if he did. Being caught kissing was nothing compared to this, even if everyone had heard about it, as the little girl claimed. She didn't know whether to believe that or not. If her mother knew, surely she wouldn't have remained silent, unless Lady Blythe was finally giving her a chance to use her own judgment. Shrugging lightly in wonderment, she dressed in a festive red woolen gown and returned to Eugenia's room. David was gone, and the child was sitting by the new mother and kittens, watching intently.

"They're so cute." Eugenia smiled.

"They are," she agreed. "All babies are darling."

"Will you have a baby someday, Miss Stephanie?"

She felt her cheeks warm. "Well, I may, Lady Eugenia. But I'll have to find a husband first."

"I want you to marry Uncle David. It would be nice if we lived all together. Then you could have a baby. Would you like that?"

"I have always wanted children," Stephanie replied evasively. "Let us go down to the kitchen now. I will begin breakfast, and I'll warm a bowl of milk for you to bring to Fluffy."

"I want to help!" Eugenia enthused, then pulled a wry smile. "But I am not dressed."

"You are a child. I believe we can make an exception, just for a short time."

"Good!" She clutched Stephanie's hand. "I feel so happy today. Do you realize I've had my first Christmas gift. The kittens are a gift from you."

Thank goodness they came, Stephanie thought. She had nothing for the little girl, nor her uncle, but presents from them were waiting for her. She couldn't shop, and there'd been no time to make anything.

It was so early that they were the only ones in the kitchen. She set about warming the milk, while the child petted old Sarum. When the liquid was lukewarm, she filled a dish for the tomcat and handed a bowl to Eugenia.

"Should I carry that up?" David appeared, framed in the doorway.

"I can do it," his niece announced confidently.

"Be very careful," Stephanie advised, "and don't forget your own breakfast."

"We have to open gifts first!" Eugenia called from the hall.

She moved to lift the coffeepot, but David caught her wrist.

"I want you to open your gift from me."

"But . . ."

"Don't avoid me, Stephanie." He tucked her hand through his arm and escorted her to the salon. "Merry Christmas, my dear, from me."

She looked at the flat package. A handkerchief, probably, meant for one of his relatives. David was lucky to have some items on hand.

"Thank you, my lord, but . . ."

"No 'buts.' And what happened to 'David'?"

"David." She smiled shyly, removed the wrapping, and opened the box. On a bed of black velvet lay a sparkling diamond necklace. Stephanie stared in shock.

"Do you like it?" he prompted.

"It is the most beautiful thing I've ever seen." Regretfully, she closed the lid. "But you know, of course, that it is too intimate and far too costly for me to accept."

"Perhaps I am doing things backward." Taking her hand, he dropped to his knee. "Marry me, Stephanie. Make me the happiest man on earth."

She was speechless.

He kissed the top of her hand, then turned it over and kissed the palm of it, too. "I am a wealthy man. You shall never want for anything, my love, nor any of your family or servants."

"But . . . do you love me, David?" she managed to whisper.

"With all my heart." He straightened and placed her hand on his chest. "Do you feel it beating for you?"

Stephanie smiled. His heart was thrumming as hard as hers. "Love is the most important thing, not wealth nor title. And I do love you!" Spontaneously, she threw her arms around his neck. "Yes, I will marry you. Yes, yes, yes!"

"My darling!" He gathered her close and kissed her long and deeply, with all his love and happiness poured into his lips.

Stephanie kissed him back, heart bursting with love. Her dream had come true. And she never thought it would be like this.

They separated, heaving for air. David laughed. "Now you can accept my gift."

She nodded eagerly. Her neck fairly burned as he placed it on her. "Does it look pretty?"

"Beautiful. But not so lovely as you." He drew her back against him, kissing the top of her head. "I did not think it possible to love someone so much."

"Nor did I." She suddenly remembered, and whirled about in his arms. "Oh, David, I have nothing for you."

"You've given me the best gift of all . . . yourself."

She touched his cheek. "Do you really feel that way?"

"Sweet darling, of course I do." He started to draw her closer, as the scent of brewing coffee floated into the room.

Stephanie stiffened. "Breakfast! I must . . ."

"No, you must not. You will remain right here with me until we make our announcement."

"But . . ."

"No 'buts' ever again, my darling." He covered her mouth with his, silencing her protest and making her legs so weak they could scarcely hold her up.

In the hall, Eugenia giggled. Very well! Now she would have all the cats and Stephanie, too. She would make sure Stephanie's aunt and uncle gave the couple old Sarum for a wedding present. They would like that very much.

Things were going to be all right. With a happy skip, she trotted down the hall to tell Betsy, then up the stairs to tell everyone else. She had such important announcements . . . the kittens *and* the betrothal. Eugenia couldn't decide just which was the greatest one.

CHRISTMAS JOY

Wilma Counts

One

Justin Wingate heaved a sigh and ran a hand over his face to rest his chin in his palm. Across from him, in his London drawing room, a concerned look on her face, sat his sister-in-law, the Marchioness of Everleigh. "I am willing to try anything, Irene. Anything."

"What did the doctor say?"

"They. There have been several here to examine her. She responds to instructions so long as they do not require speech. The doctors see no reason for her not to talk—and it has been a year now."

"Children often absorb things within themselves. She was only—what, three-and-a-half years old?—when her mother died." Irene looked thoughtful. "In the convoluted way children sometimes view events, Joy may blame herself for her mother's death."

"You think a child having fewer than five years understands death?" Justin's tone was merely curious.

"They understand far more than most adults surmise. She may not *fully* realize what happened, but she knows her mama has gone away and will not return."

"Yes, I have told her as much. And I have told her her mama is in a pleasant place now with no more pain."

"But all Joy knows is that her mother is gone, and she misses her. And she may think *she* did something to cause that."

"How did you get to be such a perceptive lady?" His

tone was teasing, but admiring. "Who would have thought
when my brother was courting the Season's Incomparable—
lo! these many years ago!—that pretty Irene Hamlin would
turn into such a fountain of wisdom?"

She laughed. "I swear, Justin, if you start *counting* the
years, I shall box your ears. But surely having produced
five children of my own qualifies me a bit."

"More than a bit. But back to my problem. What am I
to do? I have heard of a doctor in Switzerland . . ."

"Before you go haring off to the Continent for Lord
knows how long, let us try exposing her to my wild hellions
for more than the usual short visit. We shall put Joy in the
bedchamber shared by my girls and just let all the children
play freely much of the time. But mind, Justin, it may take
a while."

"I could not simply desert her for any period of time."
Justin knew very well that neither he nor Joy could bear
such a parting. Joy might not talk, but those little arms
wound around her papa's neck at bedtime bespoke volumes.

"Of course not! I am suggesting you both come to our
winter house party at Everleigh. Most of the guests will not
arrive until after the first week of December, but several
are coming earlier. So you come then, too."

"It may have escaped your notice, *my lady,* but those of
us who did not inherit great titles must work for a living."

"Oh, fiddle-dee-dee. Everleigh is only two days' ride
from London—in a comfortable coach. Less than that if
need be. I seriously doubt there is much that you cannot
handle from the country. And there *are* such things as the
mail—and couriers—you know."

He threw up his hands in mock defeat. "Very well. We
shall come in November."

"And stay till Parliament opens and we must return to
the city?"

"If you do not tire of us before then."

"Should we tire of you, we could just shut you up in
the North Tower—you, not Joy—with our resident ghost."

"It would not work. She appears only to children. Besides which, I thought she had not made an appearance in years," he said.

"Nor has she. Not really. Though every once in a while we find books or toys or things on a dresser have been rearranged. The third marchioness of Everleigh must have been a most fastidious housekeeper—unlike her latest successor!"

"Ah, but very like the latest to fill that role, she loved children."

"Yes." She paused. "But I think it will be other children—not the spectral Lady Aetherada—who might affect a change in your daughter."

"I hope so."

Irene had called at his request to discuss, once again, what he might do to help his little girl to a more normal existence. She now stood, gathered up her gloves, and prepared to leave. She settled her bonnet on her carefully coiffed blond hair and gave him a long look. "Two more things, dear brother."

"What might those be?"

"You must not expect a miracle. Joy may not respond to other children any more than she has to all your other remedies. It is *possible* that she will—given enough time. We shall have to leave it in God's hands."

"I know." He grinned. "And God knows very well that patience is not exactly one of my virtues."

She chuckled as she drew on her kidskin gloves. "No, I would not say it is." She paused a moment, then said, "You know, you might think about providing Joy a new mama."

His answer was guarded. "I *have* considered that possibility. . . ."

Her brows lifted in surprise. "Have you now? Well, there will be some very eligible females at our house party."

"Whom you just happened to have on your guest list, eh? You are too transparent by half, my dear."

"I have found," she said in the tone of one making a profound announcement, "that people—especially you infernal men—often need to be nudged in the right direction."

"Well, just see you do not nudge too forcefully. Mind you, I am not averse to remarrying, but neither am I in any great hurry to do so."

"Oh, very well." She showed mild impatience as they moved toward the door. He opened it for her and was about to bid her farewell when she turned back. "One more thing, Justin. Meghan Kenwick will be among our houseguests."

"Will she now?" He tried for a neutral tone. "Is she aware that I have been invited, too?"

"I told her you would probably be there for at least part of the time. After all, even when Belinda was alive, you always came to us for Christmas."

"Well, if Mrs. Kenwick can bear up, I suppose I can."

Irene's brown eyes twinkled. "You know? Meghan said almost exactly the same thing!"

In another part of London, the subject of this discourse sat in her own drawing room and voiced second thoughts about accepting the invitation to the house party at Everleigh.

"Why did I not just tell Irene I had made other plans?" Meghan asked.

Her cousin Eleanor laughed. "Perhaps because you know very well she would see right through such a lie."

"She would at that. She was a full two years ahead of me in school, but even then she always seemed in tune with what others thought or felt."

"Still, if you do not want to go to Everleigh, I am quite sure you may join me in Kent. My sister would welcome you most effusively."

"It is not that I do not *want* to go. I do. Truly, I do."

"Well, then . . . ?"

"I am not sure I can deal with Irene's children. Her twins are eight—the same age Stephen would have been."

Setting aside the embroidery she had been working on and tucking away a wisp of soft gray hair, Eleanor gave

Meghan a penetrating look. "Perhaps the children are just what you need. It has been well over a year since Stephen and his father died in that accident. Do you not think it time—beyond time—you rejoined the world of the living?"

"Well, yes . . ." Meghan, accustomed as she was to her cousin's plain speaking, did not take offense. "And I *have* begun to go about. I put off my mourning clothes several weeks ago—much to the dismay of Lady Kenwick."

"Your mother-in-law would find something to disapprove of if you had worn black for a decade—or—or joined a convent!"

Meghan smiled. "I suppose you are right."

"This party is the perfect setting for your return to society. The marchioness will have invited people that you know. You should have a wonderful time."

"Umm . . . maybe."

Eleanor ignored her hesitation. "Besides, you may meet a fine gentleman at such a gathering."

"Oh, Nell, not you, too," Meghan wailed softly.

"Not me, too—what?"

"Why is everyone bent on seeing me rewed? Even my brother Richard sends letters from Canada extolling the merits of such a step. I am sure Richard put that amiable captain—you know the one—up to calling on me."

"Captain Hillary, you mean? Well, and what of it? Your brother is simply trying to look out for your interests."

"*I* have no interest in marrying again—ever," Meghan said tartly.

"Surely you do not mean that."

"I do mean it, Nell. Truly, I do."

"But . . . you are so young. . . ."

Meghan smiled. "At nine-and-twenty, I would hardly be considered a treasure on the marriage mart, even were I inclined to offer myself there. However, I am not so inclined." Lord, no, she was not so inclined, Meghan thought, remembering vividly the pain associated with her marriage.

"But, but," Eleanor repeated, "what else is there for a

woman in our society? Young widows are subjected to such gossip. . . ." Her voice trailed off.

"People may gossip as they please. I doubt they will find anything of substance to condemn in my rather dull affairs. Besides"—Meghan smiled at her companion—"I have you—and luckily, I am not one of those unfortunate females who *must* marry."

"What shall you do? I always assumed once you were out of mourning—"

"Do? Why, what I do now. My work with the historical society, an occasional social outing, and maybe some traveling. I would dearly love to go to Rome!"

"Oh, Meghan, you cannot just shut yourself away with old Celtic and Roman artifacts."

Meghan laughed outright at the despair in her companion's tone. "Why not? I *enjoy* my work. And with a name like 'Meghan Minerva,' who better to deal with Celts and Romans?"

"What was your father thinking when he saddled a tiny baby with such a name?"

"Well . . ." Meghan pretended to give the matter weighty consideration. "Perhaps it was his love for his Welsh mother and his love of antique Rome?"

"Be that as it may . . ." Eleanor waved her hand dismissively, picked up her embroidery again, and returned to her original train of thought. "I still say there is sure to be an interesting group of people assembled at that house party, and you should not think twice about accepting Lady Everleigh's invitation."

"I *have* accepted it. But—"

"But what?"

"I think I told you Justin Wingate will be there, too."

"So? What has that to do with your decision to go?"

Meghan shrugged, feeling somewhat sheepish. "I am a bit embarrassed about seeing him again. I mean, after all, I very nearly accused him of *causing* the accident."

"Yes, so you told me. However, Lord Justin is a gentleman, and he surely understood you were overset at the time.

Besides, he must have been occupied with his own problems very soon afterward."

"His wife's illness, you mean?" Meghan recalled that Wingate had lost his wife scarcely six months after the boating accident that claimed her husband and son.

"Yes. So tragic that was."

"The fact remains, I behaved irrationally and I shall probably have to apologize to him."

She remembered the scene very well.

And that her animosity toward Lord Justin had its roots in events beyond the boating accident. . . .

Meghan Minerva Godwin had been luckier than many another daughter of a country vicar. Her maternal grandfather being the Earl of Falmouth had ensured her a place in society, but her upbringing had not prepared her to be swept off her feet by the handsome, charming Burton Kenwick. Caught up in the wonder of her first love, Meghan had simply ignored the possibility that one of the things Kenwick—heir to a mere baronetage—found attractive about her was her grandfather's title.

The marriage had been happy enough the first year or so. Kenwick was attentive and thoughtful and took genuine delight in his new wife—and she in him. Burton seemed to have little in common with her friends and he thoroughly disapproved of any of her male friends. Gradually, she lost contact with many people she had once enjoyed.

The biggest disappointment in their first years was their failure to have a child. There had been a miscarriage before Stephen. Kenwick had not said anything, but she sensed his blaming her, and certainly his mother had made no secret of where *she* ascribed the blame.

Then Stephen had arrived. At first—other than taking pride in proof of his virility—Burton had ignored the child. But once the baby became a little boy, he began to command his father's interest. After a terrible fall, Stephen showed little enthusiasm for riding, and even less for killing animals on a hunt. Burton accused her of making a mama's boy of his son. In that last year, Burton had insisted that the boy accompany him on strictly male outings. The boating expedition had been yet another attempt to "make a man" of the boy who had then been scarcely seven years old.

Wedded bliss had begun to sour after the failure of the first pregnancy. But in the way of many a *ton* marriage, they had muddled along. She remembered clearly the day she knew for sure her husband's interest in other women went beyond idle flirtations at every social event. At a ball a few months after her son's birth, she became tired of Burton's displays—and the inquisitive looks cast her way for a reaction. She had retreated to a secluded area of the room set aside as the ladies' withdrawing room—an L-shaped chamber—when two women came into the other section.

"Poor Meghan." Meghan recognized the insincere tones of Lady Ardith Ponsonby, who had been given to gossip even as a schoolgirl.

As soon as the other woman responded, Meghan identified Susan Buckley, once a rival for Kenwick's attentions. "True. You know, I saw that fault in Kenwick early on. I wasted little time in discouraging his suit to *me.*"

Feeling trapped, Meghan gritted her teeth. She knew very well that Susan had rather shamelessly chased the then bachelor Kenwick for an entire Season—right up until the announcement of his engagement.

Apparently Lady Ponsonby knew it, too. "Well, it hardly matters *when* you made such a discovery. Kenwick's affair with *la belle* Beatrice is beginning to raise eyebrows."

"I fail to see why. There have been any number of others whose beds he has shared since the honeymoon was over— for him, if not for Meghan," Susan said.

"But most of those were light skirts from the Covent Garden. *La belle* has a jealous husband."

"Ah, well . . . *That* could prove interesting."

There was the sound of rustling skirts and some more small talk. Meghan was so mortified she just sank further into the elegant chair she occupied and hoped they would not come into her part of the room. To her relief, they did not, but she was left shaken. She knew it was true. All the signs were there, had she admitted to them. Her husband's long absences, his evasiveness, the occasional trace of perfume on his clothing.

His usual—and quite often truthful—explanation for his absences from home were that he was engaged in some sort of sporting or gaming activity with his male friends. Most prominent among these was the powerful, influential Justin Wingate. Meghan knew her husband suffered a profound case of hero worship mixed with envy regarding Wingate. But, truth to tell, Wingate seemed to encourage it, for Burton was forever responding to this or that invitation from Wingate or a Wingate crony. A racing meet. A few days at the Wingate family's hunting box. An evening of cards at the club. And—later—a boating trip.

Hurt and embarrassed by her predicament, Meghan had nevertheless made a determined effort in the weeks after that ball to restore some stability and happiness to her marriage. However, Burton refused to discuss unresolved issues. Indeed, as far as he was concerned, there were no issues to be resolved. The existence of a mistress was not something a gentleman discussed with a wife. And, no, he was not interested in their engaging in more activities together. Furthermore, he insisted she stop associating with that ridiculous historical society. People were beginning to think he—sportsman extraordinaire—was married to some sort of bluestocking.

In the interest of preserving peace, she gave up her active support of the museum, just as she had earlier given up friends of whom Burton disapproved. Meanwhile, as her world narrowed more and more, he went about his affairs as usual.

The once-spirited Meghan Godwin had a heart-to-heart talk with the mousy, fearful Mrs. Kenwick she had become. She insisted that that pattern-card of wifely virtue confront her husband again about the state of affairs between them. He responded with impatient anger. They had what he viewed as a perfectly adequate marriage and she should accept it as such.

In the end, she had done so—for what choice had she? The law clearly gave men the upper hand in such matters, and she could not bear the thought of losing her son. She tried to keep herself occupied, and, of course, she doted on the child. She often sat in on his lessons and dreaded the day he would be sent away to school. She shared Stephen's pleasure in new discoveries. He was a total delight—eager to learn, with a teasing sense of humor. He loved both his parents and she sought to reinforce that love. So she had not objected overmuch to the boating trip.

When Wingate's sailboat encountered bad weather, both her husband and her son drowned. In her initial grief she had sought something or someone to blame for her losses. She had been rather distant when Lord Justin, along with his wife, Belinda, and his sister-in-law, Irene, called to extend their condolences.

"I simply do not understand how it happened that Kenwick and my son were the only ones lost," she had said. "Was there no way to rescue them?" She had asked this question of others, but grief prompted her ask it yet again.

"We tried," he said. "That is, Travers and Layton tried. I think Travers must have told you I was knocked unconscious when the boom swung about. I deeply regret that, madam."

"The boat was safe, was it not?" It was a challenge as much as a question. "Surely you did not knowingly invite guests onto an unsafe vessel?"

"Please, Meghan," Irene had said, "it was an accident—and in a sudden storm at that. You cannot hold Justin responsible."

"No, I suppose not, but it *was* his boat. And"—her voice caught on a barely suppressed sob—"and my son is dead. My little boy is gone!"

They had all been standing through this discussion. Belinda plucked at her husband's sleeve. "I think we should be going."

"Perhaps you are right, my dear." He bowed stiffly to Meghan. "I am very sorry for your loss, madam." He and his wife left the room.

Irene said to them, "I shall be with you in a moment." She turned to Meghan and simply opened her arms and Meghan found herself dissolving into tears yet again—this time on Irene's shoulder.

"S-Stephen was my *life*. I do not know how I am to go on without him."

"There, there, love." Irene held her tightly and there were tears in her own eyes and in her voice. "This is so very hard for you, but you must try to pull yourself together."

And she had tried.

Lord knew how she had tried. For weeks she had gone through life like one mesmerized. She would spend hours in Stephen's room, smelling his clothing, fingering his toys, trying to feel his presence. Yes, she mourned Burton's death, too, but it was Stephen for whom her heart longed and her arms ached.

After a few weeks of this, she had taken herself to task, invited the spinster cousin Eleanor to become her companion, and tried to devote herself to "improving societies" and other charity groups. She carefully avoided those involving children.

She missed Stephen achingly, missed being a mother, for that had given her life its meaning in those last years. She also missed being a wife, though the pain of her husband's infidelities and her own isolation tempered those memories. Her anger and grief there focused largely on "what might have been." She had managed to accept Burton's character, finally, by recognizing that he was not so much a "bad" person as just a weak man with little sense of honor. Still, he had been a presence in her life for nearly a decade. . . .

So, Lord Justin would attend the Everleigh house party. She no longer actually blamed him for what had happened. The fact remained, though, that had Wingate not enticed Burton off to this or that outing, he might have stayed home more. How many times had she heard "Justin says this . . ." or "Justin has invited me . . ." or "Justin is planning . . ."? She had almost come to view Wingate as yet another rival for her husband's affections.

She had, of course, met the Wingates at various *ton* soirees. Meghan knew Belinda was very aware of her social consequence. After all, she was related to a marquis. Belinda's husband appeared—paradoxically—to be both more aloof and more easygoing than his wife. Meghan thought they were rather mismatched and voiced this view to her own husband.

Burton had merely shrugged. "Not much of a secret there. They were promised in their cradles, more or less. She was a Hamlin, too. Wingates always seem to marry Hamlins."

"But the marquis and Irene were a love match. I know they were."

"Perhaps they were." Burton's bored tone seemed to question why anyone would care.

Privately, Meghan continued to wonder about the other couple from time to time. Belinda—tall, blonde, and self-assured—often appeared in public accompanied by someone other than her husband—a cousin or sister or another family member. But then so did many *ton* wives. And, judging by the amount of time Burton spent with his friend, Meghan assumed Wingate was often away from home. Belinda and Justin, then, seemed to have a marriage not unlike her own.

Moreover, Lord Justin had appeared to revel in the company of other women just as Burton had. Women found both men attractive. Kenwick's blond good looks and air of superiority had naive women flocking to him. Wingate's tall, lithe physique, dark brown hair, deep blue eyes, and a generally friendly demeanor made him a *ton* favorite.

When Belinda died, Meghan had sent a very formal note of condolence to the widower to which she had received an equally formal thank-you note.

Two

Joy lay sprawled across her father's lap as their coach bounced along. She had been asleep for the better part of an hour. Justin caressed her golden curls, twining one of them around his finger. This child had been a marvel to him from the moment she was born. Her first coherent word had been "Papa." It had not taken her long to start stringing two, then three and more words together. At first only he and the nurse—and often Belinda—had been able to understand her babble. She was soon speaking clearly and asking dozens of questions, most frequently "Why?" He had loved listening to her at play with her dolls as she carried on imaginary conversations.

It has been such a long time, he mused. "I surely hope your Aunt Irene is right about this," he said softly to the sleeping form.

Joy's eyes had glowed with pleasure when he told her of the proposed visit. They had been in the nursery and she went immediately to pick up her favorite doll, clearly asking if she could take it along.

"Of course you may bring Penelope," he had said. When she then picked up three more dolls, he had laughed and said, "No, poppet. Only one. Sarah and Becky have a closet full of dolls you may play with."

She had readily accepted this, though she had to have her "blanket"—a scrap of an old blue blanket that had been given to her for her doll's bed, but which Joy carried around as a constant attachment to her person. Even now she hugged it in her sleep. Persuading her to give it up for an occasional washing usually involved diversionary tactics like a ride in the park with her beloved papa.

Justin sighed. "Why, little one? Why do you refuse to speak?" He had asked the question hundreds of times.

He knew the surface answer.

Belinda, ordinarily a patient and loving mother, had been cranky and out of sorts intermittently for months before her death. She complained of terrible headaches. When they were upon her, she demanded total darkness and absolute quiet. She had once asked him to silence two maids who were giggling in the hallway as "their noise was killing her." He knew a little girl's chatter had probably been most unwelcome to the suffering woman. Had she said something similar to Joy?

Doctors called in to examine Belinda surmised that she suffered some sort of growth that put pressure on her brain. In any event, her pain seemed to intensify and there was little anyone could do to alleviate it. She began to take larger and larger doses of laudanum to combat the agony.

The medication seemed to help, though it often left her in a state of unconsciousness. In their concern for the mother, few noticed that, as Belinda spent more and more time in a drug-induced stupor, her daughter had begun to withdraw. Finally, Belinda had taken an unusually large dose of the medication and had simply never awakened.

Joy, arriving in her mother's chamber for their customary time together and prattling happily as she went through the door, had been the one to discover Belinda just lying there. She seemed instinctively to sense that something was terribly wrong. Servants had discovered her screaming "Mama! Mama!"

When she understood that her mama had gone away and would not come back, she had simply quit talking. Period. She no longer babbled to her dolls. Those incessant questions were silenced. Nor did she often smile.

"If only I knew what to do," Justin murmured. Never in his life had he felt so helpless.

He deliberately turned his mind to Everleigh's house party. He looked forward to renewing some old friendships. Even with Meghan Kenwick? he twitted himself. Well, maybe not Mrs. Kenwick—especially if she were still inclined to blame him for her losses.

Justin did not know her well, though he remembered dancing with her once or twice at a ball. He had liked the feel of her in his arms and her conversation in a social setting had been pleasant enough. It was a shame such an attractive woman was possessed of such a negative character. She was not an accredited beauty in the classic manner, but there was something very appealing about the petite Mrs. Kenwick. She had dark brown hair and her clear gray eyes bespoke intelligence. A rare smile transformed her appearance to a dazzling degree.

She apparently had little patience with fools. Yet she had chosen to marry one. Well, maybe not a fool, precisely, but certainly a fellow with few ideas of his own and little initiative, albeit he was an agreeable fellow. Perhaps she was just one of those controlling females who liked to run things *her* way. Kenwick had complained often enough of his wife's demands. Justin had not approved of the man's publicly airing grievances against his wife. However, hints to divert him had proved ineffective.

Mrs. Kenwick, according to her husband, was never satisfied. She belittled him, ignored him, and disapproved of his decisions regarding their son. She was, Kenwick said, always pressing him to read some treatise on chimney sweeps or some such, or attend this or that political or literary meeting. Kenwick lamented the fact that the social debutante he had married had "turned into something of a bluestocking."

With a wife so indifferent to her husband's interests, perhaps it was understandable that a man like Kenwick had sought comfort elsewhere.

* * *

Bitter cold had arrived by the time Meghan journeyed to Everleigh. When she had to break a thin sheeting of ice in the water pitcher in her room at an inn, she was thankful to have only one overnight en route. Wrapped in a hooded cloak lined with white fur, she stepped out of the inn door. The air was crisp and she noticed that everyone's speech was punctuated with misty puffs.

" 'Tis dreadful cold, ma'am." Her coachman stood back as a footman handed her and her maid into the vehicle. "We reheated the bricks, though, so it should be warm fer ye and Betsy here."

Sure enough, as the carriage door opened, she felt the warmth emanating from the bricks on the straw-covered floor.

"Thank you, Mr. Hawkins," she said.

"Leastwise, the cold will make our going easier," the talkative coachman observed. "Mud is the worst thing for slowing us. Won't have that till midday at earliest. Should practically be there by then."

"Good. You and Tony be sure to wrap yourselves tightly."

The journey itself was uneventful and the day too dreary to afford much enjoyment from passing scenery. Betsy dozed in the opposite seat and Meghan was alone with her thoughts and memories. Recalling Eleanor's comment about meeting an amiable gentleman, Meghan snorted quietly. If Eleanor only knew. . . .

Burton Kenwick had been the very epitome of "an amiable gentleman" as he courted her. She could do nothing wrong. She was a goddess to be treasured. Once she was his, however, she lost her value. Only now was she beginning to understand the extent to which she had lost herself in trying to please a man who could not be pleased.

Her friends were the wrong people. Her taste in dress was abominable. Her interests were trivial, her opinions unimportant. The more she tried to please, the more he found to criticize. No wonder sweet, accepting Stephen had become the focus of her life! How she missed him. Would that pain *ever* go away? It had been well over a year now.

As for her husband—yes, she had experienced sincere and wrenching sorrow at his death. But within a few weeks she also began to experience a growing sense of freedom— then guilt for feeling it. The guilt was followed by anger. She was angry at what Burton had done to her; she was angry that he had escaped unaware; she was angry at herself. Gradually, the anger turned to resolve.

Never again would she put herself in a position to suffer such pain. One could enjoy life and other people without allowing them opportunity to inflict pain, and she fully intended to do just that.

By the time they arrived at Everleigh in the late afternoon, the bricks had long since lost their warmth. Meghan had but to look at Betsy's reddened cheeks and nose to know how her own appeared.

Another coach drew up at Everleigh's entrance just ahead of her own. Three fashionably dressed people—two ladies and a gentleman—descended from it as Meghan was handed from her own carriage. The entranceway of the stately mansion was a beehive of activity as the arriving guests were greeted by the marquis, his wife, and his brother with handshakes, hugs, and air kisses as appropriate.

"Oh, Lord Justin, how very glad I am to see you," one of the two other female arrivals trilled, throwing back her hood. She was young—nineteen or twenty, Meghan surmised—with honey-blond, almost red hair, amber-colored eyes fringed with dark lashes, and a porcelain complexion unsullied by the cold. Meghan felt a veritable frump next to this beauty.

"Miss Hamlin." Justin acknowledged her and greeted the couple with her, who were obviously her parents.

Meghan held back slightly, then felt herself enclosed in a warm hug from Irene. "I am *so* glad you came," Irene said. "I had visions of your crying off at the last minute."

Meghan laughed. "What? And endure your censure? Oh, I think not."

Irene kept her arm around Meghan's waist as she quickly introduced her aunt and uncle, Lord and Lady Hamlin, and her cousin Georgiana. "And of course you know Justin," she finished.

"Yes. My lord." She extended her hand to him and looked into his eyes just as she had with Lord Hamlin and Robert Wingate, Marquis of Everleigh. However, with neither of the other men had she felt the tremor of excitement that ran through her body at Lord Justin's touch. She dismissed it instantly as the result of previous nervousness. Averting her gaze from his, she caught a speculative look from Miss Hamlin.

Irene gestured to an older woman who had hovered in the background. "Mrs. Ferris, our housekeeper, will show you to your rooms. You may all have a rest before the evening meal. Should you need anything, Mrs. Ferris will be happy to supply it." The housekeeper smiled and dipped a quick curtsy as Irene went on. "Come, Robert and Justin, on to the nursery. Our children await."

"Oh! May I join you?" Miss Hamlin asked. "I should love to see the children—especially darling Joy. Such a sweet child." She gave the sweet child's father a meaningful look.

"Of course. All of you are welcome." Irene gestured invitingly.

"Later, please," Meghan said. "I need to remove the road grime first."

"You young people go ahead." Lady Hamlin waved them on. Her daughter, who was quickly relieved of her cloak, fell into step with Justin Wingate as the foursome left the remaining three guests to Mrs. Ferris.

Meghan smiled ruefully at being relegated to the oldsters, but she was glad to put off facing the children just yet. She chatted amiably with Mrs. Ferris, whom she knew from previous visits. In her own room, she removed her traveling dress and washed up. Then, carefully setting a miniature of her son on the bedside table, she lay down for a few moments as Betsy disappeared with the gown she would wear later.

Well, that did not go too badly, she congratulated herself. She would still have to apologize to Lord Justin, but at least he had been cordial. To her surprise, she actually fell asleep, for suddenly Betsy was shaking her shoulder with the news that the dressing bell had sounded.

Her gown was a deep blue that intensified the blue cast to her gray eyes. The square neckline was modestly cut, revealing only a hint of rounded bosom. Betsy arranged her hair in a simple but rather severe style—one altogether fitting for a widow who intended to remain so, Meghan thought, pinning up an errant curl.

Entering the drawing room, she discovered that yet more guests had arrived in the afternoon, swelling the number to more than a dozen. Meghan's attention strayed to Lord Justin Wingate. The Hamlin mother and daughter hovered near him and seemed perfectly at ease with him, for Georgiana's trill of laughter rang out often. Meghan was not surprised when the beauty turned out to be his dinner partner, but she was surprised to find that she herself experienced a twinge of envy at this.

Later, when the ladies withdrew, Meghan had a moment of relative privacy in which to ask Irene, "Are you up to your old tricks, my friend?"

Irene spoke in mock umbrage. "I beg your pardon? Whatever do you mean?"

"Are you trying to promote a match between your husband's brother and your cousin?"

"N-not precisely. Why do you ask?"

"No reason. She is a lovely girl and I was once told that Wingates usually chose Hamlins as spouses. And you *have* been known to play matchmaker." Meghan grinned as her friend gave her a telling look.

"Not always very successfully . . . But, to answer your question—yes and no."

Meghan rolled her eyes. "Oh, that certainly answers the question."

"It is true that Belinda was also my cousin—a different branch of the family from Georgiana's. And Justin liked being married, I think, but I am not sure his interests lie in *that* direction." Irene nodded toward Georgiana.

"And hers?" The question was out before Meghan thought.

"Oh, I think there is little doubt of *her* interests. He is, after all, a very prime item on the marriage mart."

"So you *are* playing matchmaker again!"

Irene shrugged. "What will be will be. I have invited a number of persons who are unattached—including you, my dear."

"Oh, no! You are whistling into the wind if you seek to practice your craft on me again!" It had come out more vehemently than Meghan intended.

Irene's eyes were full of concern. "Was it so very bad for you, then? I am so sorry, Meghan."

Meghan shrugged. "It was no better or worse than many another pairing in our circles." She paused. "But I will *not* go through it again."

And, she thought, certainly not with another rake. Justin Wingate and Burton Kenwick were, after all, birds of a feather.

And with that thought, Meghan's little tête-à-tête with Irene was interrupted as the gentlemen rejoined the ladies and tables were set for card games. Meghan found herself partnered by her host. She had always liked Robert, whose quiet solidity contrasted with his wife's energetic gaiety. Georgiana, of course, was partnered by Justin, though Meghan did not observe whether that was by his machination or hers. Perhaps Irene had arranged it, or the girl's mother. Anyway, why should it matter?

Altogether, it had been a pleasant evening, she thought later as she blew a kiss toward the miniature of her son and turned down her lamp. So what if she felt herself more an observer than a participant? Observers paid no dues in pain.

In his own chamber, Justin leaned on pillows pushed against the headboard of his bed and reviewed this third day of the visit. So far, so good. Joy seemed relaxed with the other children, though she remained on the sidelines of

heir noisy games. She had readily allowed Irene to hug
er, though *that* bit of progress had come only this morning.

When Miss Hamlin had offered her own arms, however,
oy had turned shy, hiding herself behind her papa.

"Come, darling," Miss Hamlin had coaxed, "I would
early love to hold you."

But Joy had demurred, clutching her blanket and snuggling even closer to her father, who patted her head and
aid, "Perhaps later, Miss Hamlin."

Miss Hamlin had shrugged and murmured, "Of course."

He had supposed—from her eagerness to accompany
hem to the nursery—that Miss Hamlin was well acquainted
with the other Wingate children. This did not seem to be
he case, for the younger ones had to be reminded of who
she was, and all of them greeted her in only the most formal
manner. She had made little effort to secure the affection
of the others once Joy had rejected her overtures.

He smiled to himself. Irene was clearly up to her old
ricks. Everleigh's marchioness was so happy in her own
union that she felt it some sort of divine duty to help others
to such marital felicity. Well, give Irene credit. She had
promoted his marriage to Belinda, urging the relationship
from a vague understanding between families to getting the
principals to the altar. And it had turned out well enough.
He was not averse to being married again—sometime.

To Miss Hamlin? Hmm. A possibility. She was a trifle
young for his usual tastes though she had been "out" for
a year or more. He remembered her as an angular stick of
a thing when he had first met her—what, six? no, seven
years ago. Now here she was—a decided beauty and clearly
encouraging.

And if that did not take, his dear sister-in-law had invited
other "eligibles" in Lady Helen Bly and Miss Dierdre
Thompson, both of whom were unexceptional females of
passing good looks. And Mrs. Kenwick?

No. Even Irene would not promote quite such an impossible pairing. His inclinations had never leaned toward
women of intellect. His urges were far more primal. And

the delectable and willing Miss Hamlin, who had made such
pretty overtures to his daughter, might suit very well after
all.

Meghan knew both friendship and courtesy dictated that
she look in on the Everleigh nursery. She also knew Irene
was not one of those *ton* mothers who left the rearing of
her children to nursemaid, governess, and tutor. The marchioness took an active role in her children's upbringing
and she was rightfully proud of the results. So it was that
after breakfast the next morning, Meghan asked to visit the
nursery.

"Are you sure?" Irene asked doubtfully. "You need not
feel obliged to admire my progeny. You will probably have
your fill of them before the holiday is over."

"Of course I am sure," Meghan lied, for she was not at
all sure, but it was something she needed to do.

The Everleigh nursery was actually a suite of rooms that
included a dressing room, a schoolroom, and a large playroom, as well as various bedchambers. They found ten-year-
old Jason and his sister of eight years, Sarah, in the
well-furnished schoolroom. Meghan noted a large slate-
board and a freestanding globe, as well as numerous books.
Jason greeted his mother's friend with a very grown-up bow
and Sarah executed a practiced curtsy. They had been working intently on a model of Lord Nelson's ship, the *Victory*
and were clearly anxious to get back to it.

Irene and Meghan moved on to the playroom, which
despite its bright colors and a profusion of toys for both
genders, seemed unusually quiet. The only sound was a single adult—male—voice. The marquis was reading a story
No, it was not the marquis seated on a thick carpet in the
middle of the floor, his back to the entrance. It was Justin
Wingate! Before him sat two little boys of eight and six
and on his crossed legs sat two little girls who were of an
age—between four and five. Meghan knew the little boys

were Wally and Matthew, the latter being Sarah's twin. The little girls might have been twins as well, but she knew one to be Irene's youngest, Rebecca, and the other must have been Justin's own daughter.

Wally and Matthew looked up as their mother and her friend entered the room. This drew Lord Justin's attention, cutting into his imitation of a fierce wild bear. He started to rise on seeing the women, but Irene put a hand on his shoulder.

"No, stay put, Justin. We merely came to say hello to the children. Matthew, you remember Stephen's mama, your Auntie Meg, do you not?" Irene beamed proudly as both boys stood to bow graciously. Meghan's heart wrenched as she recalled teaching Stephen such courtesies.

Irene then touched one little girl's curls. "This is Rebecca—we call her Becky. And this"—Irene touched the other child in Justin's lap—"is Justin's Joy."

"In every way," he murmured, giving the child a quick little squeeze.

"Girls," Irene said gently, but firmly, "how does one greet a guest?"

Both little girls clambered off his lap and executed charming if clumsy curtsies.

Meghan smiled and knelt to put herself on their level. "Becky, you have grown into quite a young lady since I last saw you." Becky giggled and ducked her head. "And Miss Wingate," Meghan said, offering her hand to the child as she would to a grown-up, "I am very pleased to make your acquaintance."

Joy gazed at her silently for a moment, then took the offered hand, but she did not smile. Nor did she say anything. She merely looked at Meghan out of sky-blue eyes exactly like her father's. Meghan felt a jolt as she recognized profound loneliness in the child. Yet Joy was clearly much loved.

"Finish the story, Uncle Justin," Wally demanded, thus shifting the mood of the moment.

"You must not be rude, Wally," Irene admonished.

"I'm sorry," the boy said. "But 'tis such a good story, Mama."

His mother glanced at the book in Justin's hand and laughed. "And I daresay one you have heard only a dozen times."

Justin chuckled. "He *does* correct me if I get something wrong."

"Well, we shall leave you to it, then," Irene said.

As the two women left the room, Meghan let out a long breath she had not been aware of holding.

"There. That was not so very bad, was it?" Irene asked.

"No. Of course not. They are lovely children."

"Your Stephen would have fit right in." Irene's tone was at once matter-of-fact and sympathetic.

"I am sure he would have." Meghan had always been grateful to Irene, who never tiptoed around Stephen's death as so many others did. Irene had always encouraged her to share her thoughts and memories and seemed to understand precisely what sort of response was needed.

"You were a wonderful mother, Meghan. I doubt not you will be again one day."

"Perhaps one day," Meghan said vaguely, but she was merely placating her friend. She knew very well there would be no more children for her. Losing them hurt far too much to take that risk again. Besides, to have another child she would have to remarry—and *that* was out of the question.

That afternoon yet more guests arrived. Justin was especially glad to hear the names of Viscount Winston Travers and Mr. Melvin Layton as the butler announced new arrivals.

"I see Kenwick's widow is here," Travers said later that evening when the three of them at last had some time alone. They were in the billiards room, where they sat in comfortable armchairs after a game.

"Yes," Justin replied. "She and Irene have been close friends for years."

"Does she still harbor resentment toward the three of us about that accident?" Layton asked. "I confess I have not seen her since Travers and I called on her immediately afterward."

"Frankly, I do not know how she feels now," Justin said. "She has been polite, of course—exactly what one would expect of a lady."

"Perhaps we should have told the truth at the time." Layton shifted to refill his wineglass.

"I believe we did, did we not?" Justin looked at Travers for confirmation.

"I meant the *whole* truth," Layton insisted.

"It would serve little purpose to have a widow know her dead husband contributed to the accident that claimed him and her son," Justin said. "Dredging that up now—a year-and-a-half later—would merely cause undue suffering."

"I suppose you are right," Layton conceded.

"What is done is done," Justin added.

"Ah, but unlike Lady Macbeth's little problem, this one *can* be undone, if necessary," Layton responded.

Travers groaned. "I do hope the two of you are not going to spend the holiday challenging each other with obscure quotes from Shakespeare."

Layton winked at Justin and said to Travers, "Of course not, dear boy, for we both 'want that glib and oily art, To speak and purpose not.' "

Justin gave an exaggerated sigh. " 'Rude am I in my speech, And little bless'd with the soft phrase of peace.' "

Travers rose. "I can see *I* shall have little peace with the two of you spouting on. I believe I shall go and find some fair maiden on whom to work my wiles."

"You *will* let us know us know if they do indeed work, will you not?" Layton joked.

With the influx of additional guests, the evening meal became a more elaborate affair and the evening entertainments more varied. With careful attention to what she knew of personal preferences and to social protocol, their hostess managed to change her seating arrangements from day to day. Thus it was that Meghan found Lord Justin to be her dinner partner one evening. Irene had made her designations just prior to the butler's announcing the meal.

"La! It is like musical chairs," Dierdre Thompson observed with delight, taking the arm of Lord Travers.

"Only a marchioness could get away with bending the rules so," grumbled one gray-haired dowager, but Meghan noted this was not expressed in a tone to reach the ears of their hostess.

"Mrs. Kenwick, I hope this arrangement garners your approval?" Lord Justin said, offering her his arm.

In the confusion of the large company sorting itself out, they were afforded a moment of privacy. Did she approve? She was not sure. In any event, a guest accepted the dictates of her hostess. And she *had* been hoping for a chance to speak with him.

"As a matter of fact, my lord—"

"Justin."

"I beg your pardon?"

"Call me 'Justin.' That is how my friends address me."

His friends? He wished her to consider him a friend? "As you wish, Justin. And I do prefer 'Meghan' to the more formal means of address."

"Good." He patted her hand on his arm. "We are past that hurdle."

"As I started to say, sir"—she caught a raised eyebrow and added—"Justin—I have wished for an opportunity to extend my apology to you."

"Apology? Whatever for?" He looked down into her eyes with genuine surprise.

"F-for my rather ungracious reception when you called at the time of Kenwick's death. I am sorry for that."

"Think no more upon it. We were all overset by the accident. However, I must confess that I am glad you no longer seem to hold us responsible."

"At such times there seems always to be sufficient blame—real or imaginary—to be shared. I found it difficult—and I still do—to forgive myself for not objecting to my son's going on such a grown-up expedition." Her voice was soft and tinged with regret directed wholly at herself.

"One is always tempted to consider 'what ifs?' in such a case," he said. "I have often asked myself, 'What if I had supervised my wife's medications more closely?' But—you know—'that way madness lies. . . .' "

She looked up and held his gaze, warmed by the empathy she found there as the rest of his quotation popped into her mind. "And 'let me shun that.' Thank you. I think I needed to hear this."

"You are welcome." He smiled. "I hope you are skilled at charades."

"Charades?" she asked, surprised at the abrupt change of topic.

He leaned closer and said in a stage whisper, "I happen to know Irene has charades on the evening's agenda."

She laughed. "Well, pity he who ends with *me* on his team!"

Three

As was customary at large house parties, breakfast was a casual affair with guests coming to the dining room at their leisure. Meghan found several of the company there before her the next morning. Robert and Justin were breaking the fast with Lady Helen, the elder Hamlins, and two other gentlemen. One of these was a young dandy named David Islington, whom Meghan knew to be a Wingate connection of some sort. She waved the men back to their places as she filled a plate from the generously laden sideboard and took a seat just as Irene breezed in.

"I declare, Robert, you must do something about that heir of yours." Laughter in Irene's voice and a twinkle in her eyes belied the reproof she aimed at her husband.

Robert looked up, but calmly continued to spread jam on a muffin. "My wife is disowning our eldest—again," he announced in a mild voice. "What is it this time, my dear? Not another frog in Nurse's washbasin?"

"No. This time he has the entire nursery in an uproar over kittens."

"Kittens? In the nursery?" the marquis asked.

"No. No. In the stable, of course." She gestured impatiently. "I know Connors mentioned them to you."

"Hmm. The stable seems a reasonable place for kittens. How can that be a problem?"

"Under ordinary circumstances, my dear, it would not be." Hers was the tone one might use with a person of limited mental powers. "But *your* son visited the stables earlier this morning, and now he has the other children pestering to see the kittens."

The marquis gave an exaggerated sigh. "He is always *my* son when a problem arises. Otherwise, of course, he is his mama's 'darling boy.' "

The men at the table chuckled and the women nodded knowingly.

Robert turned to his wife. "I beg your pardon, my dear, but I still fail to see a problem."

"Oh," she said sweetly, "it is not a major crisis, but in the next hour or so *we*—that is you, my love, and Justin, and I—will be trekking out to the stables to visit the youngest additions to Everleigh."

Justin groaned. "Kittens? And you are sure *I* must accompany this adventurous expedition?"

Irene gave him a sympathetic smile. "It will not take long. You need only *look,* you know. But all the children are going, and," she added, "any of our guests is welcome to join us."

David Islington delicately wiped his lips and replaced his serviette. "What novel entertainments you offer, Cousin Irene."

Irene gave a gurgle of laughter. "Can you not just see it now? The *Morning Post* will report that the Everleighs have lost all sense of what is due their guests."

"Au contraire, my friend," Lady Helen said, joining in the joke with an exaggerated tone of hauteur. "The *Post* will write something to the effect that 'The elegant Marchioness of Everleigh once again charmed her guests with an innovative diversion designed to capture the essence of bucolic life. The marchioness is accounted one of the most clever hostesses in the realm.' However, I trust you will forgive me if I decline your kind invitation?"

There was general laughter as some agreed to the expedition and others declined. Meghan, having always found babies of any species charming, chose to join the parents.

* * *

Quite an entourage accompanied the Wingate children on their expedition. The sky was overcast; the air was crisp and cold. A wide graveled path, with now bare trees alongside, led from the rear of the mansion to the stables some distance away. The crunch of the gravel blended with the high-pitched voices of excited children. The group of younger people had grown by four with the arrival of additional guests. Three youths in their teens were apparently torn between disparaging an infantile activity and fearing they might miss something if they chose not to go. Remembering that awkward in-between stage of life, Meghan smiled.

She also smiled—somewhat less indulgently—as she observed Georgiana Hamlin appropriate Justin Wingate's arm for the trek to the stables. It was mid-morning and thus early for Miss Hamlin, who had not previously appeared before noon. Meghan surmised that Miss Hamlin's mother had carried word of this adventure to her daughter.

Meghan thoroughly enjoyed the crisp morning air as she trailed behind the group. She could observe and listen without actually taking part—yet—in the others' conversations. Nor was Meghan the only one who seemed to seek the sidelines. Justin's daughter, Joy, walked slightly apart from the rest of the young children. She clutched what appeared to be a blue scrap of blanket. Meghan remembered seeing her with it in the nursery, too.

Irene had told Meghan of the child's refusing to speak and the probable cause. Meghan's heart went out to the little girl—and to the parent trying to cope with such a problem.

"Come, darling Joy," Miss Hamlin called prettily. She held out her free hand to the child. "Come walk with me and your papa. We shall go and see the kitties," she added, stating the obvious in the deliberately childish voice that some adults thought appropriate in dealing with children.

Joy merely looked at her briefly, then away. She skipped

over to her father's other side and looked up at him questioningly.

He brushed a hand over her curls and said, "Whatever you wish, poppet."

Joy smiled up at him and returned to the sidelines where she had been previously.

Miss Hamlin smiled flirtatiously and said, "My charms do not seem to work on *all* your family, Lord Justin."

He patted her hand on his arm. "Keep trying. She will succumb as have the rest of us."

Miss Hamlin laughed gaily at this bit of superior witticism, which reinforced Meghan's view that the man was a consummate flirt. Meghan deliberately turned her attention to the other members of the party. Irene and Robert seemed to be sharing a private joke and Lord Travers and Miss Thompson talked animatedly of their favorite topic—horses. Mr. Layton had gone on ahead.

Suddenly, Meghan felt a presence at her side. She looked down into the grave expression of Joy's upturned face.

"Good morning, Joy."

Joy cocked her head and continued to look at Meghan appraisingly. Then she nodded and, shifting her blanket, Joy slipped her small hand into Meghan's.

Amazed and unsure of her own emotions, Meghan had only one thought in mind. This was a child—a small being—in terrible need and that need must not be refused at this point. She gently squeezed the little girl's hand and smiled down at her. They walked in companionable silence.

As the group reached the stable, Justin appeared to look around for his daughter. When he saw her clutching the hand of Mrs. Kenwick, he gave a start of surprise that, in turn, brought the attention of the girl on his arm.

"Joy?" He gave Meghan an inquiring glance.

"We are doing very well, thank you, sir." Meghan gave Joy's hand another little squeeze just before Joy released her grip to join the other children crowding into a stall that had been given over to two mama cats and their babies.

Meghan mentally shrugged off a look of what seemed

resentment in the eyes of Miss Hamlin. Surely the beauty would not expect one to offer rejection to a small child?

Soon the stable was alive with laughter and childish giggles at the wonder of new life. Seven kittens frolicked in loose hay. Four of them, a groomsman said, were about three weeks old and the others about four weeks. He also answered Irene's concern by assuring her that both mama cats and kittens were used to being handled by people. The kittens were fully as curious as their visitors, though the mother cats appeared more suspicious than curious.

The kittens were a mixture of various colors, attesting to very mixed parentage, Meghan observed. Two were black and white, one a striped gray, two a mixture of gray, brown, black, and ginger, and one was pure white with just a touch of black on one paw. This one seemed most shy, quickly escaping to the side when it was let loose.

Lord Travers and Miss Thompson soon lost interest in watching small humans ooh and ahh over small felines. They and two of the youths—one a younger brother of Miss Thompson—went off to look at horses. The other adults stood watching the commotion in the "kitten" stall, where Miss Hamlin had picked up one of the multicolored kittens in her gloved hands.

"Oh, are they not just the most precious creatures?" she crooned. "Look, Lord Justin, is this one not beautiful?" She held the kitten out to him.

He took a deep breath and turned away slightly. "Yes. It is . . . ah . . . charming."

"Do you not want to hold it?" she asked, thrusting it toward him again.

"No . . . I . . . ha . . . ha-choo! . . . I do not believe so." And he sneezed again.

Robert laughed. "I wondered how long you would last, little brother. Are you all right?"

"I . . . ha-choo! I will be if I just avoid handling them."

"I am so sorry," Miss Hamlin said. "I had no idea—"

"No, of course not," Justin said, his eyes watery. "Never

mind, now." He stepped back away from the center of activity, smothering another sneeze.

Meghan had stood silently observing the scene. She sympathized with Justin, for her father had suffered just such an aversion to certain plants. She picked up the gray striped kitten as it tried to escape and cuddled it briefly before turning it over to Irene's Sarah. She noticed Joy standing aside as well, her eyes agleam with enjoyment. As Joy moved around, her ubiquitous blanket hung down nearly to tops of her shoes, swaying with the child's every movement. The swishing blanket caught the white kitten's attention and it batted at this interesting phenomenon with a tiny paw. As soon as Joy became aware of it, her lips widened into the purest, most childlike smile yet that Meghan had seen on her. Joy began teasing the kitten with her trailing blanket and the kitten eagerly followed it. Suddenly, the child giggled aloud.

"Joy?" It was her father's voice, full of amazement.

The wonder of this moment was interrupted by a loud feminine wail from Miss Hamlin. Everyone's attention was immediately diverted to the beauty.

"Oh. Oh. It scratched me! Look! I am bleeding!" she cried. She had removed a glove to pet one of the kittens, crooning at it lovingly through pursed lips and altogether presenting a very pretty picture. The kitten had apparently taken exception to being held aloft and attempted to climb down the arm holding it, catching a clawhold wherever it could. Miss Hamlin cried out and dropped the kitten, which scampered away. She held out her wrist and, indeed, there *was* a scratch on her wrist and it *was* oozing red.

"Ah, it's just a little scratch," Jason said dismissively.

"But it *hurts*," Miss Hamlin whimpered.

Justin dipped his handkerchief into a nearby bucket, squeezed excess water from it, and handed it to the injured woman. "Here. This is cool and should take out the sting."

"Oh, thank you *so* much," she said.

It was, Meghan thought, a thank-you worthy of a slain dragon at the very least.

"I think it is time we returned to the house," Irene said, "and left these babies with their mamas."

There was some protest from her own children, but she soon had the whole lot of them herded toward the house. Meghan noticed that Joy had gathered up her blanket and walked along with the other children while her father commiserated with the wounded Miss Hamlin.

"I do hope I do not contract a fever," the young woman was saying. "One can have a terrible illness from such animals, you know."

"I think you need have no such fear of these," he reassured her.

"It is just that it would be such a shame when I have anticipated this holiday so very, very much."

Meghan, again walking behind the rest, saw Miss Hamlin look up and bat her long lashes at Lord Justin, but she could not see his face for a reaction to this bit of transparency. Meghan herself could not hide a small snicker of amusement, which she attempted to smother with a cough.

"I agree," said a voice at her elbow. She looked into the twinkling hazel eyes of Mr. Layton. "She *is* doing it a bit brown," he explained.

"Well—I—" Meghan was embarrassed at having her own thoughts so easily read by another.

"Never mind. Justin can take care of himself. Lord knows the Hamlin chit has been trying hard enough. Ever since her come-out this last Season."

"I am not sure—" Meghan started, but Layton talked right over her.

" 'Course he ain't tumbled yet, but she sets great store by that Hamlin-Wingate thing, you know? She must think it worked twice in one generation, it oughta work again."

His tone was merely friendly chitchat, but Meghan was uncomfortable with the substance of his remarks. "Mr. Layton, I do not think such a topic is quite proper."

He grinned. " 'Course it ain't. But 'tis interesting, what?"

She kept her expression bland, but she knew her amusement shone in her eyes as she looked at him and said sternly, "Nevertheless—"

"Quite right. Quite right. We shall discuss the weather." He held out his hand as though testing for rain. "Fine day. Cold, but dry. Just right for early December, do you not agree?"

She laughed and agreed and they returned to the house in pleasant camaraderie. She had, of course, known Mr. Layton for some years as an acquaintance of her husband. In the last couple of days, she had begun to see him in his own light and found him to be an amiable and amusing fellow.

Justin would have liked to spend the next few hours with his daughter. Other than sobs when she had fallen or a cry of fear when a huge black dog had growled at her in the park, that little giggle was the first sound he had heard from his child in months, though her nurse had told him she sometimes cried out in her sleep. Still, none of this pointed to real communication.

And what was that bit of business with her taking Meghan's hand? She had clearly refused Georgiana's. Even Irene had had difficulty establishing contact with his daughter. He remembered how Meghan had treated the little girls in the nursery. Obviously, the woman had a way with children that Miss Hamlin did not have. Well, anyone—anyone—who might help Joy would incur her father's undying gratitude.

As the children were taken above stairs, Miss Hamlin had commanded his—indeed, everyone's—notice. Lady Hamlin had been properly solicitous of her daughter's wound. Thereafter, Justin's attention had been diverted by his brother's request that Justin make up a party to go hunting in the afternoon. So, he had spent much of the rest of the day chasing rabbits.

That evening when he went to say good night to Joy he saw no change in her. She clung to him lovingly and she nodded or shook her head as he asked her about her doll and the adventure of the day. But his little chatterbox of the past said not a word.

Having returned to the adult company, he sat in the drawing room later with a number of other guests. Some had already said their good nights and retired. Those who remained sat around in quiet conversation, sipping brandy or mulled wine. Irene came into the room and spoke during a lull in his discussion with Travers and Miss Thompson.

"Justin, may I have a word with you?" She gestured to a seat in an alcove formed by a large bay window.

"What is it?" he asked quietly.

"I have just come from the nursery."

"Is something amiss there?"

"Hmm. Not precisely. Nurse discovered one of the kittens from the stable in Joy's bed."

"Wha-at?"

"A kitten. That white one. Seems she wrapped it in her blanket and carried it back with her."

"That little minx."

Irene smiled. "Nurse wants to know what to do—return the kitten to the stables or what?"

Justin ran his hand through his hair. "Is the kitten old enough to be away from its mother?"

"I think so. Yes. It is from one of the older of the two litters."

"Will her having the kitten there create havoc among the nursery set?"

"Probably not," Irene said. "We have had other animals there from time to time—fish, a turtle, even a baby squirrel in a cage last summer. Joy seems willing to share."

"Well, then . . ." He shrugged. "What do you think?"

"I think it might help Joy. And I wonder we did not consider it ourselves. In any event, a kitten in the nursery will do no harm."

"Easy for you to say," Justin said. "I cannot look forward to a fit of sneezing every time my daughter approaches with her new friend!"

Irene gave him a sympathetic smile. "Mrs. Ferris is a marvel with herbs and such. Perhaps she has a potion that will help you."

The next day, members of the enlarged household at Everleigh were engaged in a variety of activities—some in organized entertainments and others wandering about on their own. Meghan, who had once been a frequent guest, had gone to the kitchen, where she found not only the cook, but several kitchen maids and the housekeeper. Mrs. Ferris concentrated on stirring the strong-smelling contents of a pot sitting on a very modern cooker.

"Hello, Mrs. Peevey," she greeted the cook.

"Why, hello, Mrs. Kenwick. Heard you was here an' wondered if you would make it back to visit with the likes of us." The cook was a plump woman of middle years.

"You know very well I would not miss an opportunity to wheedle yet another recipe from one of England's best cooks."

"Ah, now—" Mrs. Peevey looked only slightly embarrassed at the praise. "An' which dish would it be this time?"

"That rabbit stew we had for lunch was delicious," Meghan said.

"Ah, yes. The secret there is slow cooking and a special sauce I have from a friend over in Worcestershire."

"Will your friend allow you to share?"

"Of course—but only with the likes of you. All cooks appreciate people who know good food."

Suddenly Meghan was aware that she recognized the odor emanating from the pot on the cooker. Mrs. Peevey noticed her awareness and said, "Mrs. Ferris is stirring up a special herbal remedy."

Mrs. Ferris turned and nodded. "Thought we had some on hand, but the bottle was empty."

"It smells very like an infusion my mother used to make

for my father. He suffered from an aversion to certain plants
in the spring."

"This might be similar. 'Tis for Master Justin," Mrs. Ferris said.

"*Lord* Justin," Mrs. Peevey corrected with a laugh and
explained to Meghan, "Some of us still think of the marquis
and his brother as little boys."

"Sweet lads they were—both of them," Mrs. Ferris said.
"I hope this infusion helps his lordship. He never could be
comfortable around cats."

"But neither can he deny his daughter anything she
wants. And Nurse says she won't be separated from that
little kitten." Mrs. Peevey's tone was full of indulgent goodwill for both the father and the daughter.

Meghan discussed with Mrs. Ferris the ingredients for
such an infusion while Mrs. Peevey wrote out the stew recipe for her. She finally left the kitchen with yet another
view of Justin Wingate as a caring father—a role these two
apparently found to be totally natural for him. Well, she
supposed it to be possible—if not wholly probable—for the
man to be both a rake and a good father.

Later, Meghan joined a number of ladies in the morning
room who were busily weaving branches of greenery into
long garlands to be strung around the ballroom. Several of
the younger women, including Miss Hamlin, giggled and
chatted as they fashioned kissing balls of mistletoe and
holly. These would be hung in strategic locations in the
public rooms of the house.

The morning room was on the ground floor and opened
through French doors onto a terrace and a garden beyond.
Despite the cold of the December morning, the doors were
slightly open to allow in the fresh air. The buzz of conversation in the room was accompanied by squeals of delight
from the garden, where the children played a lively game
of blindman's buff. Occasionally a mother would go to the

door to check on a child, though Meghan knew at least three nursery maids accompanied the little people.

As she rose to replenish her supply of boughs from a pile on a table in the center, Meghan glanced out toward the game in the garden. They were having such fun! She felt a twinge of longing as she imagined a certain little boy added to the group. She shook herself and looked for Joy. There she was—off to the side again, completely absorbed in the kitten in her arms. Meghan could not hear the individual words, but she saw Becky approach and obviously invite Joy to join the game. Instead, the two little girls went off to sit on the steps leading down to the garden. Becky, apparently chattering enough for the two of them, frequently reached to pet the kitten that Joy freely shared.

"What has captured your interest so?" Irene had come to stand next to Meghan.

"Those two little charmers." Meghan gestured at Becky and Joy.

"I have watched them in the nursery. The other children are remarkably protective of Joy, but it is Becky who seems to be her interpreter, as it were."

"Joy appears to be very attached to the kitten."

"Yes." Irene sighed. "Let us hope that little kitten will help bring our Joy back to us."

That evening a special entertainment was planned to include the children. A certain family in the village made their living by presenting puppet shows at market fairs in the months of good weather.

"They winter here and have kindly presented their show to us during the Christmas season for the last four years," Irene explained in announcing the presentation.

Adults who might have demurred at such a childish entertainment were quickly disabused of their attitude by others who had seen the show previously. In the event, children and adults alike poured into the ballroom, which had been turned into a temporary theater. Children sat on the floor and low benches in front of the puppet theater; adult guests occupied straight-backed chairs behind them; the rest of the audience consisted of as many servants as could be spared from their posts.

The play fare ranged from the farcical comedy of Punch and Judy to fairy tales and more sophisticated satires. One of the latter dealt with Napoleon in exile, ruling his "empire"—a barren island some six miles wide and ten miles long. Another had the audience in embarrassed stitches as a puppet prince regent was bested by his flighty wife, the out-of-royal-favor princess of Wales.

Meghan was thoroughly enjoying both the show itself and the children's delight in it. It occurred to her that this was perhaps the first time since Stephen's death that she had been able to *enjoy* watching children have fun. Yes, there was nostalgia, but not the devastating despair that customarily assailed her.

To bring their show closer to their audience, the puppeteers invited the children to take part. One female member of the troup approached the children with hand puppets fashioned as a fairy godmother and an elf who would grant wishes. She had performed thusly with two small boys and other children eagerly anticipated their turns. Joy sat silent, but her eyes shone as they followed everything. The puppeteer approached Joy.

"Ah, here we have a real princess disguised as an ordinary but very pretty little girl," the woman said in the tone of the fairy godmother. "Now, *what* do you suppose such a beauty would wish for?"

"I have no idea," the elf replied. "We must ask *her.*"

"Joy can't talk." It was young Matthew who spoke up.

"Oh, but she must want to tell me her secret wish," the fairy godmother said persuasively.

Meghan held her breath hoping the little girl would not be ridiculed. She glanced at Justin seated several places away from her. He seemed to sit straighter and very tense, waiting.

"She don't talk!" This time it was Wally who explained in an insistent tone.

"She does so!" Sarah assumed a very authoritative manner.

"Joy can talk," Becky said, clearly defending her cousin. "She talks to the kitten all the time."

Meghan saw Justin give a start at this. He cast a questioningly look of wonder in Joy's direction.

The woman puppeteer apparently perceived that she had stumbled into a delicate situation, for she had the elf say, "I am sure the pretty princess will tell us what she wants us to know in her own good time."

The two puppets then went on to involve other children, seemingly oblivious to the bombshell that exploded behind them.

Four

Justin wanted nothing so much as to jump up and find out immediately if what Sarah and Becky had said was true. *Did* Joy actually talk, or was it merely like her mumbling in her sleep? He was forced to wait until the puppet show was over. Then the children were herded back to the nursery for a snack before they were prepared for bed.

"Do you think it is possible?" he asked Irene. "Could she really be talking to the kitten? She used to talk to her dolls incessantly." He could not smother the longing in his voice.

Standing next to Meghan, Irene answered, "Yes, I think it very possible. What do you think, Meghan?"

"I agree." Meghan gave him an encouraging smile.

My God! When she smiles, she is beautiful, he thought. *A man could lose himself in the warmth of her eyes.*

Meghan continued, "Perhaps she needs to practice, as it were, with the kitten, before she opens to people again."

"I hope that is the case," he said. "I shall go and bid her good night."

Irene touched his arm. "Justin, do not press her. Allow her to set her own pace." He saw Meghan nod in agreement.

"I shall try to restrain myself."

He found Joy and her two cousins attired now in similar white cotton nightdresses. The nursery maid had just finished braiding Sarah's hair.

"Will you *wead* us a story, Uncle *Jus'in?*" Becky pleaded. "Puh-leeze?"

"Would you like that, too, Joy-of-my-life?"

Her eyes glowed as she nodded energetically.

"Very well. A short one. Hop into bed now, all three of you."

"Four," Sarah said with a giggle.

"Four?" He looked around in an exaggerated search, which brought more giggles.

"Joy's kitten," Sarah explained.

"Ah, yes. The kitten." He leaned down to tuck his daughter into bed and already felt that tickling sensation that presaged a sneeze. He gave her a quick kiss and stifled the sneeze, then pulled a chair close to the beds and began to read a familiar fairy tale.

He listened carefully, but not once did he hear Joy make a coherent sound. When all three girls were clearly asleep, he closed the book with a sigh and sat staring at his sleeping child. He felt a presence behind him. Robert and Irene had just come in. They looked at him sympathetically.

"Nothing?" Irene asked softly. "We just came to say good night. Too late here, I see." She patted Justin's shoulder. "Do not despair. There *is* progress."

"Right," he said with little conviction. He rose and accompanied them back downstairs to the on-going party.

The next day servants hung many of the decorations, including the kissing balls—small ones in the drawing room and foyer and a huge one from the middle beam in the ballroom. Meghan enjoyed tolerant amusement at watching guests be "surprised" under a kissing ball. Then, coming in from a walk with several others, she was herself surprised under the one in the foyer.

Melvin Layton laughed and caught her in his arms. "Aha! I have been hoping for just such an opportunity," he chortled, largely for the benefit of the others. As Travers and Miss Thompson and Justin and Miss Hamlin looked on, Layton kissed Meghan rather thoroughly.

Embarrassed and flustered, she was further disconcerted when she caught a decidedly amused expression on Justin's face. "We should have warned you about Layton's wicked ways," he said.

"I . . . uh . . . yes. You should have," she agreed with a soft laugh.

The truth was, she had not really minded the kiss. Such was, after all, part of the frivolity of the season. However, this was the first time she had been kissed by a man other than her brother since Burton's death. She had expected to feel somewhat more than . . . well . . . deflated. She had felt nothing—except warm friendliness.

Then she mentally chastised herself. What more could she possibly want?

In the afternoon the weather turned even colder and it began to rain. Children who were wont to play outdoors were now confined. The overflowing nursery was hard put to contain them. Irene ordered the ballroom arranged for a rollicking game of musical chairs that would involve the children and such adults as might wish to take part.

Justin noted that Miss Hamlin eagerly participated and that she tried to engage Joy in the game. Justin found a seat along the sidelines next to Meghan. Joy leaned against her father's knee, clutching her blanket-clad kitten. He and Meghan talked amiably about the players, laughing over this one's clumsiness or that one's eagerness.

As a new round of play started, Sarah grabbed Joy's hand. "Come on, Joy," she pleaded. "It's fun. You'll see."

Joy looked up at Justin as though to ask permission. "Go ahead, little one," he encouraged, whereupon she thrust the kitten at him and did just that.

He tried unsuccessfully to stifle a series of sneezes. "Oh, we-e-l-l-l . . . I had not quite counted on this, had I?"

"Here. Allow me." Meghan took the kitten from him and held it in her lap away from him.

"Thank you." He reached for his handkerchief.

"Did the infusion Mrs. Ferris prepared help you?"

"Yes, it did, surprisingly, because little has helped in the past. She said you suggested some secret ingredient. I thank you."

She flashed him that devastating smile again. "Willow bark is not much of a secret, but it always helped my father."

Irene and Robert managed to have themselves eliminated from the game and took seats near Justin and Meghan. A number of other adults had joined the spectators as well.

Soon Joy was eliminated and returned to stand at her father's side. There was a look of panic in her eyes at not seeing the kitten with him. He pointed to the animal sleeping on Meghan's lap.

Joy moved to stand between Meghan and Justin and reached to pet the kitten, but made no move to take it. The kitten looked around, its sea-green eyes a striking contrast to its white coat. It yawned, showing small teeth and a pink tongue.

"Your kitten is very pretty, Joy. Does he have a name?" Meghan asked.

Joy looked up at her and nodded. "Don't tell me," Meghan said. "Let me guess it. Hmm." She pretended to think about it very hard. "Maybe its name is Pinky for his pink nose and tongue."

Joy merely shook her head, but her eyes danced at the game.

"Well, then," Meghan said, leaning her head on her fist in a caricature of intense thought. "It must be . . . White Princess."

Again Joy shook her head vigorously.

"I know! He is the Black Knight!" Meghan declared in a tone of brilliant discovery.

Joy giggled aloud at this. Justin, who had turned away to talk with Robert, swiveled around in surprise. "No-o," Joy said in little squeal of utter delight. " 'Tis Snowflake!"

Justin's mouth dropped; Irene and Robert looked aston-

ished. Meghan, though, merely hugged Joy to her and said,
"Snowflake! What a perfect name. Why did I not think of
that?"

"Snow is white, too," Joy said.

"Yes, it is," Meghan said.

"Joy?" Justin said softly. "Joy?"

"Yes, Papa?"

"Oh, Joy." He reached for her, tears in his eyes. "You
are talking. Oh, thank God! You are talking." He hugged
her fiercely and kissed her cheek.

"Yes, Papa." She put a small hand on either side of his
face.

"But why now—so suddenly after all this time?" he
asked wonderingly over her head.

"The lady said I should," Joy explained matter-of-factly.

"The lady?" He stared at Meghan as though she were a
miracle worker, but she seemed mystified.

"No, Papa. Not Auntie Meg. The one in white last night."

"In white—last night—?" he repeated dumbly.

"She sat on my bed. She came from Mama and she said
I could speak, that it would not hurt Mama anymore."

"Lady Aetherada?" Irene asked softly.

"Did the lady do or say anything else?" Justin asked
seriously.

"She straightened my blankets," Joy said.

"Definitely her ladyship," Irene said, keeping her voice
low for only the immediate group. "What else did she say,
darling?"

"I-I can't tell," Joy said. " 'Tis a secret. And I must not
say it yet."

"Very well, my sweet." Justin hugged her again. "A lady
keeps her word."

Joy pushed herself off his lap, took her kitten from
Meghan, and went off to join Becky and another little girl.
The children seemed only momentarily surprised when Joy
spoke to them. Very soon she was but one of several in a
babbling, laughing group.

Justin turned to Meghan. "I have no idea how you did it, but thank you. Thank you."

She looked baffled and glanced from him to Irene and Robert. "But I did nothing. Nothing. It was this lady—Lady—"

"Aetherada," Irene supplied.

"What a strange name," Meghan said. "I have not met her, have I?"

"No-o. I think not." Irene's eyes twinkled.

"You had better tell her, my dear," Robert said.

"Promise you will not laugh or be shocked," Irene demanded.

"I promise—I think." Meghan's voice conveyed amused trepidation.

Justin caught her eye and winked at her.

"Well, you see," Irene began, "the Lady Aetherada is our resident ghost."

"Your ghost. Of course. I should have known."

"Sarcasm does not become you, my dear," Irene said with a laugh. "No. Truly. She was the third marchioness and she shows herself only to children."

"Though she occasionally upsets the housekeeping staff," her husband added.

Meghan's eyes widened in disbelief. "You are serious!"

"Yes, they are," Justin said.

"And she reveals herself only to children? How extraordinary."

Irene took a seat next to Meghan. "Family legend has it that Lady Aetherada lost a child of six or seven years when the holding was sacked by Vikings. She grieved terribly and later died in childbirth. Now when Everleigh children need her, she appears to help them through a time of difficulty."

"That is a wonderful story," Meghan said, "but you realize that as a family legend it may have imbedded itself in Joy's imagination."

Justin grinned at his brother. *"This* lady is a skeptic." He looked at Meghan. "Most people would take that view, but, personally, I do not care quite how it came about. I am just thankful to the lady that Joy is speaking again."

"Yes," Irene said, "though I suppose it would be best not to noise the *how* of it about too much."

"I agree," Meghan said. "I, like Joy, will respect the lady's secret."

Meghan was somewhat taken aback by the story of a ghost who protected children. However, *something* had happened to break through Joy's wall of silence and that had to be all to the good. In the days that followed, Joy laughed and played as vigorously as the other children. She no longer relegated herself to the sidelines. A stranger happening on the scene would have observed nothing unusual.

When the children were involved with adult guests, Joy seemed to gravitate toward Meghan. Outdoors, she would walk near or with Meghan and voluntarily take Meghan's hand. Indoors, Joy always sought a seat near Meghan and tended to sit closer than necessary. It was if the child needed—desperately needed—the simple human contact.

Yet she was clearly a much-loved child. Her father doted on her, picking her up, nuzzling her, caressing. He could not seem to be near her without touching her. Irene did not discriminate among the children when she was passing out hugs. Nor did Robert.

At first Meghan was disconcerted by Joy's obvious preference for her. Was she not determined to withhold herself from excessive involvement with children? Moreover, Justin seemed slightly embarrassed by his daughter's behavior, and Miss Hamlin, who had tried so hard to befriend Justin's child, was downright resentful.

It took Joy almost no time at all to wriggle her way into Meghan's heart. Meghan found herself welcoming the child with a smile and looking forward to seeing her. Whenever Joy came to stand at Meghan's knee, Meghan readily lifted the little girl onto her lap, with no regard for what such action did to freshly ironed muslin.

One afternoon Meghan stepped into the library to find Justin the only other person in the room. He appeared to be absorbed in some papers at his brother's huge mahogany desk.

"Oh! I beg your pardon," she said. "I merely came for a book, but I can return later."

"No. No. Come ahead. Truth to tell, I would welcome a distraction." He rose and came from behind the desk. "May I help you find something?"

"Robert told me he had a copy of Chapman's translation of *The Iliad*."

Justin's brows lifted in surprise. "*The Iliad?*"

"Yes. *The Iliad.* Oh, please do not tell me you are one of those gentlemen who think women should never read anything more serious than a fashion magazine." *Like my late husband,* she thought bitterly, but she did not say so aloud.

His brow lifted even higher. "No. Not at all. However, I must admit that few women have asked me lately for copies of Greek epics." He paused. "Few men have either, for that matter."

She laughed. "I wanted to see what all the fuss was about."

"You refer to the poem by that fellow Keats, I take it?"

"Yes!" She was delighted to find another familiar with this poet whom she had but lately discovered. " 'Much have I traveled in the realms of gold—' "

" 'Which bards in fealty to Apollo hold,' " He finished the lines for her, and then added, "And have you?"

"Have I what?"

"Traveled much in the ancient world?"

She shook her head regretfully. "I have never been off this 'sceptered isle.' But now that things are truly settled on the Continent, I hope to see a bit of it."

"I am sure you will enjoy it," he said politely as he

pursued the search for the book she wanted. "Ah, here it is."

As she took the volume, their fingers touched. She looked into his clear blue eyes and felt a tremor run through her. "Thank you," she murmured and turned to leave.

"Uh . . . Mrs. Kenwick."

She turned back.

"Meghan, that is." He smiled. "I wanted to thank you for being so kind to Joy."

"One could scarcely be otherwise to Joy."

"Still, I would suspect that you might find her attentions somewhat . . . uh . . . less than welcome, shall we say?"

"Why ever would you suspect that?" she asked, surprised.

"Well . . ." He ran his hand through his hair and shifted from one foot to another. Incongruously, Meghan recalled Stephen's doing the same thing when he was uncomfortable. She smiled at the memory. "Well," he went on, "Irene said you were reluctant to be too involved with the children and I thought . . ." His voice trailed off in obvious embarrassment.

"Well, don't think." It came out more sharply than she intended. "I mean, Joy is a very sweet little girl. How could anyone have the heart to hurt her?"

He grinned. "Quite naturally, I share that sentiment. All the same, I do thank you."

"You are most welcome." She held his gaze for a moment, then added softly, "In the end, I may be thanking you."

Now what on earth had she meant by that? she asked herself as the door clicked shut behind her. Somehow her mind always seemed to become befuddled around that man.

Five

Justin was aware of Joy's seeking out Mrs. Kenwick, but he did not understand it, for Meghan did not seem to encourage her in any way. Neither did she reject the child's overtures—and for *that* he was grateful.

Their discussion of the poet Keats had startled him. He recalled Kenwick's complaints about his wife, but so far he had seen none of the narrowminded pedantry Burton had laid at her doorstep. In truth, that bit of repartee, along with her quick response on the "madness" quotation earlier—brief as they both were—had brought to mind some of his discussions with Layton.

This, in turn, brought to mind his observing Layton seek out the widow several times. He frowned at this thought. Was Layton actually pursuing Mrs. Kenwick? And if so, to what end? And why should it matter to *him?*

But it did.

In keeping with the gaiety of the event, he had been amused when Layton trapped Meghan under the kissing ball. And she had been very sporting about it. Or had she anticipated the "entrapment"? Perhaps she even encouraged it? This idea brought another frown.

He immediately chastised himself for his greedy dog kind of jealousy. After all, *he* had no interest in the woman and if his friend Layton did . . . Well, they were grown-up people and Layton was an honorable man. So are we all—all honorable men, he thought, giving Shakespeare's line a slight twist.

Justin and his two honorable friends were having a night-cap in the library one evening. The three of them sprawled on two settees in front of the fireplace.

"Wonderful thing—Joy's talking again," Layton observed.

"It is, indeed," Justin agreed.

"So, does that give you more time to pursue the lovely Miss Hamlin?" Travers ask with a grin.

Layton gave a bark of laughter. "You mean succumb to the pursuit do you not? That young lady seems to know very well what she wants. And so does her mama."

"You *are* looking to marry again, are you not, Justin?" Travers asked. "Or did the marchioness just happen to pepper her guest list with eligible females?"

"If that is the case," Layton said, clearly teasing, "what are *you* doing cutting out our friend here with Miss Thompson?"

Travers, who never seemed fully aware when his friends were roasting him, said, "Oh, I say. I never meant . . . It just never occurred to me . . . it is just that Dierdre and I—"

"Ah—'Dierdre' is it?" Layton interjected.

Travers colored up and mumbled, "We agreed on Christian names." He paused. "She knows an uncommon lot about horses."

"Always a priority when one considers a woman's attributes, would you not agree, Justin?" Layton said with a wink.

Justin decided to take pity on Travers and responded with, "It helps to have something in common with a woman one hopes to wed—or bed."

Travers drew himself up. "Oh, I say." His tone was both defensive and pompous. "I have no dishonorable intentions regarding Miss Thompson. Quite the contrary."

"Really?" Layton was serious now. "Have you offered for her?"

Travers ran a finger around his neckcloth. "Well . . . not exactly. Have to speak with her father first—and he ain't due to arrive for a few days yet."

"This is good news, indeed," Justin said. "Her father is not likely to have any objections to *you*."

"You don't mind, then?" Travers asked earnestly.

"Why should *I* mind?" Justin asked. "Miss Thompson has no interest in me, nor I in her. No. I congratulate you on a fine match."

"Well, it ain't done yet," Travers said cautiously.

"When it is, the marchioness will rejoice that her efforts have not been *wholly* fruitless." Justin raised his glass to his friend.

"So, those wiles you worked were successful," Layton observed.

"Rather unexpectedly," Travers said, and he added in a sly tone, "and I noticed I am not the only one who has had some success with a lady of late."

Layton shrugged. "Ah, Justin has always had uncommonly good luck with females."

"I was not referring to Justin. I have seen you cozying up to Mrs. Kenwick."

It was Layton's turn to color up. Justin found himself waiting intently for Layton's reply. When it came after a pause, it was guarded.

"Mrs. Kenwick is a very attractive woman. A man would be lucky to engage her interest."

"She does not appear to be the sort of person Kenwick said she was," Travers said.

"Not at all." Layton was vehement. "She is witty and has a good sense of humor. A lovely woman. It was criminal for him to keep her hidden away in recent years."

"Kenwick did not always have the right of things," Justin said and changed the subject to a pugilistic contest the gentlemen planned to attend the next day.

He was uncomfortable discussing Meghan with the others. It occurred to him now that, yes, they knew even then that Kenwick's views were likely to be distorted, yet none of them had questioned the picture he had presented of his wife. Justin was also uncomfortable with the fact that Layton was so clearly attracted to her. Was the attraction mutual?

As the Christmas season drew closer and more hectic, Meghan found herself being drawn into the activities far more than she had expected. Moreover, she was participating with far more enthusiasm than she had dreamed. Irene had adopted her as a sounding board and partner as she planned activities for the guests.

One morning the two of them sat in Irene's private sitting room, reviewing plans and writing invitations for a grand Christmas ball at Everleigh. An annual event, it was mere days away.

"I am so glad you decided to join us this year," Irene said for what Meghan thought must surely be the twentieth time. "This is so much more fun than doing it all alone as I usually do—though I must say Robert and Justin *do* do their share."

Meghan smiled. "As I have said before, I am very happy to be here. Nell—my cousin Eleanor—said it would be good for me. And she was right."

"You *are* having a good time, then?" Irene sounded anxious.

Meghan reached across the small table at which they were writing to pat her friend's hand. "You must not worry about me. I am having a wonderful time."

"But I do worry about you. Even before the accident you had withdrawn so. And then you went into *such* a decline after losing Stephen. . . ."

"I know. I could not seem to help myself."

"One could hardly blame you," Irene went on. "I just do not know what I would do if I lost one of my babies."

"You would do exactly as I have done—rage against the injustice of it even as you muddle through and survive." She paused and added, "With the help of friends like that marvelous Marchioness of Everleigh!"

Irene's eyes were bright with unshed tears of sympathy.

Meghan went on. "I miss Stephen. I will never not miss him. And I have such regrets about the life Kenwick and I had. But one can only go forward. . . ."

"You do seem more at ease around the children than you did when you first arrived," Irene observed.

"Oh, yes. Children are hard to resist. They are so inherently open and honest."

"Painfully so at times. I nearly died the other day when Becky asked Mrs. Seagraves why she had two chins!"

Meghan laughed. "Luckily, Mrs. Seagraves has a good sense of humor."

"And understands children." Irene straightened her stack of invitations and gave her friend a speculative look. "So, are you going to tell me about you and Mr. Layton?"

"About me and—" Meghan was genuinely startled by the question. "Why, there is nothing to tell."

"He has been very marked in his attentions to you. I heard about his kissing you, you know."

"Oh, that." Meghan waved her hand dismissively. " 'Twas nothing. Just seasonal nonsense."

"I am not so sure. . . ." Irene's voice rose on a teasing note.

Meghan laid down her pen and sat straighter. "Now, look. Mr. Layton is a very amiable fellow, easy to talk with—but I am not—I repeat, *not*—looking to remarry. Nor to cultivate a reputation as a willing widow."

"You may find yourself changing your mind."

Meghan laughed. "About marrying? Or the 'willing widow' business?"

Irene rolled her eyes. "You know very well what I meant."

"Neither is likely." Meghan turned back to the task at hand and a moment later said, "There. I have finished my list."

"Good timing! So have I."

* * *

Meghan knew very well she had not answered Irene's question fully. She also knew she had not done so because she was not as sure of her feelings as she wanted Irene to believe. The next day she was forced to confront those feelings.

After breakfast Mr. Layton invited her for a walk in the garden in one section of which a previous marquis had laid out an elaborate maze. In the center of the maze was a small gazebo. Layton guided her to a bench there.

"I hope you do not plan to leave me here to find my own way back." Meghan laughed nervously, keenly aware of how alone the two of them were.

"Never, my lady." He sat next to her. "I merely wanted a private word with you and this seemed the perfect place for such."

"Well, it *is* private, what with this continuous tall hedge."

He took her gloved hand in his own. "Mrs. Kenwick— Meghan—I know that our acquaintance has so far been rather brief. . . ."

Oh, Lord, Meghan thought, *Irene was right!* Aloud, she said with a laugh of forced merriment, "Why, Mr. Layton, I am sure we met several years ago. If I remember correctly, I danced with you at my betrothal ball."

"But I did not really come to know and admire you as I have these last few days."

Striving for a lighter mood, she said, "Renewing old friendships is one of the functions of a house party, I think." He still held her hand and she did not want to offend him by jerking away.

"What I am trying to say in my inept way is that I should like to see our acquaintance grow beyond mere friendship."

"I see . . . ," she said slowly, not seeing, really.

"Can you offer any hope for me?" His hazel eyes earnestly studied her face.

"I . . . I . . . I am not sure. . . ." She looked away, unable to bear that intense scrutiny any longer. Finally, she freed her hand and clasped her hands in her lap. "What is it, exactly, that you are asking of me? I must warn you, I shall be truly insulted if it is a 'slip on the shoulder.' "

"Meghan! No! Never!" His tone was sincere shock. "I . . . I . . . well, I had in mind to propose marriage one day—though I had not expected to spring *that* idea on you now."

She was silent for several moments. What could she say? How *should* she respond?

"Mrs. Kenwick? Meghan?" He put his hand to her chin to turn her gently to face him.

"I . . . I am honored, Mr. Layton. "Truly, I am. However, I do not intend to marry again—ever."

"I . . . I apologize. I had not realized the strength of your feelings for Kenwick. I assumed since you are out of mourning . . ."

"No, you do not understand." She floundered. She had no intention of discussing her marriage with Layton as she had with Irene. On the other hand, she did not want him to view her as one of those pining widows who gloried in the attention perpetual grief brought them. "I . . . I have long since become reconciled to Kenwick's death."

"Your son?" he asked softly.

"I am—lately—learning to accept that, as well, though, that is harder. You see, I should never have agreed to his going that day. I shall never forgive myself."

"Surely you cannot be blaming yourself?"

"To some degree, yes."

"If anyone were to blame for that accident, 'twas your husband—certainly not *you,* miles way in London."

"Wha . . . What do you mean, Kenwick was to blame?" she asked, shocked at this idea.

"Oh, Lord. I never meant to burst out with that."

Her tone was sharp. "But you did. And I want to know—now, if you please—precisely what you meant."

"Oh, Lord," he repeated. He looked away and then back to hold her gaze. His expression was bleak. "You are not a sailor, are you?" She shook her head and he went on. "When the storm came up, we were hit by one of those sudden, unpredictable wind shifts and the main sail jibed—"

She frowned in consternation.

"It caught the wind and flapped out of control," he explained. "When that happens, everyone has to react quickly to keep the boat upright. Kenwick and his boy were at the tiller and we think he overcompensated. The boom swung around and caught Justin, knocking him flat. When the boat tipped, Kenwick and the child were washed overboard. I really thought we were all goners—knew Justin was. We looked and looked—maybe two hours—for Kenwick and the boy, but never saw a sign of them."

Again she lapsed into silence, overset by the horror he described. She closed her eyes against the vision, but it was still there—the wind, the rushing water, the chaos, and the fear her child must have experienced.

Layton took her hands in his. "I am sorry, Meghan. I know this is painful for you. Perhaps if Kenwick had reacted sooner—or less forcefully . . . But who knows with a freak accident?"

Suddenly she understood what he had not said. "Kenwick was intoxicated, wasn't he?"

Layton looked uncomfortable. "Well, he was perhaps a bit bosky, but he was not drunk by any means."

"Just enough to impair his reactions," she said bitterly. Trying to absorb this information, she could not keep the edge of anger from her voice. "Why was I not told this before? You—you, Lord Travers, and Lord Justin—you should have told me!"

"Justin—that is, we—thought it might upset you. We . . . We did not want to add to your grief."

This mollified her a bit, but she would consider it more thoroughly later. "I am not some fragile flower that wants protection."

"Yes. We—I—know that now, but none of us was well acquainted with Kenwick's wife, then."

Kenwick's wife—that silly mouse of a creature, she thought. They were both silent now, each seemingly lost in thought. Finally, Layton gave her hands a final pat and re-leased them.

"I wish, my dear, that you would reconsider my offer and let me hope for a more agreeable response at some future date."

She looked into his eyes and gave him a sad smile. "I am sorry. I cannot entertain such an idea. My life is really quite, quite satisfactory as it is."

He studied her expression for a long moment, then said, "So be it. You do not strike me as the sort who would keep a man dangling with no, no, no and then a yes."

"I should hope not."

"May we continue as friends at least?"

"Of course. I have enjoyed your company far too much to want to give it up."

He leaned toward her and kissed her cheek. "You are a fine lady, Meghan Kenwick. And I think one day someone will break through that resolve of yours. Would that it could have been I who did so."

Gentleman that he was, Layton did not broach the subject again. Meghan found their friendship took on a new dimen-sion of camaraderie with their understanding. Still, she felt some residual anger over not having learned the full truth of the accident until now. She found it discomforting to have to reexamine previous notions of an unsafe boat and inept sailors.

Privately she took herself to task for leaping to conclu-sions at the time—and for her own subterfuge of late. First, she had not been wholly honest with Irene and now she had repeated that faux pas with Mr. Layton. For the truth—which she barely admitted to herself—was that her life was not as satisfactory as she wanted him to believe. She rec-ognized the longing, the need, that was at the core of her disquietude. However, a bit of disquiet was a small price to pay to be free of pain.

* * *

Justin noticed that Meghan and Layton dealt with each other with greater ease. Obviously, Layton had managed to push the relationship beyond the first stages of getting to know another. He found to his mild surprise that he rather envied his friend.

This feeling intensified as Layton drew her more and more into their circle. In the drawing room one evening, he and Layton were engaged in one-upping each other with Shakespearean wit. They were off in a corner of the room with Travers, Miss Thompson, Miss Hamlin, Lady Helen, two other gentlemen, and Mrs. Kenwick. Other conversations whirled elsewhere in the room.

Justin had traded a couple of barbs with Layton already. When he saw that Miss Hamlin looked confused, Justin thought it time to put an end to the game.

"I confess I am not following this discussion. I mean, I just never read such things," Miss Hamlin said, then added, "but I truly admire gentlemen who do."

Travers groaned. "Do not—I pray you—encourage them, Miss Hamlin. They will prose on for hours."

"I am sure you slander these fine gentlemen," Lady Helen said.

"Yes." Justin, who could not resist teasing Travers, raised an eyebrow in challenge to Layton. " 'Slander, whose edge is sharper than the sword . . .' "

Layton picked up, " 'Whose tongue outvenoms all the worms of Nile . . .' "

" 'Whose breath rides on the posting winds and doth belie all corners of the world.' " It was Meghan's voice.

Justin and Layton both turned in surprise to see her cast the group a smile that was at once sheepish and smug.

"Oh, no-o!" Travers said in an exaggeration of great pain. "Not another one!"

"Aha!" Justin said approvingly. "There's language in her conversation as well as 'in her eye, her cheek, her lip.' "

She blushed. "Now it is the gentleman that 'doth protest too much.' "

Justin would have enjoyed even more of such verbal sparring, but he could see that Miss Thompson had as little interest in it as Travers. Miss Hamlin appeared to resent being left out, and others showed varying degrees of disinterest.

"Come," he said. "To the music room. I believe Irene has arranged to have several of the ladies play for us."

"I do hope I may rely upon you to turn my pages for me," Miss Hamlin said, giving him a coy look.

"Of course," he said politely.

Six

The Everleigh Christmas ball was to be an elegant production of major proportions. Besides the resident house guests, invitations had gone out to a vast number of local people—anyone who was anyone for miles around. Few had returned regrets.

For this grand affair—the first ball she had attended since coming out of mourning—Meghan wore a simple but elegant gown of deep green velveteen. Its only trimming was very narrow strips of soft gray fur at the neck and hem. Kid gloves of the same soft gray color and a single strand of pearls with matching ear bobs completed the outfit.

"Betsy, you have outdone yourself!" Meghan exclaimed when the maid had finished with her hair. It was a freer style than she usually wore, with curled tendrils framing her face.

"I have, haven't I?" Betsy's pride was obvious.

The ballroom presented a rich feast for the senses. The piney scent of the green decorations blended with a spicy aroma from discreetly placed potpourri. The rich colors of the ladies' gowns showed to good advantage against the starker evening dress of the gentlemen. Music called forth merriment in everyone. The central decoration was the huge kissing ball in the middle of the room. Two elaborate chandeliers as well as candelabrums on the sides reflected light from framed mirrors placed between window niches.

Despite the elegance of the surroundings and dress, the spirit of the ball was one of sheer fun. Every dance was interrupted with an abrupt pause in the music of that dance. Dancers were to stand still at that signal. The orchestra would then swing into a merry little tune to which the company chanted

Everleigh Hall, Everleigh Hall
    Come one, come one, come all, come all,
See who's under the kissing ball!

Then amidst laughter and cheering, the couple caught in that strategic location fulfilled the purpose of the room's most elaborate adornment.

Meghan thought a number of young ladies and gentlemen contrived their being so caught—but that, too, was part of the fun. It was late into the festivities when it happened to her. In thinking about it later, she suspected Irene had contrived her entrapment, for the marchioness had been standing near the orchestra leader.

It was a waltz and she was dancing with Justin. From the moment he enclosed her in his arms, she had felt her senses heightened. She was already mildly annoyed with herself for, from the very beginning, she had been more aware of *his* elegant evening attire—and the way he wore it—than that of other gentlemen.

Then her impatience with herself intensified. During an earlier dance Miss Hamlin had seemed to manipulate Justin under the kissing ball. With a delighted smile, the beauty twined her arms around his neck and leaned into him dramatically for her kiss. Justin laughed and gave her a quick kiss. Was he laughing *at* the girl? Was the lovely Georgiana disappointed at the brevity of the connection? And just why did she, Meghan Kenwick, feel a twinge of pain at watching this pair? She had had no such reaction to other couples.

Now, here she was—in the arms of a man whose influence on her life she had once resented. And somehow it felt totally right, eminently comfortable. Lost in thought, she was startled to hear his voice—and the laughter in it.

"I have a penny."

"I beg your pardon?"

"I have a penny," he repeated. "For your thoughts."

"Oh!" She felt herself blushing furiously—and her mind went blank.

He laughed outright now. "That bad, eh?" He pulled her slightly closer and said in a conspiratorial tone, "Never fear. A lady cannot be expected to share her thoughts, especially if they happen to be naughty ones."

Recovering, she replied with a challenge. "How can you be sure they were naughty?"

"That blush, perhaps?"

"A true gentleman," she said, her laughing tone belying her pompous reprimand, "would never single out a lady's involuntary reaction for comment."

"Oh, my," he said in a groan of mock despair. "I thought I had hidden it so well, but you have discovered the ugly truth—I am no gentleman."

"Now you add untruths to your litany of faults."

"Untruths?"

Before she could respond, the music stopped. They stood statuelike and the chanting started. Meghan looked around to see who was the focus of fun this time only to find all eyes on her and her partner.

"Oh, dear," she murmured.

His eyes danced with amusement as he enfolded her more tightly in his arms. She braced her hands against his upper arms, but as soon as his lips brushed hers, any idea of resisting his embrace was lost in the torrent of sensations that rocked through her. At first his lips explored softly, but then they became firm and demanding. She lost all sense of time and place as she responded with the hungry yearning she had not willingly admitted to before—even to herself.

The laughter and cheering finally penetrated and the waltz music resumed. She looked into Justin's eyes, which now held something other than amused merriment. He looked fully as stunned as she felt, but he swung her gracefully into the dance. They were both silent until the dance ended. He thanked her and walked away. Moments later, both took the floor with other partners.

It was not until the wee hours of the morning when she finally climbed into bed, that she had time to try to make some sense of that kiss. To no avail. She finally gave up, half joking with herself that were she not careful she might very well turn into that "willing widow" after all—at least where Justin Wingate was concerned.

Justin was shaken to his very core by his encounter with Meghan. He could not recall ever reacting so to a mere kiss. Hungry for more, he had also felt a need to cherish and protect. He sensed a deep vulnerability in her that belied the image of a woman in control and sure of herself.

He admitted his deep attraction to her. However, despite his assertion to her that he was no gentleman, he had no intention of trying to edge out his friend Layton. He frowned at the image in his shaving mirror the next morning. He had observed Meghan and Layton closely. They laughed and chatted with ease, but he could not recall in the last few days their seeming to seek time alone together, as, for instance, Travers and Miss Thompson did.

Miss Thompson's parents had arrived a few days before and happily approved Lord Travers's suit, as Justin had known they would. Travers was clearly besotted, and Justin found himself envying a man toward whom his usual feeling was indulgent tolerance.

He straightened his waistcoat and prepared to go down to breakfast when there was a knock at his door. He opened it to find Irene looking very concerned.

"Joy's kitten has gone missing," she said immediately. "She is inconsolable. We have looked everywhere in the nursery. We now have people checking elsewhere—even the stables. But perhaps you should speak to Joy to reassure her."

"Right away."

He accompanied Irene back to the nursery, where he found Joy, her face reddened and stained with tears. She began to sob anew as her father picked her up and held her to him.

"Don't cry, poppet," he soothed. "We shall find your Snowflake. You'll see."

Her sobs were heartbreaking and then she wrenched his heart even more when she cried, "I tried to be good, Papa. I tried not to be bad. Really, I did."

"There. There." He patted her back and kissed her cheek, tasting the salt of her tears. "You must not cry anymore, my sweet. He will be found. I promise."

She took several deep breaths and her crying eased off. She had cried herself into an exhausted state.

"I shall take her now, sir, if you'd like," the nursemaid said, holding out her arms. "Let us go and wash your face, Miss Joy, and see about some breakfast for you."

"Thank you, Cookson," Justin said.

Joy seemed listless, but she went willingly with the maid and Justin went to check the progress of the hunt for the missing feline.

By noon the kitten had still not been found and Joy had once again drawn a cloak of silence about herself.

The following morning, Justin faced far more devastating news.

Joy herself was missing.

Again, it was Irene who brought the word. The maid charged with getting the three girls readied of a morning had brought the news even before Irene had dressed. She had obviously merely tossed on a dressing gown and gone immediately with the maid to tell Justin.

"What do you mean, she is gone?" Justin's voice rose in alarm. He had barely awakened and had not yet arisen when they came. He stood in the doorway barefooted and wearing only a hastily donned dressing gown.

"She was not in her bed when the others awoke," the maid said. "I checked on the girls soon after midnight and she was sound asleep. All three of them were. But now she is gone. So is her blanket."

"We thought perhaps she came to you," Irene said.

"No, she did not." His mind produced images of kidnappings and children attacked by wild beasts, but he quickly quelled such ridiculous notions. "Let me get properly dressed and I shall join you in the search. She cannot have gone far. And she is bigger than that infernal kitten, so should be easier to find."

An hour later, she had still not been found and fear was beginning to gnaw at his innards. *When* had she left the nursery? The weather had turned bitter cold of late and a light snow had fallen in the night. A small child, clad only in a nightdress, would not fare well in the elements. He refused to consider all the possibilities.

Meghan, along with the other guests, had been informed the day before of the crisis in the nursery produced by the missing kitten. Irene had minimized the incident for the company at large, but privately she shared her concern with Meghan.

"Joy is beside herself—nearly hysterical. I have never seen a child so distraught."

"Is there anything I can do to help?" Her heart went out to the little girl who had lost her mother and now a beloved pet. Meghan knew a thing or two about loss.

"She seems to like you," Irene said. "Maybe you could speak to her. Reassure her about the kitten?"

"I shall do what I can."

She went to the playroom, where she found the loss of the kitten had produced a rather subdued atmosphere. Joy sat in a window seat clutching her blanket and merely watching some of the younger children engaged in a game of pickup-sticks. Others were in the neighboring schoolroom.

Meghan greeted the other children, then went to sit on the window seat next to Joy.

"Hello, Joy," she said softly. "I heard about your kitten."

Joy turned stricken eyes toward Meghan, but did not say anything. Meghan decided to go on as though this were a totally natural reaction. She spoke in a conversational tone.

"You know, when I was a little girl, I, too, had a kitten. Her name was Clara. I named her for my favorite doll, but then I used to get them mixed up." She gave a self-deprecating laugh and looked down to see a shade of amusement in Joy's eyes. So she went on, "And, do you know? Clara used to disappear on me, just as Snowflake has. I truly think she was playing hide-and-seek with me!"

Joy smiled at that idea, but then looked serious again.

"Sometimes," Meghan continued, silently hoping she was saying the right thing, "my Clara would be gone for a *very* long time. Once, I think it was over two *days!* Of course, I was very worried, as I am sure you are for Snowflake."

Joy looked up and nodded. Then she moved closer and Meghan put her arm around her to hug her. She felt her heart full to bursting with love for this small, hurting child. The door to the playroom opened and Justin came striding in.

Joy looked at him, her eyes full of hope. He squatted on his heels before the two in the window seat. He took one of Joy's little hands in his and shook his head sorrowfully.

"No. I am sorry, poppet. We have not found him yet. But everyone is still looking. He is sure to turn up."

Meghan thought there was more hope than conviction in this assertion.

He then looked at Meghan and said, "Thank you, Mrs. Kenwick. I appreciate your trying to help."

She gave the little girl a gentle squeeze. "Joy and I have become friends, and it is important for friends to stand by each other."

"I see," he said gravely, looking from one to the other. It was late afternoon now and in keeping with short December days, it grew dark quite early. Nurse came to light the lamps in the playroom. Joy glanced out the window and seemed alarmed to realize how dark it was. Panic shone in her eyes as she looked from Justin to Meghan.

"He will be fine, I am sure," Justin said, patting Joy's hand and apparently trying to sound confident.

"He probably decided to visit his brothers and sisters," Meghan said, keeping her voice even. "Maybe they are *all* playing hide-and-seek with us."

Joy smiled, but it was a sad little smile. Nurse soon came to announce it was time for the children to prepare for their supper, and Justin and Meghan took their leave.

He thanked her again and he spoke of the search as they descended the stairs to the floor on which their own rooms were located. Occasionally, their arms brushed and she was intensely aware of him.

The rest of the evening progressed rather quietly through dinner and card games, music, and scattered conversations afterward. Meghan retired early to write some letters and then she went to bed to read "for just a little while" but quickly became engrossed in the Chapman translation of *The Iliad*. It was well after midnight and she was empathizing with Achilles' grief over the death of his friend Patroclos, when she heard a sound in the hall. Wondering, she got up and opened her door. There stood Joy, holding her blanket and shivering in a thin nightdress in the cold hallway. She simply gazed at Meghan for a moment; then she pushed into the room, and climbed into Meghan's bed. Meghan closed the door and stood in amazement as the child scooted over and patted the bed, clearly inviting Meghan into her own bed!

"Joy! What are you doing here? You should be in your own bed."

Joy shook her head, looked imploringly at Meghan, and again patted the bed.

"Very well. You may stay for a few minutes," Meghan said slowly, thinking that as soon as Joy fell asleep she would return the child to her own bed. "But I have only this one book, so you will just have to endure the Greeks with me."

She began to read aloud and soon enough she saw Joy's eyelids begin to droop. As soon as she was well and fast asleep, Meghan would take her up to the nursery. Meanwhile, she would just finish this next section.

It was morning when Meghan awoke to great commotion in the hall and then a knock at her door. She came out of her sleep somewhat groggily and was suddenly conscious of the small body snuggled close to hers.

"One moment," she called as she reached for her dressing gown. She opened the door to find Irene looking very distracted.

"Joy has disappeared," Irene said. "We have looked everywhere for her. Have you any idea where she might have gone?"

Meghan stepped back and pointed to her bed.

"Oh, thank heavens!" Irene murmured, then stepped back into the hall and called, "Justin! We have found her. She is here."

A moment later Justin Wingate thundered into Meghan's bedchamber, seemingly oblivious to the impropriety of his being there.

"What in God's name is she doing *here?*" he shouted, clearly angry.

Meghan felt her hackles rising at his tone. "She *was* sleeping. We both were."

He spoke through a clenched jaw. "I ask you again, madam, how did she get here?"

Meghan looked helplessly at Irene. "I—we—fell asleep. She appeared at my door . . . after midnight, I think it was. And she . . . She just climbed into my bed."

"And you lacked the good sense it would have required to take her back to the nursery?" he shot at her with no apparent attempt to keep his voice under control.

A noise from the bed drew their attention. Joy looked frightened and began to sob.

"Oh, now just see what you have done." Meghan glared at him and they both moved to comfort the child, but it was in Meghan's arms that Joy sought refuge. "Don't cry, darling. Your papa is not angry with *you*. He is just a big brute who became afraid when he could not find you."

She heard Justin snort in disgust at her shoulder, but he patted Joy's back. "That's right, Joy-of-my-life. Papa was just worried."

Joy sniffed and became calmer and Justin said, "Come, let Papa take you back to the nursery."

Meghan kissed her cheek and said softly, "It's all right. Everything will be fine. I shall come to see you later." She released the child into the arms of her father, who immediately took her from the room.

Meghan stood for moment feeling decidedly bereft. She looked at Irene, who was considering her with a very bemused expression on her face.

"Never mind," Irene said. "He will get over it. You were right. He was just frightened."

Seven

Later in the morning, Justin sought Meghan out to beg her pardon for his anger at her earlier. She could tell that he was a man unaccustomed to rendering apologies. She accepted his and tried not to harbor resentment at his having immediately found her at fault over the incident. Nevertheless, there was a certain stiffness between them that she regretted but could not seem to get beyond.

In the afternoon, having finished the Chapman book, Meghan went to the library to return it. Seeking something else to amuse her, she found three volumes that looked interesting. She took them over to a high-backed settee that faced away from the door and settled into her decision-making process.

A few minutes later she heard the door open and someone entered. Perhaps it was merely someone wanting to return or retrieve a book. But whoever it was seemed to linger near the desk. She peered around the back of the settee. Justin. Well, he was the last person she wanted to confront at the moment. If he did not leave in a matter of minutes, though, she *would* make her presence known to him.

The door opened again and then closed. Had he left then? She started to look and quickly drew back when she heard the dulcet tones of Georgiana Hamlin.

"Oh, Justin. I am *so* glad we have this moment together."

"Miss Hamlin? Was there something particular you wanted? It is not quite proper for you to be here alone with me. But then you probably know that, do you not?" There was a touch of irony in his voice.

"Pooh." Meghan heard her snap her fingers. "I care *that* much for such silly conventions."

"Perhaps," he said. "But I am quite sure your parents—especially your mama—have a much healthier respect for the niceties by which society lives." Meghan heard a movement and thought he was moving toward the door.

There was the sound of a swishing skirt and then the girl's throaty voice. "Oh, but Justin, my darling, do you not welcome the opportunity to be alone with me?"

Meghan sank lower on the settee. Why had she not let him know immediately that she was here? What an embarrassment for everyone if she revealed herself now!

"Miss Hamlin. Georgiana." His voice sounded muffled. Meghan thought he might be trying to disentangle himself from the girl.

"Do you not want to kiss me?" Miss Hamlin sounded as though she were pouting now. "Our kiss at the ball the other night held such promise. . . ."

"Miss Hamlin. Please." Again, his voice sounded muffled. "You misunderstand. That was not . . . that is to say . . . no one takes such matters seriously."

Is that so? Meghan thought, but she held her breath and hoped he would make his escape soon, since that did seem to be what he intended.

Suddenly the library door banged open and the abrasive voice of Lady Hamlin was heard. "I say. Exactly what is going on here? Georgiana? Lord Justin?"

"Oh, Mama . . . I . . . Justin and I were merely . . ."

" 'Justin' is it? You were merely *what?* I am shocked by your behavior. I hope you are planning to offer for her, Lord Justin, after leading an innocent into such appalling indiscretion. This conduct is most distasteful."

"*Offer* for her?" Justin's voice sounded strangled. "Why, she has been here less than five minutes. Even I need longer than that for what you apparently have in mind."

"How am I to know how long the two you have been closeted alone together?" Lady Hamlin asked.

"Oh, Justin, I fear we are truly caught, my love," Georgiana cried in a voice not entirely devoid of triumph.

Meghan flinched at the sound of what seemed to be a fist being slammed against solid wood. "Now, see here," Justin growled, "I have no intention of offering for your daughter, madam. Even had I seriously entertained any such idea before, this little scene would have surely scotched it."

"Please, Justin, darling," Georgiana pleaded. "I shall be ruined. And we could be so happy. . . ."

"Happy?" He sounded disgusted. "I could be *happy* with a scheming little trollop? I think not, miss."

"Mama!"

Lady Hamlin's voice was hard and threatening. "I believe you will want to rethink your decision, Lord Justin. After all, your brother's position with the current government is not exactly sound. My husband's standing in the House of Lords could very easily thwart any of Lord Everleigh's reformist plans. Not to mention that my brother, Lord Angley, has the prime minister's ear."

Before Justin could reply, Meghan decided she had heard quite enough. She stood, knocking one of her books to the floor with a loud thud.

"I think," she said with scathing looks at mother and daughter, "that once word of this tawdry little plot reaches the ears of the prime minister or anyone in Lords, you will have made your husband and father the laughingstock of the political world."

Lady Hamlin was shocked into mere sputtering. Georgiana kept opening and closing her mouth.

"Moreover," Meghan continued, "I doubt either of you would find yourselves welcomed in many *ton* drawing rooms."

Georgiana finally found her voice. "Justin! You were in here with *her?*"

"Well, I never!" Lady Hamlin huffed. "Come, Georgiana."

The two Hamlin women left the room, one in high dudgeon and the other with a wistful backward look. The door slammed shut behind them.

Justin was momentarily speechless. Then he looked at Meghan, who still had the fire of battle in her eyes. *God! she is magnificent,* he thought, noting her determined stance and the spots of color on her cheeks. He clapped his hands, applauding her.

"Brava! I *could* have handled that, but not quite so expeditiously, perhaps."

Suddenly the whole scene seemed to hit her and she looked sheepish. "I . . . uh . . . It is just that I do detest a bully—and they did seem to be trying to bully you."

"I had no idea you were back there."

"I . . . I was about to make myself known to you when Miss Hamlin came in. And then I did not want to embarrass any of us." She turned slightly away.

He strode over to her and touched her shoulder. She turned, and with a small cry, she was suddenly in his arms. He held her in a tight embrace, her head just under his chin. Finally, he lifted her head to gaze into her eyes. He marveled at what a truly beautiful color gray could be.

"You were wonderful. My lady knight in shining armor," he whispered and lowered his mouth to hers. Georgiana was right, he thought. That kiss at the ball was just a promise, for Meghan was searing herself into his very soul with her response.

When he pulled away, he was breathing heavily and she seemed disconcerted.

"Should I apologize—again?" he asked, holding her gaze.

"No. This was my fault as much as yours. But it must not happen again."

So. She *did* have an understanding with Layton. Yet she had returned his kiss as though she meant it. Perhaps her response was merely the aftermath of an emotional scene, though. He suppressed a flash of disappointment at that idea.

"Come," he said. "I think we need to tell Irene what

transpired here. She and Robert may be counted on to control any damage done by the Hamlin women."

They found Irene in her sitting room. She laughed aloud at their tale of Meghan's rescue.

"You were miscast in that school play, Meghan," Irene said with another gurgle of laughter. "You should have been Robin Hood, not the meek maid Marian."

"It is all well and good for you to have a hearty laugh, dear sister-in-law, mine, but what can be done to forestall the damage those two females may wreak?"

"Never mind," Irene said airily. "Lady Hamlin was just here. She told me Hamlin has received a message of an emergency at home and they will be leaving within the hour, despite the weather."

Justin waved his hand in a gesture of impatience. "Their leaving here today will not preclude their besmirching Meghan's name in town."

Irene rose. "I rather think I can prevent that."

"How?" he challenged.

"Lady Hamlin will be reminded that Sally Jersey is a close friend of mine. If she wants her daughter to continue to be admitted to the exclusive precincts of Almack's next season . . ."

He looked from Irene to Meghan and grinned. "Blackmail and extortion. Remind me not to cross you two in future."

Meghan knew the search for the missing kitten had continued. She visited the playroom briefly before dinner to find Joy still immersed in silence. She had been offered another kitten but refused it.

After dinner the company in the drawing room was somewhat subdued. The snow had begun again, so much of the conversation centered on the weather. There were some whispers of curiosity about the departure of the Hamlins, but everyone accepted—or pretended to accept—the explanation that had been given.

When the gentlemen rejoined the ladies, Justin was not with them. He came in a few minutes later and drifted toward the group that included Meghan. He looked concerned. She turned away from the others to give him an inquiring look.

"I have just come from bidding Joy good night," he told her.

"Still nothing of Snowflake?" she asked softly.

"Nothing. One of the grooms thought he saw that particular kitten, but he could not be sure."

"This is the second day," she observed.

"I know. And I promised her it would be found."

"Has she . . . said anything yet?"

"No." His eyes took on an even bleaker look. "She believes the kitten disappeared because she was bad."

"Did she misbehave?"

"Not that I know of. But that is what she thought about her mother's leaving, too. In some ways this is worse—because it is such a setback."

"Oh, Justin, I am so sorry." She placed a hand on his forearm and gave it a sympathetic squeeze.

"Thank you." He patted her hand and the physical contact sent a flood of warmth through her.

As she rejoined the group and Justin took up a thread of conversation with someone else, she saw Layton glance quizzically from her to Justin and back.

Later, when Meghan had retired, she was again reading in bed when she heard the now familiar sound at her door.

"Oh, Joy, darling, you should be in your own bed."

Joy just stood there looking forlorn and shook her head no.

Meghan sighed and stepped back. "Very well. It would take a far harder heart than mine to refuse you."

Meghan tugged the bellpull and when a maid answered the summons, she sent word to the nursery and to Justin that Joy had again slipped the nursery bonds.

"At least they will know where you are this time," she muttered as she went back to bed. Joy snuggled close to her and Meghan felt such a flood of affection for the little girl that her eyes began to water. Shaking her head, she placed a comforting arm around the child. "I do not know how you have achieved it," she murmured, "but you—and your father—have certainly managed to upset *my* emotional applecart!"

The next morning the nursery maid came to Meghan's room to fetch Joy just as though it were a routinely natural thing to do.

The snowstorm during the night had turned the world of Everleigh into a wonderland. Children's sleds appeared from storage in the lumber room. A dependable draft horse was hitched to an ancient sleigh and kept busy for much of the day, providing sightseeing trips around the grounds.

The children with the sleds and a number of adults reported to a hill some distance from the manor house. With a silent tug, Joy had insisted that Meghan join the sledding expedition. The child glanced at her from time to time, as if to reassure herself that Meghan was still there. Justin, along with Robert and another father, had been recruited to pull the sleds loaded with children.

Irene, who walked at Meghan's side, said, "Joy has become very attached to you."

"I know," Meghan said. "And while that is very flattering, it is also worrisome."

"Do you find her presence annoying, then?"

"Oh, no. Never. I have grown very fond of Joy. But what happens when I return to the city and drop out of her life, too?"

"What is to say that you must do so?" Irene asked. "In any event, your return is weeks away yet. Much can happen in that time."

The sledding hill was located near a fruit orchard, which the group now approached. A dark evergreen forest formed a backdrop for the orchard. The sun had emerged to create a world of rich black shadows against the sparkling snow.

Justin came up beside Irene and Meghan, breathing hard from the exertion of pulling a sled with three children on it uphill. As Irene set about the business of organizing the children to take turns sliding down the hill, he and Meghan were somewhat apart from the others.

"Even leafless, these trees are beautiful," Meghan said conversationally. "Just look at the marvelous designs their shadows create on the snow!"

" 'Bare ruined choirs,' " Justin quoted.

" 'Where late the sweet birds sang,' " Meghan finished, delighted that he had thought of the line. "That is one of my favorite sonnets."

"It is a melancholy thing, dealing as it does with old age," Justin said.

"No," she argued. "It is really quite positive, for it deals with the enduring power of love."

"Do you believe in that?"

"In what?"

"The enduring power of love."

"I think" she said slowly, "that we would all *like* to believe in it."

" 'Tis a fantasy, then?"

"For some." And some of us have the fantasy destroyed by betrayal, she thought, but there was no point in bringing *that* bit of ugliness into such a marvelous day.

By now Irene and Robert had the adventure fully organized and Justin was to be a "pusher," to give the sled extra momentum as it started down the low hill.

Waiting her turn, Joy came to stand near Meghan, a bit to the side of the waiting line. She had taken Meghan's hand when, suddenly, they heard a barking dog and saw a streak of movement. A midsized dog emerged from the forest, chasing a kitten—Joy's Snowflake!

Joy uttered an unintelligible cry, dropped Meghan's hand, and ran after the two animals. Meghan followed her, keeping an eye on the child and the animals. They were some distance into the bare trees of the orchard when the kitten darted up a tree. The dog dashed around the tree, clawed at the trunk, and gave a few more halfhearted yips that sent the kitten higher into the branches. Finally, the dog gave up and ran off in the direction of the stables.

The kitten sat on a high branch, gazing down at them with its sea green eyes. Its fur was wet and ruffled and it mewed plaintively.

Joy gestured for it to come down, and Meghan called, "Here, kitty. Here, Snowflake. Come down."

The kitten clung to its branch, obviously afraid to descend.

Meghan studied the tree. It had a number of low branches, but dressed in heavy winter attire, how could she manage it? Still, for Joy's sake, she had to make the attempt.

"You stay right here," she told Joy. "I shall try to reach him."

She managed the first few branches easily enough. "Come on, Snowflake," she crooned, and the kitten—amazingly—seemed to understand and moved along its branch closer to the trunk. "That's it. Come on," she said softly so as not to scare it.

When it came closer, she reached for it and heard the branch on which she stood crack. Suddenly, she lost her balance and fell backward, her arms flailing. She felt her head hit something hard. She had a fleeting thought of its being another branch, and then darkness enveloped her.

Eight

Justin had just trudged back to the top of the hill pulling a child-laden sled when he saw Joy come running from the orchard.

"Papa! Papa! Come quick! She's hurted."

Responding to the urgency in her voice, he had no time to marvel at the fact that his daughter was speaking again. He grabbed Joy's hand. "Come. Show me."

She led him to tree under which lay a blue heap. Meghan. *Oh, God, no.*

"She fell, Papa," Joy explained needlessly.

He knelt beside Meghan, afraid to move her, lest he injure her further. She was lying on her side, one leg curled under her. She groaned and thrashed about some. Well, apparently she had not broken one of her limbs. As she turned her head, he saw a spot of blood on the snow. He felt beneath her head and touched a lump already forming there. She groaned in protest.

"She will be all right," he assured Joy, not at all sure of the truth of that. Joy nodded.

He picked up Meghan and stood holding her inert body close to his chest as Robert and Irene came up.

"What happened?" Robert demanded.

"How bad is it?" Irene asked.

"As nearly as I can tell," Justin explained, "she was trying to rescue that kitten." He gestured with a movement of his head to the white ball of fur still clinging to a branch.

"She hit her head, but I do not think there are other injuries."

"You go on," Robert told him. "I shall get the kitten, and Irene and I will bring Joy back with us."

In a flash of insight as he carried Meghan back to the house, Justin realized how much she had come to mean to him. *Please, God,* he prayed silently, *do not let me lose her.*

He carried her to her room, shouting at a footman to go for the doctor as he went. Meghan's maid and another maid arrived and he helped them remove her cloak and then left them to the business of getting her into bed. She had groaned a time or two, but remained unconscious.

He was pacing outside the door to her chamber when Robert and Irene arrived with Joy. "She is still unconscious," he told them. "I sent for the doctor."

Irene disappeared into Meghan's room. Joy stood looking rather forlorn and holding her precious kitten close to her.

"Don't worry, Papa. Auntie Meg will be all right. The lady told me."

"The lady?" he echoed, not comprehending at first. "Oh. The lady. Of course." And somehow Joy's reassurance comforted him. He hugged her to him and immediately broke into a fit of sneezes.

The Everleigh maid emerged from the room. "Her ladyship said as how I should take Miss Joy to the nursery."

"Good idea," Justin said, reaching for his handkerchief and eyeing the kitten askance.

Meghan became conscious slowly. She knew instinctively that she lay in her bed and then she recalled the fall. She opened her eyes and was startled to see Justin sitting in a chair by her bed. He was asleep. She turned her head to see Betsy on the other side and felt a twinge of pain.

"Oh, ma'am, you're awake!"

Betsy's exclamation awakened Justin, who sat up straight and ran a hand over his face.

"How do you feel?" he asked as Betsy left the room.

"As though I were hit on the head." She reached to touch her head and felt a bandage. She winced.

"The doctor said you will have a headache, but he found no other injury," Justin assured her.

"How long have I—"

"Been unconscious? About three-and-a-half or four hours."

"Have you been here all that time?"

"Intermittently. They chased me out when the doctor examined you, but Irene was here."

Meghan smiled at the thought of such care being extended to her. It had been years since she felt so cherished.

Justin went on, "Do you feel up to having Joy come to say good night? I told her she could come see you if you awoke before her bedtime."

"Of course."

He left as Betsy returned, bearing a tray. "I know you must be starving, ma'am."

Meghan pushed herself to a sitting position, aware of her throbbing head as she did so. "I would welcome a cup of tea, certainly."

Betsy set the tray over her lap, poured the tea for her, and removed the cover from the plate to reveal an appetizing serving of fish in a white sauce with side vegetables. Meghan drank the tea and nibbled at the food only briefly before pushing it away. Betsy removed the tray, straightened the covers, and fluffed her pillows before leaving.

Joy came bounding into the room with the kitten peeping from the folds of her ever-present blanket. Her father strolled in behind her.

"Are you all well now, Auntie Meg?"

"My head hurts, but I will be fine," Meghan assured her, reaching to touch the kitten.

"And you, missy, are to stay in your own room tonight," Justin said to Joy. "Do you ha-h-h-achoo! Do you hear me?" His voice sounded rather watery.

Meghan gave him a sympathetic look and smiled at Joy. "You have Snowflake for company tonight, though, right?"

Joy nodded. "Hm-mm. Snowflake is very sorry he ran away. He was so scared of that dog an' he was quite hungry, I must say."

Justin and Meghan shared a smile at what was obviously an attempt to sound very grown up.

Justin nudged his daughter. "It is time to say good night, poppet."

Joy thrust the blanket-clad kitten into Justin's hands and climbed upon the bed to give Meghan a clumsy hug. "I love you, Auntie Meg."

Meghan felt tears spring to her eyes. She hugged the child fiercely and kissed her cheek. "I love you, too, dearest Joy."

She looked over Joy's head at Justin, but she could not read his expression. She heard him draw in two strong breaths and then let forth a powerful sneeze.

"Come, Joy." He helped her off the bed and hastily handed her the kitten as another sneeze came upon him.

"G'night, Auntie Meg."

"Good night, dear."

"We shall see you in the morning," Justin said from the doorway and promptly sneezed again.

Meghan lay back against her pillows. It was true. She *did* love that child—with the same kind of protective warmth with which she had loved Stephen. Despite her conviction that such would never again be possible, here she was, loving a child wholly, without reservation. She had not *learned* to love Joy; it had just happened. Yes, she was fond of Irene's children, too, but she *loved* Joy.

And if she were capable of loving a child again, could she also love a man?

Justin Wingate's image flashed across her mind.

No. Children were innately open, not given to dishonesty and betrayal, as adults were.

Oh, for heaven's sake, came an impatient voice from

within. *How can you possibly dump all adults into a box like a bunch of broken toys?*

You know *many* people of deepest integrity. Richard. Irene. Robert. Eleanor—to name only the most obvious. Mr. Layton undoubtedly belonged in such company.

And Justin Wingate?

And Justin Wingate.

She had seen nothing in the last few weeks that put him into the mold she had previously fashioned for him from her own misinformation.

But, no!

She could never again subject herself to possible humiliation and betrayal, to the pain of rejection.

The next morning Justin was surprised to find Meghan already seated at the breakfast table when he came down. She sat next to Layton and was clearly the focus of attention as others asked after her welfare and how the accident had happened.

"Should you be up and about so soon?" Lady Helen asked.

"I feel fine," Meghan insisted. "I have lump on my head and having my hair combed was a bit of an experience, but I am sure the inconvenience is only temporary."

"Gel's got stamina," Travers observed to his betrothed, but in a voice heard by everyone at the table. "A real thoroughbred."

This brought a general laugh, and Justin smiled at Meghan, holding her gaze momentarily. He quickly filled his plate and took an open place at the other end of the table.

"Our goal for the day," Irene announced, "for whichever of you gentlemen who might care to participate, is to bring in the Yule log. But first, of course, you must *find* it."

"Never fear, my dear," her husband assured her. "One has already been found. 'Tis only a matter of dragging it in. However, we shall take our guns and see if there is any game left in our woods, too."

"I strongly suspect there will be a jug of brandy involved, as well," Irene said in an aside intended for the ladies.

"In that case, I shall gladly participate," young Islington said playfully.

"Just see you do not overdo it, son," his usually quiet mother admonished. This, too, brought general laughter, especially among the gentlemen. It was well known that David Islington had been sent down from Oxford after a prodigious drinking bout. He took their teasing with equanimity and gave them all a cheeky grin.

It was some time before the excursion got underway, and Justin observed that Meghan and Layton lingered over extra cups of coffee in animated conversation. He tried to avoid making too much of this in his own mind. Out on the trail, he and Layton ended up some distance behind the others.

"So," Justin said, a shade too heartily perhaps, "is Travers the only man we shall be wishing happy this holiday season?"

"I don't know. *Is* he?" Layton challenged,

"You and Mrs. Kenwick—maybe?"

"Me and Mrs. Kenwick? Doing it too brown, Justin," Layton said harshly. He paused and then added in a tone tinged with regret. "I tried. But it just was not there for her."

"Oh?"

"Meghan has sworn off marriage. Or so she says. She probably really believes it. I think Kenwick hurt her very deeply."

"Are you saying he abused her?" The idea infuriated Justin.

"I don't think he beat her or physically mistreated her. But, you know, we rarely saw her after her marriage, though she often went about during her Season before. And from little things she has let drop, I believe he belittled her both in company and privately."

"He could be a mean-spirited fellow at times."

"I think," Layton said, seemingly working it out as he spoke, "that Kenwick married the prettiest belle of the Season. Then he found himself leg-shackled to a woman with far more depth and intelligence than he possessed."

"And he could not endure being second best. Is that it?" Justin asked.

"That's what I think," Layton agreed. *Especially* to a woman. He just ground her down and robbed her of her spirit—which she has only recently regained."

"That bastard!" Too late, Justin realized how much his vehemence must have revealed.

Layton gave him a knowing look. "Just so. Whatever you do, don't hurt her, Wingate."

Justin squelched the flippant reply he might have made and gave his friend a look of understanding and sympathy. "I shall try not to."

The Christmas festivities proceeded on course with the Yule log, mummers' show, and carolers. Father Christmas made his appearance in a long red robe trimmed with fur and passed out sweetmeats, nuts, and oranges. As an added treat, he had a small toy or a puzzle or a book for each child, that had been selected for that particular young person. Joy's gift was a small ceramic kitten that bore a strong resemblance to her Snowflake.

Justin surprised Meghan by inviting her to meet him in the library, where he privately presented her with a duplicate of Joy's ceramic kitten.

"To remind you not to go around climbing trees," he teased.

"I should rather think of that incident as a good deed gone awry," she replied.

"Some good did come of it," he said. "Whether it was the return of her beloved kitten or the shock of seeing her beloved Auntie Meg in danger, Joy started talking again."

"Yes. Then, indeed, some good did come of it. And I thank you for this charming memento."

He wanted nothing so much as to take her in his arms and kiss her till they were both senseless. But for the first time since he was a stammering, awkward youth in his teen years, Justin Wingate was unsure of himself around a woman. He had promised not to hurt her, and he sensed a vulnerability in her that fairly tore at his heart.

So the moment passed. She excused herself to continue helping Irene prepare baskets to be distributed on St. Stephen's Day, the day after Christmas. And he was left to chastise himself for a missed opportunity.

Having discovered his error in thinking there was a romance brewing between Meghan and Layton, Justin had set about quietly wooing the widow himself. He deliberately sought her company—for a walk in the garden or a sleigh ride. They talked endlessly during these excursions, their topics ranging from the trivial to the profound. He was shameless in using Joy to spend time with Meghan. He timed his outings with Joy and the other children when he knew Meghan would be available to join them.

He had supposed his courtship to be subtle enough not to draw undue attention from others. He should have known better. That is, he should have known Irene better.

"Might I have a word with you, Justin?" she asked the second morning of his "campaign." She ushered him into her sitting room and gestured to a seat as she took a chair opposite.

"What is it?" he asked, expecting a topic having to do with the nursery.

"What are you up to with my friend?" she asked bluntly.

"Your friend?"

"Don't you play the fool with me, Justin Wingate. You know very well I refer to Meghan."

He grinned. "Are you demanding to know whether my intentions are honorable?"

"In a manner of speaking—yes."

"Well, in a manner of speaking—yes. They are. Why do you ask?"

"Because I would not have her hurt. Not again."

"Nor would I," he said simply.

Irene gave him a long, penetrating look, which he returned. "Good heavens! You are truly in love with her, aren't you?"

"Yes, I fear I am."

"Oh, Justin . . ." Her tone was more sad than glad.

"What? Is it so wrong?"

"Not wrong at all, but I am not sure Meghan is ready to love again."

"She already loves Joy."

"That's different and you know it," Irene said.

"Well, I am not Burton Kenwick," he ground out.

"And Meghan is not Belinda."

"What does that mean?"

"Belinda was a charmer. She loved the social scene, pretty clothes, her status as a belle of the *ton*. None of those things means much to Meghan. With Belinda what you saw was what there was. Megan has more . . . more . . ."

"Depth?" he supplied.

"Yes. And thus greater capacity for pain."

"Or love," he said quietly.

"Or love."

For Megan, these days were idyllic. Her headache was gone after the first day. She enjoyed the Christmas preparations with the other ladies and her moments of companionship with Irene. She looked forward to time each day with Joy—even, or especially, to the child's incessant questions. She took part enthusiastically in the games and singalongs of an evening. She found the mummers vastly amusing and the carolers' songs very moving.

But most of all, she looked forward to moments with Justin. Merely being in the same room with him would send her spirits soaring. Chance physical contacts stirred her senses.

One evening during a sing-along session, Meghan sat on the sidelines with Layton as Justin and Mrs. Seagraves sang a duet, his baritone blending perfectly with the older woman's soprano. The two singers enjoyed enthusiastic applause at the end.

"You should give him a chance," Layton said quietly.

"Give whom, what?"

Layton nodded toward Justin. "He *is* interested, you know. And since you won't have me, you might as well have second best." He grinned.

"Arrogant beast," she said with a laugh. "But I have told you—"

"I know. I know. You *say* you aren't interested, but then Justin comes into a room and you can't take your eyes off him."

"Oh, come now. I do not behave quite so ridiculously."

"Well," he conceded, "I doubt many others notice it as I do."

"I admit that Justin Wingate is a very attractive man, but . . ." Her voice trailed off.

"He is not like Kenwick."

"What do you mean?"

Layton gave her hand a gentle squeeze. "I don't say this to hurt you, Meghan. *Justin* was unfailingly faithful to *his* wife—though Lord knows he had ample opportunity not to be. Nor was he—is he—the gamester Kenwick often led you to believe Justin to be."

"How do you know—"

"How do I know what Kenwick told you?" Layton gave a harsh, mirthless laugh. "Because he used to tell us what excuses he had given you."

She gazed into his eyes for a moment, then sighed. "You must have all thought me the veriest fool."

"No. We thought *him* a fool for thinking he could behave that way with impunity. Now we *know* him to have been pathetically stupid in not recognizing what a treasure he had in you."

She smiled at that. "Careful. You will make me hopelessly conceited."

Later, she thought over what Layton had said.

It was true that Justin had singled her out for attention of late. It was also true that her own observations of the man belied her previous view of him. Had her father not taught her years ago that one could judge a man by the people who loved him? With the exception of her own husband, Justin's friends were of the highest caliber—and, in this regard, she accorded Robert and Irene as his friends as well as his relatives.

Yes. She could love him. She *did* love him. But had she not sworn she would not be open to more pain?

What a cowardly approach, that devilish inner voice chided. *Yes, cowardly. Being alive means to feel. One must be vulnerable to pain in order to appreciate life's pleasures.*

Had she not learned as much from the unconditional love Joy gave her—and which she returned in kind?

Love always carried a risk of pain, but it had to be offered unconditionally despite that risk.

With this revelation giving her the most optimistic outlook she had had in years, she finally drifted off to sleep.

The next morning she discovered Justin had returned to London.

Nine

He had left her a note asking *her* to explain to Joy that he would be gone for three or four days, that urgent business called him back to town.

Meghan feared that having her father leave so precipitously would cast Joy back into her world of silence. Thus she was surprised when the Joy accepted the news with great equanimity.

"Yes, I know," Joy said. "The lady told me not to worry."

"The lady?"

"The lady in white. She said when Papa comes back something wonderful will happen."

"Something wonderful?" Meghan felt foolish merely echoing the child's patter.

"It's a secret, though," Joy said very matter-of-factly.

"A secret. Very well. Then, shall we continue our journey to the stables so that Snowflake may visit his brothers and sisters?"

"Oh, yes, please."

"Can you really credit this nonsense about 'the lady'?" Meghan asked wonderingly of Irene later.

"Yes, I can."

"Irene! Surely you do not believe in ghosts?"

"I think I believe in this one, though she never shows herself to adults. Robert swears she came separately to him and Justin when their mother died. Robert was only five and Justin was three. Justin barely remembers it."

Meghan shrugged. "Well, if 'the lady' comforts Joy, so be it."

"At least Joy is continuing to talk. That awful silence in a child . . ."

"Joy has the idea her father will return with some wonderful surprise," Meghan said. "Have you any idea what it could be?"

"Well, not another kitten, I am sure."

"Oh, be serious."

"Hmm." Irene thought for a moment. Then her eyes opened wide in surprise and she grinned.

"What?" Meghan demanded.

"I am not positive—but if I am right—it is a secret."

"Are you quite sure *you* are not masquerading as Joy's lady in white?"

True to his word, Justin returned late one afternoon, two days before the new year. He seemed exhausted from what amounted to nearly four days in the saddle.

He greeted Meghan warmly and seemed vastly amused when she failed to conceal the fact that she was somewhat miffed over his abrupt departure.

"Come with me," he demanded, drawing her hand into the curve of his elbow and propelling her from the drawing room to the neighboring—empty—music room.

He closed the door firmly and took her in his arms.

"Justin! What has come over you? Do you realize what a scene you just created?"

He smothered her last syllable with his lips on hers. It was an unexpected, but not unwelcomed action. She put her arms around his neck to draw him closer and leaned into the kiss.

"Ah. You *did* miss me," he murmured into her hair.

"Well, of course I did," she said, impatient with a statement of the obvious. "And so did Joy. You might have given us some warning."

"Show me again," he whispered against her lips.

And she did. His lips were firm and demanding, his tongue gently probing. All her senses leaped to full awareness, and her response mirrored the yearning and passion he offered.

"I love you, Meghan."

"I love you, too, Justin. But I really think we had better return to the others, lest our absence be remarked upon—and lest we both lose what little common sense we may have left."

He laughed. "Are you going to prove to be a managing female?"

"Perhaps," she said, pleased by the implied future together in his question.

She led the way back to the drawing room from which he then retired rather early.

When Justin had gone, Irene casually strolled over to where Meghan was standing, momentarily alone. "Hmm," Irene said in a low, knowing voice. "I always did wonder what a 'thoroughly kissed woman' looked like."

Meghan rolled her eyes. "Irene—"

The next morning, Meghan sat in the nursery with Joy in her lap as she read to the younger children, when Justin came into the room. She gave him a smile and finished the tale as he waited.

"Read it again, Auntie Meg," Becky demanded.

"Tomorrow, perhaps."

"Joy," Justin said, "Papa needs to talk with you. Do you think you could leave Snowflake with Auntie Meg for a while?"

"Yes, Papa."

She dutifully climbed down from Meghan's lap, and with

a parting caress for the kitten, put her small hand in his.
He turned to Meghan.

"Will you join us in the library in—say—twenty minutes?"

"Of course," She was puzzled by his behavior, but as
she made her way to her own chamber, she conjectured that
his communication with Joy must have something to do
with his hurried trip to the city.

Twenty minutes later she and Snowflake arrived in the
library to find not only Justin and Joy, but also Robert and
Irene and their children all gathered there. Irene looked
amused and Joy's eyes fairly sparkled, but Robert and the
other children looked as mystified as Meghan felt.

She was directed to a wing-backed chair. Joy stood in
front of her and reached for the kitten. Justin squatted on
his heels, his arm around his daughter's waist.

"Go on. Ask her," he prompted.

"Auntie Meg," Joy said, "will you marry us?"

Meghan felt tears threaten. "You want me to marry you
and Snowflake?" she asked, deliberately teasing Justin.

"Me and Snowflake and Papa."

"Yes, darling, I will. I will marry your papa—and you
and Snowflake."

Justin stood and drew her to her feet. "And you get the
whole Wingate clan, as well." He kissed her soundly as the
"whole clan" erupted with joyful cheers.

"The next question," Justin said when the din had sub-
sided, "is—will you do it tomorrow?"

"Tomorrow?" She felt her eyes widen in astonishment.

"What better way to start a brand-new year?"

"But . . . but—"

"I made the trip to Doctor's Commons for a special li-
cense," he pleaded.

"That was why you went to London?"

"For that—and for this." He reached into his pocket and
presented her with a small box. Inside was a ring, a sapphire
surrounded by diamonds.

"Oh, Justin, how beautiful," she murmured as he placed it on her finger. He kissed her again—to more cheers.

Meghan looked at Irene. "You knew?"

"I *guessed*—after Joy's discussion with Lady Aetherada."

"Joy?" Meghan asked wonderingly.

"The lady said you would be my mama, but it was a secret until Papa said I could tell."

"And Papa wants to shout it to the whole world," Justin said. He picked up Joy and Snowflake to hold them in one arm as he returned the other to its proper place around Meghan's waist. He looked into her eyes. "Tomorrow?"

"Tomorrow," she agreed.

Gleeful cries blended with Justin's sneezes.

CHRISTMAS MIRACLE

Debbie Raleigh

One

"There, it is not so horrid, Grace," the plump dowager chirped as she glanced about the cramped cottage.

The slender maiden with a riot of fiery curls and brilliant emerald eyes slapped her hands onto her hips. Although not precisely pretty, there was a certain charm to Miss Grace Honeywell's small features when she smiled. Her smile, however, was decidedly absent at the moment.

Really, she thought in exasperation, her mother had always been one to seek the best in any situation, but this was absurd. Everything about the cottage was horrid, from the lingering stench of the dank darkness to the scurry of mice that could be heard with alarming frequency. It was hardly fit to house the livestock, let alone two gentle-born ladies.

"It is ghastly," Grace retorted, barely keeping herself from shivering as the November wind howled through the ill-fitted windows and door. "The chimneys smoke, the floor is damp, and the roof leaks. We might as well have been tossed into the stables."

A hint of sympathy entered Arlene's eyes. "You will feel better when we have unpacked our belongings. It is never truly home without a few familiar things about."

Grace thought of the pristine beauty of Chalfried standing just beyond the woods. Until that morning it had been her home. Now, because of one arrogant command from Mr. Dalford they had been tossed out like so much garbage.

"This will never be home."

"Grace, we must accept our circumstances, however unpleasant they might be."

"But it is so unfair," Grace protested. "Mr. Dalford possesses a half dozen homes. Why must he force a poor widow into a decrepit cottage all because he wishes to spend a few days in the country?"

"Because it is his right," Arlene said softly.

"Fah. You were married to Mr. Crosswald. It is your home."

"We both knew when I married Edward that Chalfried in time would go to Mr. Dalford. We were allowed to remain far longer than I dared hoped."

Of course Grace had known this day would come. Although Mr. Dalford was no more than a distant cousin to Mr. Crosswald, he had been given everything after the older gentleman's death a year ago simply because he possessed the good sense to be born a male.

"Oh, yes, so generous of Mr. Dalford." Grace restlessly paced toward the tiny window. "He sits up there surrounded by comfort while we freeze to death."

"Grace."

Suddenly realizing she sounded more like a petulant child than a woman of nineteen, she abruptly turned with a rueful smile. "I am sorry, Mother. I just hate to see you in this place. It cannot be good for your health."

"I shall be just fine," Arlene assured her, although she had to be as aware as Grace that her habit of succumbing to chills was bound to be worsened in such a drafty place. "Why do you not help Liza in the kitchen?"

Grace stifled the urge to continue her complaints. Her mother was right. There was nothing to be gained by moaning at fate. For the moment all she could do was make them as comfortable as possible.

"Very well."

Attempting to ignore the dust that was ruining her simple gray gown, Grace moved the short distance from the main room to the kitchen. She stifled a sneeze and rued her impetuous anger. She was not by nature a bitter or vengeful maiden. In fact, she possessed a generous heart and a desire to make others happy. But even her generosity had been sorely pressed over the past years. First by a father who had abandoned his family and managed to lose the family fortune at the gaming tables before his death, and now by a heartless Russian emigrant who had decided upon a whim to visit the estate he had not seen in years. Mr. Dalford was clearly indifferent to the knowledge that his fleeting visit had relegated an elderly widow to this squalid cottage.

Entering the narrow room that passed as a kitchen Grace gave a violent shiver. Hardly surprising, she swiftly concluded, since the young maid was standing in an open doorway.

"Liza."

Turning, the timid girl raised a hand to her mouth. "Oh . . ."

Grace felt a twinge of unease at the obvious guilt etched on the spotted face. Liza might be a good-hearted girl, but she possessed a most distressing habit of creating catastrophes no matter how simple the task. That was the only reason the detestable Boswan, chief steward of Chalfried, had allowed her to come with his former mistress.

"Is something amiss?"

"I was just out a moment, miss, I swear."

Grace's foreboding deepened. "Did something happen?"

"I fear the door did not latch properly."

Grace gave a relieved sigh, assuming the girl was simply referring to the frost in the air. At least the roof was still standing and nothing was on fire.

"Do not fret. It could not be much colder with the door open or shut."

"It is not that, miss," Liza confessed. "It is the kittens."

"Oh, no." Grace's heart twisted with distress. Only weeks before, her beloved cat had given birth to a litter of kittens. Now she moved to the corner where she had made a small bed.

"I found all but one," Liza stammered.

It took Grace only a moment to account for all but one pure black kitten. "Byron . . ." she breathed. "Of course."

"I am so sorry, miss."

"It is fine, Liza." With brisk motions Grace straightened and reached for the heavy cloak hanging on a peg. Byron had proven to be far more adventurous than the other kittens, with a habit of sneaking off when the opportunity presented itself. "I will find the rogue."

"But it is snowing."

"I shall soon return."

Stepping through the doorway Grace began her search. As Liza had warned, a soft snow was falling, but while Grace shivered at the cold, she discovered herself counting the snow as a blessing as she spotted the tiny tracks leading from the house to the woods. It would make discovering the kitten decidedly more simple.

Keeping her gaze firmly on the trail, Grace hurried through the woods. It took little time for her to realize the kitten was headed directly for its former home. Her steps hurried as she felt a stirring of fear. Boswan had already threatened to have her pets drowned should he see them about, and Grace had no doubt the evil man would make good on his promise should he stumble across Byron.

Breaking from the woods her heart sank as the tracks clearly continued across the parkland and into the square manor house. No doubt becoming lost in the woods, the kitten had returned to the only home he knew, and Grace very much feared he would even now be hidden in the master bedchamber where he had been born.

"Oh . . . botheration."

Although a solidly built house with four towering columns topped by elegant statues and arched windows that flanked the double wooden doors, Chalfried made no pretensions to rival the more stately mansions throughout the neighborhood.

Still, it was well tended, with a small parkland and elegant garden.

Stepping out of his carriage, Mr. Alexander Dalford regarded his acquisition with a narrowed gaze. It had been years since his last visit to Chalfried, but not a stone or tree appeared to have been altered. Cousin Edward was nothing if not fiercely devoted to tradition.

"Alexander, it is lovely," Lady Falwell breathed, her astonishingly beautiful countenance wreathed with a smile.

Alexander could not halt a smile of his own. He had known Rosalind since she was a child and had maintained a close friendship with her even after her marriage to the much older Lord Falwell.

Not that it was a friendship without its trials, he acknowledged with a grimace. Especially of late, when their vast amount of time spent together had started viscious tongues wagging.

Which was precisely why he had devised this excursion to the country. Bringing both Lord and Lady Falwell along with the *ton*'s most notorious rattle-monger, Mr. Wallace, he intended to prove over the next several weeks that the innuendoes were groundless.

Almost on cue, the short, overly plump form of Mr. Wallace struggled from his carriage. Attired in a ridiculous velvet coat with a profusion of lace at his neck and wrists, he minced his way toward Alexander with a smirking smile.

"Egad, how drearily rustic. Hardly the setting I would have expected for the Russian Fox."

Alexander gritted his teeth at the name he had acquired during the war. It had originated from his sly attacks and swift retreats that had driven Napoleon mad with rage. And with his Russian-born mother's close relationship with the czar it had been an appropriate title. Unfortunately, it had followed him on his return to London, and even the prince regent was known to refer to him as Fox.

It was not that Alexander was ashamed of his Russian heritage. Far from it. From his mother he had inherited his large stature, midnight-black hair, and brilliant blue eyes.

Even his narrow countenance, high Slavic cheekbones, and strong nose showed little hint of his English father. But Alexander had swiftly learned that the London aristocrats held a hint of superiority over anyone with the ill fortune to possess foreign blood. It was only his large wealth and connections to the most noble families that allowed them to overlook his diluted blood.

That, of course, and his undoubted success among the ladies.

With an effort, he conjured a mocking smile. He would not allow the nasty twit to rile his temper. There was too much at stake.

"That only proves how little you know me, Wally."

The shorter man thinned his lips, but at that moment the door was pulled open to reveal an ancient butler. "Welcome, sir."

"Thank you. Would you be so good as to show my guests to their rooms?"

The servant gave a creaking bow. "Of course. This way, please."

The tall, silver-haired Lord Falwell readily escorted Rosalind up the steps, followed by a reluctant Mr. Wallace. Alexander waited for them to disappear into the house before he followed in their wake.

It felt odd to realize that this estate now belonged to him. He had barely known Edward, except for the handful of occasions he had made his mandatory visits. But when he had sought a place to bring Mr. Wallace, Chalfried had seemed the perfect location. In part because it was the one spot no one knew him or Rosalind, and more importantly, it was far from the secret they kept at his family estate in Surrey.

Hoping that the presence of Mr. Wallace did not forever taint the rather charming home, Alexander mounted the steps and entered the narrow foyer. He had just turned toward the curving staircase when a thin, beady-eyed gentleman suddenly appeared.

"Mr. Dalford." The stranger gave a rather awkward bow. "I am Boswan."

It took a moment for Alexander to place the name. "Ah . . . the steward."

"Yes, sir. I hope you find the estate in order."

There was something in the ingratiating smile and hard glitter in the deeply set eyes that Alexander instinctively disliked. "I am hardly in a position to say as of yet, although it appears to be in no danger of tumbling about my head."

The sharp features hardened, but the practiced smile remained intact. "No, indeed, sir."

"We will speak later, eh, Boswan?" Alexander dismissed the servant, inwardly deciding to spend a bit of his time discovering more of the man. There was something untrustworthy about him.

"Very good."

With a decisive movement Alexander continued his path to the stairs, using his vague memories to lead him past the landing and to the door of the master chamber. He was in dire need of a bath and a change of clothing before facing Mr. Wallace once again. He shuddered. An entire month with the man would no doubt send him batty.

Alexander pushed open the door and stepped into the shuttered room. He moved forward, then halted and bent slowly downward.

He had seen many things in his eight-and-twenty years, but never had he entered his room to discover a most delightful posterior sticking from beneath his bed. Wide-eyed, he watched as the posterior wiggled in a most fascinating fashion, then began to move backward. At last he could determine the slender bottom was attached to a young woman who was carefully scooting from beneath the bed, clutching a black ball of fur.

She slowly straightened; then noticing his tall frame, she gave a theatrical shriek.

For a moment he could only gaze at the maiden in disbelief. At first glance there was nothing more remarkable about her than an untidy halo of flame-red hair. Her eyes were fine enough, although her features plain and her cloak a hideous gray. But on closer inspection there was a decided character in the strong features and a hint of sweetness in the full lips.

Abruptly shaking off the sense of disbelief, Alexander sharply reminded himself of the other women who had attempted just such a ploy. The supposedly demur debutante who had plotted like a seasoned general to compromise him into marriage, the widow who had crept into his bed in the dark of night, and the wife of his closest friend who arrived at his home attired as a servant.

Good Lord, he had been hunted, lured, and mobbed since coming of age. Would they never cease to plague him?

"What the devil do you think you are doing?" he rasped.

Pretending to be startled by his appearance, she pressed the ball of fur to her bosom. "I came to get Byron."

Alexander blinked. Well, that was an unusual excuse in any event. Did he suppose that he kept dreary poets stored beneath his bed?

"Byron?"

"My kitten."

So, the ball of fur was explained, but Alexander was no fool. That cat was no more than a feeble reason to invade his home. "How very convenient."

She frowned at his mocking words. "I beg your pardon?"

"Do not suppose you are the first maiden to go to such shocking measures to be alone with me." His nose flared with distaste. "Although I must admit not even the boldest tart possessed the audacity to hide beneath my bed."

He thought he heard her suck in a sharp breath. "You believe I wish to be alone with you?"

"Of course."

"Why would I wish for such an absurd thing?"

He was not amused by her pretense of innocence. Clearly a forward jade, even if she did have a delectable backside. "To trap me into marriage, of course."

"Marriage?"

Surprisingly, a flush of color suddenly stained her pale cheeks, and her emerald eyes flashed with fire.

"Why, I wouldn't have you if you were the king of England."

He gave a mocking laugh. "I cannot say that I blame you, considering he is reputedly mad. I, on the other hand, am in perfect health and in constant threat of being compromised by forward harpies who have no shame and no dignity."

She made a most convincing display of outrage as she gave a sudden stomp of her foot. "Compromise you? Why . . . I despise you. I despise you more than anyone I have met in my entire life."

"Is that so?"

"Yes."

He strolled slowly forward, his blue eyes glittering with a wicked glint. The chit was clearly furious that her ploy had been seen through so easily. It was equally clear she hoped to pass her outrageous behavior off as a mere misunderstanding. Well, he would teach her not to trifle with a gentleman's reputation.

"Do you skulk in the bedchambers of every gentleman you despise?"

"I came for Byron," she gritted.

"So you have said." He halted directly in front of her, reaching out to wrap his arms about her waist and pull her close. "I think it is more likely you came for this. . . ."

She arched backward, but Alexander relentlessly pursued the elusive lips, claiming them in a bold kiss. His plan was to ensure that she never attempted such a dangerous folly again.

Unfortunately, it was a plan that was swiftly forgotten as the soft lips trembled beneath his touch. He had been right, he inanely thought as a delicious heat spread through his body. Her lips were as sweet as a fine liqueur and just as swift to cloud a gentleman's judgment. His arms tightened as he gently parted her lips with the tip of his tongue.

Delectable . . .

Delectable and utterly irresistible.

The odd realization flared through his mind at the same moment she decided to pull away. But not before the door to the chamber was thrust open and the astonished voice of Mr. Wallace jolted through the air.

"Good God . . ."

Two

For a crazed moment Grace discovered herself lost in the searing kiss. It was nothing at all like she had envisioned a kiss to be. It was not soft or tender. Instead it had been fiercely possessive and it had evoked a sharp pleasure that had tingled from the tip of her head to the toes that had curled in the privacy of her boots.

It had taken the sharp pangs in the region of her heart to bring her to her senses. Not the pangs of Cupid's arrow, she realized with an absurd flare of relief, but the pang of tiny claws digging through her gown.

Unlike her, Byron had taken instant exception to Mr. Dalford's outrageous behavior.

Unfortunately, the same moment she pulled back in horror was the same moment a voice had echoed through the room and she had turned her head to view a portly gentleman inspecting her with malicious enjoyment. In the blink of an eye the intruder had whisked shut the door, but not before Grace had felt a chill of horror at his expression.

Clutching the decidedly vexed kitten to her chest she glared at the astonishingly handsome gentleman. She wished to slay him with the furious edge of her tongue. To make him cringe beneath the righteous humiliation that flowed through her rigid body. Instead she stammered like a simpleton.

"How dare you?"

A slender hand raised to shove its way through the raven satin of his hair.

"It seemed a perfect means of teaching you a lesson at the time." He grimaced. "Now we are certainly in the bumble broth."

Teaching her a lesson? She shivered as she recalled the heat that had swirled through the pit of her stomach. She had no desire for such lessons. At least not from the gentleman who had tossed her from her own home.

"Why, you arrogant lout! I suppose you presume every maiden in England is desperate to become your wife?"

He merely shrugged. "It is not arrogance. I assure you there is nothing particularly pleasant in being pursued by rabid fortune hunters."

She steadied her quivering knees. *Oh, yes, the poor soul,* she inwardly seethed. *It must be so difficult to be rich, handsome, and the toast of London.*

"And I assure you that there is nothing pleasant about being labeled a liar and then mauled like a common light skirt. I came for Byron and now I intend to leave."

Surprisingly he firmly moved to block her path to the door. "Oh, no. Not until you tell me who you are."

Grace momentarily glared at him in silence. It was none of his bloody business who she was. But the realization that she could not very well dislodge a six-foot male from her path made her swallow her pride.

"Miss Honeywell," she reluctantly confessed.

His brows snapped together. "Do you work for me?"

Her mouth dropped open in outrage. Why the . . .

"Certainly not. I was Mr. Crosswald's stepdaughter."

A decidedly satisfying flare of shock rippled over his proud countenance. "Good lord. What are you doing here?"

"I was living here until we were forced to move to a cottage not fit for a pig so you could host your little party."

He gave a slow shake of his head. "You live on the estate?"

She regarded him as if he were unendurably slow. "Where else would we go, sir?"

Without warning, he abruptly threw his hands in the air. "Well, this is a bloody mess."

"I fail to see how our inconvenience affects you."

He possessed the nerve to appear exasperated at her ill fortune.

"I did not even realize you were living at the estate when I decided to come to Kent. I presumed you would return to your former home."

A hint of color stained her cheeks. "We were forced to sell our home to pay off my father's debts."

"Why the devil didn't Boswan tell me?"

Grace began to slowly suspect that she may have been a bit hasty in laying full blame for their eviction upon this gentleman's shoulders. He seemed quite sincere in his surprise that they were still in the area. Her lips tightened. Blast, Boswan. She should have suspected his devious hand had somehow been involved.

"Because he has always resented my presence at Chalfried. I have no doubt he was robbing the estate blind until I took over the books. When he realized you were coming he obviously assumed it was a perfect opportunity to have his revenge, although Mr. Crosswald at least ensured we would have the cottage."

His expression darkened at her words. "Damn."

If she had hoped for sympathy for her predicament, she was sorely disappointed. "Is that all you can say, Mr. Dalford?"

Her chastisement only caused his frown to deepen. "Do you not realize the mess we are in?"

"What mess?"

"We were seen in my bedchamber in a very intimate embrace."

Grace abruptly recalled the oddly repellent gentleman who had entered the chamber. "You will simply have to confess your scandalous behavior to your guest. I am certainly innocent."

"That was no mere guest," he informed her, his magnificent blue eyes darkening with dislike. "Mr. Wallace is a very nasty rattle who loves nothing more than to spread scandal to whomever will listen. I have no doubt the entire household has already learned that I was seducing a flame-haired, green-eyed minx. Your description is bound to be recognized by the servants and will be the source of village gossip by the end of the day."

Her heart faltered at his words even as she gave a shake of her head. "That is . . . absurd."

He moved to tower over her, speaking with slow emphasis. "By the end of the week it will be throughout London and on its way to the Continent."

No. It could not be. Not even her luck was that ill.

"Once you've explained the truth . . ."

He gave a humorless laugh. "Wally has no interest in the truth. He is out to destroy my reputation, and now I have handed him the perfect opportunity on a silver platter. Da . . . Blast the liver-hearted scoundrel."

"Why would he wish to destroy your reputation?"

"Because I have the ear of the prince and I have advised him strongly against placing certain undesirable gentlemen in key positions in the government. Those gentlemen would pay a great deal to have my position undermined."

She wished to dismiss his words as grandiose bragging. He would not be the first gentleman to claim to have the ear of the prince. But something in his dark countenance made her stomach twist with dread.

"There is no certainty that I will be recognized." She unconsciously clutched Byron tighter, only to be rewarded with another stab from those sharp claws. "You could always claim that I was a servant. There seems to be no scandal in seducing a poor maid."

With a faint shake of his head he reached out to gently untangle the kitten from her tender skin. Annoyingly, Byron curled onto his arm and fell asleep.

"Mr. Wallace will not rest until he has found you again. Hardly a difficult task with your brilliant hair and the fact that you live on the grounds."

The sense of dread hardened to genuine fear. Heavens above, were things not bad enough? Her poor mother was reduced to a life of penury in a decrepit cottage. Her own future was hardly brimming with glorious promise. The last thing she needed was the further burden of being branded a tart.

"This is all your fault," she hissed.

"I realize that," he shocked her by admitting. "What we have to decide is how we are to get out of this deuced dilemma."

She drew in a deep breath. Why had she come to Chalfried? The traitorous Byron would have found his way back to the cottage. Now, she had not only encountered the gentleman she had sworn to avoid at all cost, but she had been labeled a scheming minx, thoroughly kissed, and now threatened with a scandal that would break any mother's heart. And all before tea.

"You could return to London," she suggested hopefully. "Mr. Wallace would never discover who I am."

"And if one of the servants has already recognized your description?"

"Then I will deny being here."

"And Boswan will no doubt be just as swift to claim that he saw you enter the house," he pointed out with cool logic. "What better means of punishing you?"

Botheration. He was right. Boswan had detested her from the moment she had taken an interest in the management of Chalfried. And no wonder, she had eventually discovered. Although he had claimed to have lost several ledgers, it had only taken Grace a few days to realize the steward had been lining his own pocket from Edward's rents for years. Of course, without the ledgers it had been impossible to make her accusations. Instead she had personally taken charge of the books. And in the process she had gained a very dangerous enemy.

Now she realized he would indeed take great pleasure in marring her reputation. If Wallace did mention that there had been a redheaded wench in Mr. Dalford's chambers, he would leap at the opportunity to implicate her in a scandal.

"Then what do you suggest?" she demanded. "I have no more desire than you to be the center of gossip."

He studied her pale features for a long moment, as if coming to a decision. "It appears that we have no choice."

Grace was quite certain that she did not like the wicked glint that entered his dark blue eyes. "What do you mean?"

"We are too late to halt the gossip, but we can turn it to our advantage."

"I can hardly see any advantage in having others know I was in your bedchamber," she retorted with a blush.

"Well, you were impetuous." He slowly smiled. "Hardly surprising for a maiden in your condition."

She regarded him warily. "My condition?"

"A woman betrothed to a handsome, charming, and utterly devoted gentleman."

Feeling unconscionably dense, she gave a slow shake of her head. "I am not engaged."

"Of course we are, my dear. And beginning today we are going to announce it to anyone who will listen."

For the first time in her life, Grace deeply regretted the fact that she had never developed the maidenly skill of swooning on cue. It would have been so very befitting for the melodramatic scene.

Instead she regarded Mr. Dalford with wide eyes. Quite clearly he was one sheet short of a full sail.

Three

After pouring himself a generous measure of brandy, Alexander swallowed it in one gulp. He just as swiftly poured himself another shot. He felt no guilt for his unusual consumption of the fiery spirit. Miss Grace Honeywell could drive any gentleman to drink. She had to be the most aggravating minx in all of England.

For heaven's sake, it had taken him over an hour to convince the stubborn chit that becoming his fiancée was the only solution to their difficulties. An hour during which she had managed to make him feel the lowest excuse for a gentleman that had ever had the misfortune to be born. He had never regretted a kiss more in his life. Even if it had evoked the most astonishing sensations in the pit of his stomach.

Of course, he had to concede that once he had managed to wrench a promise of compliance from Miss Honeywell and sent her and her kitten on their way, he had been suddenly struck by the irony of the situation.

He had come to Chalfried to convince Mr. Wallace that Lady Falwell was not his mistress. What better means of convincing him than to produce a fiancée? One who could be easily disposed of at the proper time?

Determined to turn the exasperating dilemma to his own advantage, Alexander had sought out Rosalind and together they had plotted the best means to proceed. Now he waited in the elegant blue-and-green salon for his prey to arrive.

He did not have to wait long. He had just polished off

his second drink when the overpowering scent of citrus cologne warned him that Mr. Wallace had made his entrance.

Turning slowly, he regarded the striped plum coat and
absurdly high collar points with an inward shudder. At least
the lace was gone, he acknowledged, although the enormous
buckles on the dainty slippers were just as ghastly. A puffed
up popinjay with few scruples and a talent for being where
he was least wanted.

With an effort, Alexander summoned a lazy smile as he
poured his guest a brandy and thrust it into his pudgy white
fingers. Wallace's own smile held an edge of lewd enjoyment.

"Well, well, Fox. I must apologize for intruding at such
an . . . inopportune moment."

Alexander waved a dismissive hand. "Think nothing of
it, Wally."

"A lovely wench. Who is she?"

Alexander allowed himself a dramatic pause. "Actually,
that is a rather delicate subject."

Wallace gave a nasty laugh. "Yes, I am sure it is."

"More brandy?"

"No, thank you. I am all agog with curiosity. Are you
going to confess?"

Alexander pretended to consider his request with a faint
frown. "Only if you promise not to repeat what I tell you."

"You have my word."

Which was no doubt worth as much as the chip of glass
he attempted to pass off as a diamond in his stickpin, Alexander acknowledged wryly.

"The young lady you saw in my arms is Miss Honeywell . . . my fiancée."

There was a choked sound of disbelief. "You must be
jesting."

"Not at all."

"This is absurd. I have never heard mention of any fiancée."

"Miss Honeywell has been in mourning for her stepfather. We were forced to keep our arrangement between ourselves until after the New Year."

The oily smile faltered. "Indeed?"

"Yes."

"And what was she doing in your chambers?"

Alexander had prepared carefully for the obvious question. "She had decided to surprise me with a miniature she had commissioned from a local artist, but I arrived before she expected and I caught her placing it upon my bed. Rather impetuously, I was overcome at the sight of my beloved after such a length of time apart, and I allowed my feelings to overcome my good sense."

An ugly expression descended upon the pudgy countenance. "Good God, Fox, you spin a pretty tale, but you cannot expect me to believe such a banbury story?"

An imperial ice descended upon Alexander's thin features. When he wished, he could be as arrogant and commanding as his distant cousin the czar. He deliberately glared down his long nose at the much shorter gentleman. "Frankly, Mr. Wallace, I am supremely indifferent to what you may or may not believe. You asked for the truth and that is what I have given you."

For a moment Wallace wavered beneath the intimidating glare; then clearly remembering he stood to gain a great deal if he could destroy his host, he stiffened his spine and withdrew a lace handkerchief to lightly dab at his large nose.

"That woman is no more your fiancée than I am the prince regent," he scoffed.

They regarded each other in silence for long moments, like two fencers waiting for their opponent to reveal an opening. Then, on cue, Lady Falwell swept into the room, appearing inordinately lovely in a buttercup silk gown with an amber necklace draped about her neck.

"Am I intruding?" she demanded.

A sly smile suddenly curved the thick lips. "Not at all, my lady. Fox was just telling me of his mysterious fiancée."

Alexander grimaced. So much for Wallace's pledge of

silence. He said nothing, however, as Rosalind artfully widened her eyes with shock.

"You told him of Miss Honeywell?" she demanded of Alexander. "I thought your engagement was still a secret?"

Wallace was obviously taken aback. "You knew?"

"Of course, although Lord Falwell and I were sworn to secrecy."

"As was Wally," Alexander pointed out in sardonic tones.

Like any rat, Wallace was wise enough to realize when it was time to scuttle back to the shadows. With a forced laugh he raised his glass in a mocking toast. "It seems congratulations are in order."

The next morning Alexander rose at a most unreasonable hour to ensure he would discover Miss Honeywell at home.

Of course the minx had already disappeared to the local village. Determined to speak with her before Wallace could discover her whereabouts, Alexander had nevertheless lingered long enough to become better acquainted with her most charming mother. And long enough to realize that she had not been exaggerating when she had claimed that their cottage was not fit for a pig.

At least he now understood that prickly dislike that had shimmered in those emerald eyes. What maiden wouldn't resent losing her home to a gentleman whom hadn't the least need for yet another estate?

Returning to the gig that he had discovered in the stables, Alexander urged the plodding mare in the direction of the village. His eyes rolled heavenward at the uneven pace. He was quite certain that his grandmother could outdistance the nag. Eventually, however, he pulled onto the narrow High Street. For once his luck was in and he had traveled only a few feet when he caught sight of those fiery locks peeking from beneath a plain black bonnet. The rest of her was swathed in a heavy black cape that did nothing to complement her pale countenance.

Still, Alexander felt the oddest prick as he watched her storm down the street, the light of battle in those green eyes.

This was no milk-and-toast miss. She was a woman of passion. Decidedly angry passion at the moment.

Battling the uncooperative mare, Alexander at last managed to pull up beside his fiancée. "Ah, Miss Honeywell, I have been searching for you."

"Go away."

Alexander couldn't prevent a startled chuckle. In all his years a young maiden had never, ever told him to go away. "Is that any way to greet your fiancé?"

She stomped her foot in frustration. "How dare you make light of this . . . this catastrophe? Do you know what I have endured this past hour?"

Glancing down the street to where a dozen locals had halted their activities to openly ogle the two of them, Alexander gave a rueful grimace. "I can well imagine."

"I have never been so humiliated in my entire life."

"Get into the gig and I will take you home."

She instantly stepped away. "No, thank you. I prefer to walk."

He allowed a smile to curve his lips. "If you wish, but I believe there are a handful of dragons waiting to speak with you just down the street."

Against her will she turned to note the clutch of disapproving matrons standing beside the stone church. She visibly stiffened with dread of being at the mercy of their shrill tongues.

"Oh, bother." With a harsh sigh, Grace awkwardly climbed onto the seat beside Alexander, keeping her gaze staunchly trained on the clenched fists in her lap as he maneuvered them out of town and onto the road that led to the estate.

Once away from prying eyes he turned to regard her rigid profile. "May I say you are looking particularly fetching this morning?"

"Fah, I look hideous in black," she promptly retorted,

then her eyes widened as he pulled to a halt beneath the shelter of a towering oak. "What are you doing?"

"We must speak."

Her chin jutted out. "I do not see why."

He heaved an exasperated sigh. Out of thousands of maidens who would have bartered their own grandmother to become his fiancée, he had to choose the one female who considered him as appealing as the plague.

"You are clearly determined to make this as difficult as possible."

Her tiny gasp echoed through the chilled air. "You are the one who has made this difficult, sir. It was bad enough to be forced from my home to that wretched cottage, but now you have made me a source of gossip and ridicule throughout the entire village."

An unwelcome prick of guilt brought a hint of color to his high cheeks. Good heavens, you would think he had created this disaster on purpose.

"First of all, I have already explained that I had no notion that my arrival in Kent would in any way inconvenience you, and I assure you that I will have your accommodations seen to as soon as possible. And I also assure you that I am no more pleased than you by the gossip, although I have gone to great lengths to ensure that by the end of the day the gossip will be centered upon our impending marriage rather than our impetuous kiss."

The green eyes never wavered.

"If you are attempting to lighten my mood, sir, you are doing a shockingly poor job of it."

A reluctant laugh was wrenched from his throat. By gads the chit had brass.

"Listen you aggravating minx. I am attempting to salvage our reputations from a very nasty situation. Are you going to help me, or do you prefer to have all of England believing you are a light skirt?"

A hectic color stained her cheeks, adding a hint of beauty to her plain features.

"Oh, if I were a man I would plant you a facer."

Without conscious thought, Alexander abruptly leaned forward to snatch a brief, utterly heart-stopping kiss. Pulling back he gazed deep into her startled eyes.

"If you were a man we would not be in this interesting predicament, would we?"

Four

Grace wanted to be outraged. This was the second occasion this gentleman had taken shameless advantage of her. And this time he did not even have the excuse of believing she was angling to trap him into marriage.

But while her mind might assure her that she should be furious, the rest of her was trembling with the oddest sensations. Heavens above, if this was what kisses did to a maiden, it was little wonder they were eager to attract the attentions of a gentleman.

Decidedly unnerved by her shocking thoughts, Grace found her anger floundering. What was she thinking? This was no time to moon over a gentleman's kisses. Not when she was clearly trapped.

As much as she disliked the notion, he was right. This morning proved that the entire village was aware of her presence in Mr. Dalford's bedchamber. The only solution appeared to be pretending to be his fiancée. It was that or being branded the local tart. A most unbearable alternative.

"What do you want from me?" she at last managed to croak.

Alexander appeared remarkably unaffected by the kiss, unless one counted the strange glow in his blue eyes.

"First we must have our respective stories the same," he informed her. "Wallace is already suspicious about my sudden announcement of an engagement and is bound to attempt to trip us up."

His words made sense, she grudgingly conceded. They would have to know something of each other. "Very well."

"I thought it best that we claim to have met somewhere besides Kent, since I have already admitted that it has been years since I was last at Chalfried." He regarded her closely. "Have you traveled?"

"I spend a portion of the year with my grandmother in Leicestershire."

"Good, I have a hunting lodge near there. We can claim to have met during one of your visits. I discovered your connection to Edward and we became friends. Naturally I was bewitched by your beauty and sweet nature and declared for your hand." A smile twitched at his lips as he uttered the words, making a dangerous glint return to Grace's eyes. She did not need to read his thoughts to realize that he found her anything but beautiful and sweet natured. Thankfully, she resisted the urge to tumble him out of the gig. "Unfortunately, Edward died before our engagement could be announced and so we were forced to keep our understanding a secret until you were finished with your mourning."

"You seem to have it all worked out."

"Except for the fact that we are perfect strangers to each other," he pointed out with exaggerated patience. "I think it best that we become better acquainted with all possible speed."

Grace gave a faint shrug. "What do you wish to know?"

He turned slightly, allowing his leg to press intimately against her own. "Everything. Your name, age, what you like, your favorite color."

"This is absurd," she protested, wishing she could move from his disturbing touch.

He gave a chiding click of his tongue. "Fine, I will go first. I am Alexander Dalford, better known as the Russian Fox or Fox to those in London. I am just turned eight-and-twenty. I enjoy the usual pursuits, although I prefer an evening of intellectual debate to the endless social rounds. Both my parents died when I was but a child and I was shuttled between my English and Russian grandparents who were both determined to teach me my proper heritage. Very confusing for a young boy. My favorite color . . ." He paused as a wicked glint entered his eyes. "Well, it is swiftly becoming emerald green with delicious flecks of gold. Your turn."

Her heart gave a sharp kick at his provocative words. She was unaccustomed to such flirtatious banter and it was embarrassing to discover she appeared no more immune than the most hen-witted miss.

With an effort she thrust her ludicrous fancies aside. This annoying man had tossed her life upside down. He had made her the source of village gossip. She might be forced to pretend to be his fiancée, but she wouldn't like it.

"My name is Grace. I am nineteen and until my mother's marriage to Edward we lived in Bath with my great-aunt. Before that we lived with my father, who was a hardened gamester who managed to lose what few possessions we had. As I said, I spend a portion of the year with my grandmother. There is little else."

The dark head tilted to one side. "What do you enjoy?"

Grace took a moment to consider her words. In truth, her life had been so secluded that her pleasures were out of necessity simple. But she had never felt deprived. She had been happy with her mother and the opportunity to compose her music.

Now her music was gone.

She ignored the stab of pain as she met his searching gaze.

"I like taking walks with my cat, reading a good book, and playing upon the pianoforte."

Half expecting him to smirk at her dull pleasures she was relieved when he offered her a warm smile.

"It sounds very peaceful."

Once again she felt that tiny tingle as his gaze swept over her tiny face and she instinctively stiffened her spine. "Is that all?" she demanded in sharp tones.

He heaved an audible sigh. "We clearly need to discuss your rather prickly attitude."

"Do you blame me?"

"No, but it is bound to arouse precisely the sort of speculation that I am hoping to dismiss."

He was right, of course, but it all seemed utterly unfair. Although he was not the ogre she had imagined him to be, he still managed to disturb her in a manner she found difficult to comprehend.

Why did he have to be so blasted charming?

"You can hardly expect me to fawn over you like some dim-witted schoolgirl," she protested.

He grasped her chin with a gentle insistence. "That is precisely what I expect until I leave Kent and you announce your decision that we are not suited after all."

She felt lost in his gaze as she struggled to breathe. "It is impossible."

"You wish the alternative?"

It was shockingly difficult to think at all, but the memories of her morning in town were still raw. How horrid it had been to know she was being covertly watched as she had gone about her business. With every step she had encountered disapproving expressions, or worse, rude giggles as she had walked past. There had even been a few brazen enough to give her the cut direct as she had entered the butcher shop. How could she possibly remain here if she did not concede to Alexander's demands?

"Why did you ever come here?" she muttered in frustration.

His gaze slowly lowered to the soft curve of her lips. "Perhaps it was fate." There was a tense silence before he was reluctantly pulling away and lifting the reins. "Now, I should get you home before some fool comes along and we stir up even more scandal."

Although Alexander could never compare Chalfried to his sprawling country seat in Surrey, nor his elegant London town house, he had managed to shift through the numerous rooms to locate a few commendable furnishings that he had moved to the formal salon. He had also hired a number of local women to give the entire house a thorough cleaning.

Within a week he had declared Chalfried prepared to host a small gathering.

A very small gathering, he acknowledged as he glanced about the salon. Standing beside the fire, Lord and Lady Falwell entertained Grace's mother, while Grace smoothly sidestepped a determined Mr. Wallace.

A tiny smile curved his mouth as he regarded her small form outlined by the simple gray gown with black trim. Despite the stiffness of her body and the glitter in her eyes, she had been on her best behavior the entire evening. Rather surprising considering the amount of effort it had taken to convince her that it was necessary for her to attend.

His smile widened. He had discovered over the past few days that nothing was easy with Grace Honeywell. And oddly enough, he had to admit he was quite enjoying the effort to charm his way into her goodwill.

Watching her halt to pretend an engrossing interest in a ghastly portrait of Edward's mother, he smoothly moved to stand beside her. "You are doing remarkably well, my dear," he murmured in low tones.

She reluctantly turned to face him. "Thank you."

"And you mother is most charming."

Her smile was edged. "Although we may not be the leaders of society, we are not without manners."

Alexander was slowly learning to ignore those sharp thrusts. She was like those kittens she adored, given to producing a great deal of hissing when someone came close.

"Leave the claws for Byron," he chided. "What do you think of my guests?"

Her lips thinned, but she gave a faint shrug. "Lord and Lady Falwell are charming."

"And Mr. Wallace?"

"He is a vulgar twit with a nasty habit of finding his enjoyment in others' misery," she promptly retorted.

"A perfect description," he congratulated, "but do not

underestimate him. He is as cunning as a fox and as heart-less as an adder. He would love nothing more than to prove we are lying."

She gave a small shudder. "Yes, he has already quizzed me on how we met. I told him that you came to my rescue when I twisted my ankle walking to my grandmother's home from the local church."

"I sound quite the dashing hero," he could not resist teasing. "Did I kiss you?"

He was rewarded with a frown. "Certainly not."

"A pity," he mourned, his gaze dropping to her full lips. He had devoted more than one moment to recalling the sweet delight of that mouth. In truth, he was quite anxious to repeat the experience. Odd considering he was accustomed to kissing the most beautiful women in England and Russia and not one had made him lie awake at night.

"If you recall, that is what got us into trouble in the first place."

"Actually, I have recalled it with alarming frequency."

Her breath caught in her throat as she gazed at him with wide eyes. For a crazed moment Alexander nearly pulled her into his arms and kissed her then and there, but the unwelcome interruption of Mr. Wallace brought him abruptly to his senses.

"Egad, Fox, you cannot flirt with your own fiancée," he drawled, his eyes hard with suspicion. "Bad *ton,* you know."

Alexander gritted his teeth. "Actually, I was attempting to convince Grace to display her considerable talents upon the pianoforte."

"How delightful," Wally cried. "I must add my entreaties to Fox's."

There was a brittle pause before Grace managed a smile. "How could I possibly decline?"

After escorting Grace to the lovely instrument and en-suring she was comfortable, Alexander deliberately headed toward the group beside the fire. Lady Falwell moved forward to meet him as the delicate strains of music floated through the air.

"She is lovely," Rosalind murmured as they both turned to regard the maiden at the pianoforte.

Lovely?

Not a classic beauty. Not an exotic beauty. Not even a winsome beauty.

But there was . . . something.

"Yes," he murmured, feeling the decided magic in the melody that held them all spellbound.

"And she plays exquisitely." Rosalind turned to Grace's mother. "I am unfamiliar with the piece she is playing."

Arlene smiled with obvious pride. "Grace arranged it herself. She is quite talented."

Alexander drew in a slow, deep breath. "Extraordinary. Quite extraordinary."

Five

Grace was reluctantly becoming accustomed to the un-accustomed.

In the past fortnight she had been tossed from her home, received her first kiss, branded a tart, and then celebrated throughout the village for capturing the Russian Fox.

One would think she was impervious to the unexpected.

But upon returning to the cottage from the local vicarage she discovered herself stumbling to a halt at the sight of wagons pulled close to the front door.

"What the devil . . ." she muttered, her eyes widening as the elegant form of Alexander cloaked in a caped driving coat descended from the front wagon.

"Good morning, Grace."

For a brief moment she was distracted by his sheer magnificence. Raven hair that glinted with a blue sheen in the pale winter sunlight, dark features that had been chiseled by a master's hand, and shocking blue eyes that shimmered with a warmth that would make any woman's heart skip a beat.

It was little wonder she still trembled each time she recalled those wicked kisses.

With an effort she returned her thoughts to the matter at hand. She was becoming as noddy as her great-aunt Lucinda.

"What is this?" she demanded.

"Wagons," he assured her solemnly.

She gave a wry shake of her head. Really, this gentleman

had the most provoking habit of making her forget that she should be furious with him. "I can see that. What are they for?"

"I am having you moved back to Chalfried."

She took an impulsive step backward, nearly tripping over the thick cloak she had wrapped about her to protect her from the sharp December wind. "What?"

"I did assure you that I would seek you new accommodations."

He had of course, but Grace had presumed he was simply hoping to placate her until he could return to London and forget her. It was what her father would have done.

"But . . . we cannot move into Chalfried."

"Why not?"

"It would not be proper," she said, pointing out the obvious.

He appeared thoroughly indifferent to her logic.

"Your mother will be there as a chaperon, and it would be even less proper for my fiancée to remain in this squalid cottage."

Grace attempted to remain firm against his persuasive charm. "We cannot just move back in."

He stepped closer, reaching up to brush back a flaming curl that had escaped her bonnet. "I thought you wished to be rid of this place?"

"Of course I do." She attempted to ignore his tender touch. "It is horrid, but I see little use in moving our belongings only to move them back when you return to London."

Alexander shrugged. "We shall concern ourselves with that later. For now we should concentrate on getting your mother in far more comfortable quarters."

Grace wavered. He knew precisely where she was most vulnerable. Only this morning she had been cursing the frigid air that had made her mother shiver even as she sat beside the fire. How tempting it would be to return her mother to the comforts of Chalfried, even if only for a few weeks.

Still, she was not entirely certain that she should allow this gentleman to simply arrive on her doorstep and disrupt her life once again. "You are becoming far too fond of taking command of my life," she charged.

His gloved fingers moved to brush over her cheek and then cupped her determined chin. "I am only attempting to be sensible."

His grasp was light, barely noticeable, and yet it sent a jolt of awareness through her entire body.

"I only wish this were over."

His low chuckle floated through the chilled air. "I do not know. I have found it rather intriguing to possess a fiancée."

"You must be jesting."

"You are beautiful and talented, and when you are not breathing fire you possess a certain charm. Besides, having you as my fiancée allows me to do this."

The fingers on her chin tightened as he swooped downward to claim her lips in a brief, scalding kiss.

It took far more effort than Grace wished to confess to pull from his grasp. If she were not quite convinced she was destined to become a staid old spinster she would fear she enjoyed these kisses more than was proper for a maiden.

"Really, sir, you must halt this," she forced herself to protest.

"Why? It is so excessively enjoyable."

"Someone will see."

His blue eyes flashed with humor. "That was precisely my intent. If you will look closely you will discover Wallace skulking just at the fringe of the woods."

A flare of disgust shivered through her body as she carefully bent to pluck the persistent Byron from the hem of her cloak and at the same moment glanced toward the trees beside the cottage. It took only a moment to spot the round form ridiculously attempting to hide behind a narrow trunk.

Grace straightened, pressing the satisfied kitten to her racing heart. "He is spying upon us . . . the toad."

"Of course." Alexander appeared remarkably unconcerned by the unseemly habits of his guest. "He has no desire to believe that we are indeed engaged."

"Why did you invite him to Chalfried?"

Surprisingly, Alexander seemed to hesitate at the sudden question before his charming smile returned.

"I have discovered that it is best to keep a close eye on my enemies."

Grace shivered at the thought of the vile man spying upon them. "I wish you would have kept a close eye on him in London."

He tilted his head to one side. "But then we might never have met."

A small pang plucked at her heart, but on this occasion Grace could not blame it upon the sleeping Byron. Hoping to disguise the absurd reaction, she offered him a small smile. "Yes."

Alexander gave a sudden laugh. "Minx."

Lost in each other, neither noticed the door to the cottage being pulled open, and it was not until a small gasp broke the silence that they turned to view Arlene framed in the doorway.

"Oh, my," Arlene muttered.

Taking Grace by the arm, Alexander led her toward the bemused matron. "Mrs. Crosswald. Good morning."

Arlene regarded him with wide eyes. "What is occurring?"

"I am having you moved back to Chalfried."

"Moved back?"

Alexander was at his most persuasive. "Cousin Edward would not have wished his family to live in such surroundings."

Arlene lifted a hand to her heart, a sudden light entering her pale eyes.

"No . . . but the entail."

Alexander waved a dismissive hand. "The entail means that I can have whomever I wish live at Chalfried."

Grace's lingering unease at disrupting her mother's life

with yet another move fled at the unmistakable relief that rippled across her mother's countenance.

"That is so kind," Arlene breathed.

"Not at all." A mysterious smile played about his mouth. "I have my own motives."

Arlene's happiness briefly dimmed. "Oh, yes. Mr. Wallace."

Alexander gave a soft chuckle. "Actually I was thinking more of my desire to hear Grace's beautiful music."

Grace experienced a peculiar flare of warmth at his words, even as she told herself she was being a goose.

"Yes, she does play quite lovely," Arlene predictably agreed.

Alexander slid his gaze toward Grace. "Like an angel."

Thoroughly discomforted, Grace pulled together her tattered common sense. If she did not take care, she would be behaving like the veriest simpleton. "Mother, we should begin packing," she retorted in crisp tones.

"Of course." With a brilliant smile for Alexander, Arlene bustled back into the cottage.

About to follow her mother, Grace was halted as Alexander reached out to grasp her hand and raise it to his lips.

"I very much look forward to having you near, Grace. And, of course, you must bring Byron. I owe him a great deal."

Six

While walking down the long hall, Grace paused to re-arrange the flowers in a large vase. From there she moved to straighten the ghastly watercolor and was on the point of checking for dust on the ivory inlaid table when she abruptly realized what she was doing.

For heaven's sake, one would think that she was mistress of Chalfried rather than a temporary guest.

Her hand pulled back as if she had been scalded.

Drat, Alexander.

It was all his fault.

Ever since her arrival at Chalfried he had made her feel as if it were more her home than his own. He consulted her on the daily menu; he requested that she choose the flowers from the hothouse, and he even insisted that she be the one to explain the estate ledgers during their long afternoons together. It was little wonder she occasionally forgot that she was not the lady of the manor.

Rather disturbed by her thoughts, Grace staunchly resolved to keep closer guard on her wayward fancies. Any domestic tendencies would be better served in making the cottage more habitable, she told herself sternly. That was, after all, her true home.

Deciding she was in need of a bit of distraction, Grace was on the point of seeking out her mother when she was abruptly halted by the distinct sounds of Byron's cries.

With a frown, she attempted to determine where the sound came from.

"Byron." She moved further down the hall, slowly pushing open the door to the study. "Byron."

Her heart shuddered to a halt as Boswan rose to his feet, holding out Byron by the scruff of his tiny neck. From the moment she had moved to Kent she had not liked the wretched man. Now she would gladly have smacked his smiling face.

"What are you doing?" she demanded.

"I thought you would come looking for this rat."

"Hand him over immediately."

He smirked at her imperious tone. "Not so fast, Miss Honeywell."

Something in his oily tone sent a chill down Grace's spine. She might detest Boswan, but she would be a fool to underestimate him. He had obviously lured her into the study for some nefarious purpose. A purpose she was certain to dislike.

"What do you want?"

He slowly moved from behind the desk, dangling the protesting Byron with a callous indifference. Grace could only grit her teeth in frustration.

"I've been thinking there's something mighty queer in this supposed engagement," he taunted.

Grace sucked in a sharp breath. Good heavens. She should have suspected that it was only a matter of time before Boswan revealed his disbelief. In truth, it was a wonder he had not confronted her the moment the news of her engagement was announced.

"I do not comprehend why," she attempted to bluff.

"I ain't no sod," he warned. "Not a month ago you were cursing the name of Dalford. Now you say that you're engaged? Fah."

Grace struggled to maintain her stern frown. She could not very well deny his accusations. She had made little effort to conceal her feelings toward the gentleman who was responsible for taking her home.

"My engagement is none of your concern."

His smile revealed blackened teeth. "Mayhap not, but I

figure that there might be a few interested in knowing there be something queer in the air."

Courage, Grace, she silently chastised herself. She would not be bullied by this ruffian.

"If you have something to say to me, Boswan, then please just say it."

His smile disappeared as a cunning expression settled on his razor features.

"I be thinking I would be willing to keep my lips tied if you were to hand over a few hundred pounds."

Grace felt her mouth drop. So, that was the reason he had not brazenly scoffed the notion of an engagement between herself and Alexander, she seethed. His devious mind had clearly concluded the situation could be used for his own gain. A very, very large gain.

"Have you gone mad?" she gritted.

He took another step closer, and for the first time Grace could smell the scent of brandy on his breath. She shuddered in revulsion. How could Edward have ever hired such a sorry man?

"I be figuring that is what you cost me by sticking your nose in where it bloody well doesn't belong."

She faced him with a stubborn tilt of her chin. "Money that did not belong to you."

"Says you," he growled, angered by her accusation. "By my reckoning, that old skinflint owed me twice as much. Money that I intend to get one way or another."

A tiny voice in the back of her mind urged her to flee. Nothing could be served by arguing with the ridiculous man. But the knowledge that he was indeed vengeful enough to spread a rumor that there was something odd in her engagement kept her feet firmly planted upon the carpet.

And, of course, she could not leave Byron with the monstrous brute.

She placed her hands on her hips as she glared into his cold eyes. "Surely you do not believe that I have a few hundred pounds lying about?"

"No, but I believe Mr. Dalford is certain to have," he said slyly.

Grace gave an abrupt shake of her head. "This is absurd. I will give you nothing."

With an ugly snarl Boswan stepped closer. Close enough that Grace could smell the sweat of his body.

"Oh, I believe you will. . . ."

"Do not take another step, Boswan," a voice from the doorway commanded.

Grace's knees nearly buckled with relief as Alexander moved to her side, his expression as harsh and icy as a Russian winter. Boswan on the other hand was not nearly so pleased with the interruption. The smug confidence wilted to a sickly smile.

"Mr. Dalford, I was just . . ."

"Spare me whatever lie you are attempting to utter. I have heard every word," Alexander cut in ruthlessly.

With an effort Boswan attempted to regain command of his faltering composure.

"This here be between Miss Honeywell and myself."

"Not anymore," Alexander assured him in dangerous tones; then, turning, he regarded the silent woman at his side. "Grace, will you please return to your chambers?"

Although anxious to be away from Boswan, Grace found herself hesitating. Absurdly, she discovered herself reluctant to leave Alexander alone with the scoundrel. What if he became violent? She could not bear for him to be harmed.

"Perhaps I should remain," she said softly.

"Please." Reaching out, Alexander plucked Byron from Boswan's grasp and pressed the maltreated kitten into Grace's hands. He smiled tenderly at her anxious expression. "Byron is no doubt wishing to return to his mother."

She met his dark blue gaze for a long moment, then realizing she would only be in the way, she gave a slow nod of her head.

"Very well."

She allowed herself to be led out of the room and even took a few steps down the hall before she halted at the sound of the door closing. Although it might be ridiculous to suppose that a gentleman with Alexander's firm muscles and swift intelligence would need her aid, she could not make herself walk away.

He did not know Boswan as she did, she told herself. He had not seen him furiously attack a groom or beat a poor hound that had the ill fortune to cross his path. For all she knew Boswan might even have a gun hidden in his coat.

The unwelcome thought sent a sharp pain through her heart. She could not leave until she knew Alexander was safe.

Pacing from the pedestal cupboard to the sideboard table, Grace listened intently to the muffled sounds resounding from the study.

After what might have been an eternity, the door to the study was abruptly thrown open. Grace turned to be confronted by a furious Boswan.

"Oh."

Halting in midstride he regarded her with a feral grimace. "This is the second occasion you have ruined a plum chance for me," he grated. "I'll be back, and when I come you'll be sorry for it."

Grace instinctively held Byron closer to her bosom, a motion that was not lost on Boswan. Thankfully, at that moment Alexander stepped into the hallway and pointed a slender finger in Boswan's face.

"Out."

It was one word, but it sent the older man scurrying down the hall like a rat fleeing from a burning barn. Once alone Alexander turned to face her with a hint of resigned amusement.

"I thought I requested that you return to your chamber?"

She waved aside his words. "What occurred?"

His expression hardened as he recalled the encounter. "I have requested that Boswan pack his belongings and leave before sundown."

"Just like that?"

"Yes."

Grace frowned with concern. "What if he speaks with Mr. Wallace?"

A hint of ice was visible in Alexander's blue eyes. "Then I have assured him he will swiftly discover himself on a boat sailing for the Indies."

"Can you do that?"

"Of course."

Grace gave a tiny sigh. What a relief it would be to know that Boswan was gone from Chalfried forever.

"Can you be certain he will leave?"

"I will have my groom keep a close watch on him."

"Wretched man," she breathed, shivering in spite of herself.

Moving closer, Alexander lifted a hand to gently brush her cheek. "He will not be allowed to harm you. I will make quite certain of that," he promised in low tones.

For a breathless moment Grace swayed toward the strength of his large form. Never had she had anyone to depend upon. Her father had been no more than a stranger, and Edward had never encouraged more than a distant acknowledgment of each other. How often had she longed to feel secure? To know that regardless of what occurred there would be someone who would ensure that all would be well?

Then abruptly she stiffened her spine. What was she thinking? She was no helpless miss having to depend upon others. And even if she were, she would be a fool to depend upon a gentleman who would soon be returning to London without one spare thought for his pretend fiancée.

"You do not need to protect me." She forced herself to step from his lingering touch.

"No." His lips twitched with reluctant humor. "You are remarkably independent, and I have no doubt that you would have soon bullied Boswan into submission. But I wish to protect you."

She regarded him with a faint frown. "Why?"

"Because the gentlemen in your life have been a shocking disappointment thus far," he retorted. "And because you are my fiancée."

A week ago those words would have made her bristle with antagonism. Now a peculiar sensation inched down her spine.

"You are not my fiancé," she said as much for herself as for Alexander.

"Of course I am." He gave a low laugh. "And I for one intend to enjoy our brief engagement."

That tingle once again followed the curve of her spine. Really, it was most unaccountable. "What do you mean?"

His amusement only deepened at her breathless words.

"Nothing more devious than the pleasure of your company." He held out his arm. "Come. I have something I wish to show you."

Seven

Alexander glanced down at the maiden by his side. At his insistence she had muffled herself in a heavy cloak and bonnet, but only a few moments in the brisk breeze had reddened her tiny nose and teased a handful of fiery curls about her pale features.

A familiar warmth flooded his chilled body. It was odd, he acknowledged. He had met the most beautiful, the most exotic, the most sophisticated, and the most charming women that London and St. Petersburg had to offer. But while he had indulged himself with an occasional mistress, none of them had made him go to such efforts to be at her side or caused him to lay awake nights, pondering a means of bringing a smile to her face.

Indeed, he had to remind himself more than once that their engagement was a mere farce to protect both their reputations.

His sense of contentment was briefly disturbed as he recalled his encounter with Boswan.

The bloody fool. Had he truly expected Alexander to stand meekly aside and allow Grace to be bullied by a common thief? Boswan was fortunate that he had not wrung his scrawny neck. That had certainly been his first thought when he had entered the study. Only the knowledge that the local magistrate was bound to take a dim view of him shedding blood within his first month of arriving in Kent made him hesitate. In the end he could only hope that his threats would be enough to convince Boswan that remaining near Chalfried was a very unhealthy proposition.

"Where are we going?" Grace said suddenly intruding upon his brooding.

Alexander gave a shake of his head. He would not allow Boswan to ruin this all too fleeting moment alone with his fiancée.

"It is not far," he promised. He led her toward the woods and then he halted at a small pine. "Here we are."

She glanced upward with a startled expression. "It is a tree."

"No," he corrected. "It is a Yelka."

"What does that mean?"

Alexander allowed a reminiscent smile to touch his lips. Although he lived most of the year in England, he never forgot his mother's heritage nor the warm memories of his life in Russia. Somehow it seemed important that he share that part of his life with this woman.

"Yelka. It is a tree to celebrate the New Year. We will have it brought inside on the eve of Christmas and decorate it with fruit and tiny baubles."

Her eyes brightened with pleasure. "I have heard of that, although we have never had one at Chalfried."

"I hope to combine the best of English and Russian traditions for Christmas."

"Are they so different?" she demanded.

"Well, to begin with, we celebrate Christmas in January not December, although we will choose the English date. And it is believed that it is Babouschka who delivers the gifts to the children."

She tilted her head to one side. "Babouschka?"

He nodded his head, barely aware of the snow that had once again begun to fall. Indeed, he was aware of precious little beyond the sparkle in her eyes.

"It is told that she failed to give shelter to the Magi on their travels to find the baby Jesus, so now she is bound to wander the countryside in search of the Christ child. She always manages to visit the home of children."

A hint of anticipation could be detected on her tiny features. "Do you think she will visit here?"

"Most certainly," he assured her.

"What else?"

Her obvious interest made Alexander chuckle. He had learned over the past weeks that Grace possessed a questioning mind along with her astonishing musical talent. He had often thought it was a sin that she had been buried in the country with no one to appreciate her rare qualities.

Of course, he acknowledged, she would no doubt have been swiftly engaged had she been in a position to travel to London. He might never have met her. It was a thought he found strangely distressful.

With an effort, he thrust aside the unwelcome thought. "It is also a tradition to fast on the day before Christmas, until the first star appears," he said in answer to her question. "Only then is the table laid and the Kutya served."

She mouthed the unfamiliar word with a faint smile. "I do not suppose that is Christmas pudding?"

"Actually, it is a porridge."

She couldn't prevent her grimace. "For dinner?"

"It is quite important," he informed her, recalling his grandmother's solemn explanation of the evening dinner. "It possesses grain to represent hope and honey with poppy seeds for success and happiness. It also must be eaten from the same dish for unity."

"How lovely," she breathed, her fiery curls dusted by the falling snow. "Is that all?"

"Oh, no. There is one other very important tradition, but I shall allow that to remain a secret until the festivities," he impulsively retorted. Let her be surprised when he revealed his grandmother's favorite part of the evening.

She narrowed her gaze, but a hint of amusement remained in her emerald eyes.

"You are being very mysterious."

"Yes, I am," he agreed, waggling his brows in a ridiculous fashion. "Do you like it?"

She gave a sudden laugh at his absurdity. "Should I?"

"Of course. Ladies always prefer those brooding, elusive gentlemen that spout tragic poetry. Shall I offer you a verse?"

She held up her hands in mock horror. "No, thank you."

Thoroughly enjoying their banter, Alexander reached out to tug her into his arms. Feeling her next to him, he was quite certain that he could spend the rest of his days holding her close.

"Come," he teased. "Allow me to whisper sweet secrets in your ear." For a moment she stiffened at his brazen grasp; then, much to his delight, she melted against him. It was not until he felt the icy sting of snow upon his neck that he realized she had deviously used his distraction to reach out and grasp a handful of snow from the nearby tree. With a gasp he pulled back to regard her with amusement. "Minx."

She appeared smugly pleased with her trick until Alexander reached out to grasp his own handful of snow.

"No . . ." Her eyes widened. "You wouldn't."

Her concern appeared so genuine that Alexander instantly dropped his frozen weapon.

"Of course not."

With lightning speed she bent downward to gather another handful of snow and lobbed it at his disbelieving expression. Just as swiftly she turned on her heel and began scurrying toward the house. Briefly startled by the assault Alexander gave a loud laugh.

Why the cunning chit. It was not often he was caught off guard.

A flare of excitement raced through his body and with a swift grace he was in pursuit. It was, of course, an unfair race. Hampered by her heavy skirts and the icy ground, she had gone only a short distance when he caught her in his arms. Turning her about, he gazed down at her laughing face.

Just for a moment he felt bewitched. It was unexplainable. With women he had always felt lust or friendship. Not this peculiar combination that made him uncertain whether to kiss her or simply hear the magic of her voice.

"How beautiful you are when you smile," he murmured.

Her breath was released on a sigh as they gazed at each other, indifferent to the cold and even the knowledge that they were visible from the house. It was the sound of footsteps hurrying in their direction that finally forced them apart.

Alexander lifted his head to view Rosalind quickly moving toward them. He hid a rueful grimace at the obvious signs of distress. Although the last thing in the world he wished was to have this moment with Grace interrupted, he realized that Rosalind was clearly upset.

"Oh . . . Alexander," Rosalind breathed, her lovely face stained with tears.

"Good afternoon, Lady Falwell."

She hesitantly glanced toward the blushing Grace. "I am sorry to intrude."

"Is there something that you need?" he prodded.

She twisted her hands together until Alexander feared that they might become entangled.

"I did hope that I could have a few moments with you."

Alexander hesitated. Damnation. Grace was already regarding him with a faint frown. He wanted to command Rosalind to leave and return that smile to Grace's face. But even as the pleasant notion entered his mind he was thrusting it aside.

Rosalind was not a strong woman. And she depended upon him. It would be unfair to turn his back simply because he discovered he preferred the companionship of Miss Honeywell.

"Of course," he forced himself to say. Then he raised Grace's hand and pressed his lips to her gloved fingers. "We will speak later."

For a moment a question seemed to flicker deep in her emerald eyes. A question Alexander was forbidden to answer. Then with a reluctant nod she turned and slowly made her way back toward the house. Alexander's hand instinctively lifted, only to drop when he realized what he was doing.

What could he say to her?

"I am sorry, Alexander," Rosalind said softly.

Reluctantly Alexander turned to face the distraught woman. "What has occurred?"

She lifted a hand to her lips to muffle the soft sob. "Thomas discovered the letter you gave me."

Alexander bit back a resigned sigh. On how many occasions had he warned Rosalind to burn the letters he gave to her? It was far too dangerous to leave them lying about.

"How do you know?"

"I came into my chambers and he held it in his hands."

"What did you tell him?"

Her white face flushed with painful color. "That it must have been left in the chamber by some forgetful maid."

Alexander curbed his flare of impatience. Rosalind was not made to live a life full of lies, he reminded himself. She was too transparent, too easily rattled for deception. It was remarkable that they had managed to conceal the truth for so long.

"Did he believe you?"

Rosalind fumbled for a handkerchief to dab at her nose. "He made a show of believing, but he could not hide the suspicion in his eyes."

Alexander gave a slow shake of his head. "Ah, Rosalind, I have warned you to be careful. Those letters should be destroyed as soon as you receive them."

"How can I?" she cried, her eyes glittering with tears. She appeared as lovely as an angel. "They are so precious to me. Oh, what am I to do?"

Most men would no doubt have swept her into their arms and assured her that everything would be well. Rosalind had an air of fragile indecision that appealed to the opposite sex. But Alexander resisted his instinctive reaction to comfort her. Rosalind could not run to him forever.

With great care he reached out to take her hands in his own, gazing down at her frightened eyes.

"Tell Thomas the truth," he said firmly. "It is the only way."

"No . . ." Rosalind wrenched her hands free, her face a deathly white. "No, I cannot."

With a cry, she turned and hurried toward the nearby trees. Alexander heaved an exasperated sigh.

Women.

A gentleman would have more luck pondering the nature of the universe than the workings of the female mind.

Eight

Grace regarded her reflection with a hint of surprise. The gown was lovely. Pale lemon with a pattern of tiny pearls along the hem, it floated about her slender form with a lustrous sheen. About her neck she placed the pearl necklace she had received from her grandmother.

Certainly the gown was not sophisticated or particularly daring, but after a year of nothing but black and plain gray, it appeared startlingly brilliant.

And why not? she told herself, trying to still the pesky sense of unease in the bottom of her stomach. It was the eve of Christmas, and the day promised to be filled with festivities. Her choice had nothing at all to do with a raven-haired blue-eyed gentleman.

The reassurance fell flat as an image of Alexander rose to her mind. He really was a most uncommon gentleman, she grudgingly conceded. He never made her feel awkward or plain, as other gentlemen had done. Indeed, when they were together she felt as if she must be the most fascinating woman in all of England.

A talent that no doubt made any number of females swoon, she warned herself sternly. She might have allowed herself to forget all those reasons why she had meant to be furious with him, but she would be a fool to allow herself to dream that his flirtations were any more than an act.

Of course, there was no reason she could not enjoy the next few days, she silently argued. It had been years since she had been surrounded by guests with enticing gossip of

London and stories of their travels abroad. Once Alexander was gone, her life would return to it's dull routine, with little relief beyond her visit to Leicestershire.

In the midst of arranging a fiery curl that lay against her cheek, Grace was startled when the door to the chamber was pushed open. With a lift of her brow she turned to watch her mother cross toward her.

"My dear, how lovely you look," Arlene complimented.

Grace glanced down at her dress. "You do not believe that it is too soon to wear such a gown?"

"Certainly not. We have been in mourning long enough. And it is nice to see you in bright colors." A rather sly expression settled on the older woman's countenance. "Although I do not believe it is the bright color that has brought that glow to your eyes."

A blush that would have made a schoolgirl proud rose to her cheeks.

Drat.

What was the matter with her?

"It is the eve of Christmas," she said with a shrug.

Her attempt to distract her mother was sadly wasted. "And it has nothing to do with Mr. Dalford?"

Unbelievably, her blush deepened. "Why should it have anything to do with Alexander?"

Arlene's smile was smug. "You two have spent a great deal of time together."

"We have had little option after he forced us to pretend that we are engaged."

"But it has not been so ghastly, has it? We were allowed to return to Chalfried."

Really, what was her mother thinking?

"As guests only," Grace felt compelled to point out. "After the New Year Alexander is bound to return to London and we will once again be back at the cottage."

Arlene merely smiled in a complacent fashion. "I do not believe so. Mr. Dalford is a very kind gentleman. Far more kind than I dared hope."

A gathering frown marred Grace's wide brow. "Yes."

"You could do far worse than have him for a fiancé."

So this is where her mother was leading, Grace acknowledged with a pang of unease. Perhaps it was only to be expected. Grace had never attracted many suitors, and those who had shown an interest had either been doddering fools or local tradesmen who hoped to acquire a hint of aristocracy to their family. Certainly there had never been a gentleman such as Alexander. What mother would not eagerly begin weaving hopes in her mind?

It was important that Grace squash such lofty notions with all possible speed. She had no desire for her mother's heart to be broken when Alexander left and she was firmly placed upon the shelf.

"Oh, Mother, I hope that you have not allowed this foolishness to sway your common sense," she said softly. "Alexander could have his choice of the most beautiful and wealthy maidens in all of England and no doubt Russia. He is not about to throw himself away on an ill-tempered spinster without a quid to her name."

Predictably, her mother bristled with annoyance at the harsh truth. She had never wished to accept that Grace was anything but perfect.

"You happen to be a lovely, very talented young miss," she protested with a sniff. "It is entirely my fault for not being able to send you to London for a Season that you are not already wed to a duke or at least an earl."

Grace gave a sudden laugh at the notion of herself in London. It was one thing to childishly dream of entering a crowded ballroom and causing every gentleman to swoon in delight. It was quite another to realize that she was far more likely to enter the ballroom and tumble over her own feet.

"Fiddlesticks. I should have made a perfect cake of myself, and the dukes and earls would have fled in terror. Besides, if I ever do wed, it will be for love."

Like a hound on the scent, Arlene refused to be distracted. "Perhaps Mr. Dalford will fall in love with you and all our troubles will be solved."

Grace gave a resigned shake of her head. "Mother."

"Very well." Realizing she had pressed as far as she dared, Arlene gave a shrug. "I will say no more."

"That I very much doubt," Grace retorted dryly, moving forward to grasp her mother's arm. "Come, it is time for the celebrations."

As a favorite of both the czar and the prince regent, Alexander had enjoyed the most lavish entertainments that society could offer. There had been extravagant masked balls, treasure hunts that had led him from London to Paris to Vienna, moonlit dinners upon the Thames, and private evenings with the most beautiful courtesans in the world. But in all of his vast experiences he could not recall enjoying a day more than he had today.

With a sense of contentment he glanced about the vast salon. Throughout the day this room had been filled with countless children who had enthusiastically helped to decorate the standing tree with the fruit and various baubles they had tied onto strings. They had been equally delighted with the piles of tiny cakes and bags of coins he had helped to distribute. In the background Grace had provided festive music upon the pianoforte, her face astonishingly beautiful as she smiled with obvious satisfaction.

The joyish atmosphere lingered into dinner, where they had shared the Kuyta and toasted the future.

All in all it had proven to be a most successful day.

With a determined step Alexander moved to where Grace was tidying her music upon the pianoforte. His heart gave an odd quiver at the sight of her tiny countenance still flushed with the excitement of the day. Halting beside her, he waited for her to turn and face him.

"Did you enjoy your day?" he asked softly.

"Very much." She offered him a warm smile. "It was very festive. The children will not soon forget your generosity."

He gave a wave of his slender hand. "It was a trifle."

"Hardly a trifle. Your tree alone will be the talk of the village for years to come."

Alexander glanced toward the tree that was barely visible beneath the flurry of decorations. "Perhaps not a thing of beauty, but it was great fun."

"You are very different from your cousin."

He turned back to meet her searching gaze. "How so?"

She paused as if carefully considering her words. "Edward was very somber and very aware of his position in the neighborhood. He would never have opened his home in such a fashion. Certainly not to his tenants."

Alexander recalled enough of his cousin to be certain Grace was not exaggerating. Although not a cruel gentleman, Edward had always been rather humorless and disliked what he considered frivolous pursuits. He would no doubt have staunchly disapproved of the loud and rather messy party.

"It would not have been a success without you."

Her long lashes fluttered with embarrassment. "I enjoy children."

Alexander's heart gave a sudden jolt. This was a woman who should have a dozen children. She would be warm and loving, with a great sense of fun. Like his own mother, who had shunned nurses and insisted that he be at her side.

A delicious warmth crawled through his body at the image of Grace with a child in her arms.

"At least we have managed to convince one and all that we are happily engaged," he retorted softly.

"Not all." She pointedly glanced toward the brightly dressed dandy in the corner.

Alexander was not at all surprised to discover Mr. Wallace closely watching them. The twit was no doubt gnashing his teeth in frustration at the fear he would have no scandal to sell to his powerful friends. With his numerous debts, he had to be smelling the cells of Newgate in his dreams.

"Then we shall have to work harder," he murmured, reaching out to pull her arm firmly through his own. "Come."

Although she had little choice but to fall into step beside him, she glanced at him in protest. "Alexander."

"What?"

"We cannot just leave."

"Of course we can," he assured her, pulling her through the open doors that led to the library. "We will be gone just a moment."

"Where are we going?"

He smiled down at her upturned face. "I told you that there was another tradition on this eve."

He halted beside a small table with a candle burning on a dish and beside it a bowl of water. Grace glanced up in surprise.

"What is this?"

Alexander pulled out a chair. "Sit here." He waited until she had settled on the satinwood chair and then took his own seat next to her. Carefully, he grasped the candle and tipped it until the hot wax had dripped into the bowl of water. "Now we shall begin."

"What are you doing?"

He watched the wax harden in the water. "I am going to tell your future."

Grace gave a startled laugh. "Absurd."

"Not at all. My grandmother would tell my future every year."

"And what did she foresee?"

Alexander remembered back to those moments with his grandmother, when she would make a great show of preparing for her reading. It was all very mysterious for a young boy.

"Love, happiness . . ." His voice trailed away as he was struck by a poignant memory. "And oddly enough, a life filled with music."

It was difficult to determine in the firelight, but Alexander suspected a soft blush had stolen to her cheeks.

"You are merely jesting."

He gazed deep into her wide eyes. "Not at all."

For a moment they stared at each other in silence; then Grace turned toward the water on the table.

"And what of my future?" she said, attempting to distract him.

Alexander obligingly glanced at the wax. "I see a gentleman. Tall, dark haired, and extraordinarily attractive."

"Obviously a stranger," she retorted in dry tones.

He ignored her thrust as he continued to stare at the wax. "That is odd."

"What?"

"I see true love and some danger that seems to have to do with water."

"Perhaps my true love is a sailor," she suggested.

All thoughts of the strange vision of the water were abruptly forgotten as he lifted his head. "That would be unfortunate," he said with soft emphasis.

"Why?"

"Because you are my fiancée."

Unable to prevent himself, Alexander leaned forward and captured her soft mouth in a fierce, wholly possessive kiss. He would drive all thoughts of other men from her mind, he told himself, only to have his own thoughts scatter like leaves in an autumn wind as sweet pleasure spiraled to the pit of his stomach. A soft moan was captured in his throat as he lifted his hand to stroke the line of her jaw. The pleasure was almost unbearable, but even as he leaned forward to deepen the kiss, a sharp pang in his thigh had him pulling back with a gasp. Glancing down, he discovered a black kitten hanging on to his thigh with its front paws. With a resigned sigh he plucked the intruder from his ill-treated leg and allowed it to curl upon his arm.

"I believe Byron is attempting to warn me that we have been gone long enough."

Clearly flustered Grace rose to her feet, her eyes as brilliant as gems. "Oh."

Alexander also rose, deeply regretting their moment alone was over. "Grace . . ."

It took a moment before she could force herself to meet his gaze. "Yes?"

"Happy Christmas, my dear."

Nine

Although Grace had been placed in the same chambers she had used while her mother was married to Edward, she had never taken excessive notice of her surroundings. Now, after a sleepless night, she could confidently state that the ceiling mural possessed precisely six angels, four harps, twelve clouds, and Eve holding an apple. The paneling acquired a rose tint at the break of dawn. And the tick of the clock was only drowned by the barking of the dog outside her window.

At last weary of courting her elusive sleep, she had risen from her bed and attired herself in a warm woolen gown a shade of cinnamon. Then she headed downstairs and made a straight path for the library.

She had no desire to join those in the breakfast room. Not until she had managed to sort through the coiled emotions that had plagued her through the long night.

It was all most aggravating, she acknowledged. Before Alexander had arrived at Chalfried she had never tossed in her bed all night or been tormented with images of being held in a gentleman's arms. But of course, before Alexander came to Chalfried she had never sung Russian love songs or played in the snow or spent hours talking about herself. And she certainly had never spent so much time laughing.

If this were occurring to another woman Grace would have accused her of being in love. But she was far too sensible to tumble into love with a gentleman who could never possibly return such love.

Wasn't she?

With a faint shake of her head, Grace stepped into the library only to falter at the sight of Mr. Wallace.

"Oh." She suppressed a shiver at his soft form encased in a tight coat of pink satin with a burgundy waistcoat. He appeared more a piece of confectionery candy than a gentleman of breeding. Unfortunately, he was far more dangerous than a bit of sweets, unless one added a dash of poison.

Seeming to be unaccountably pleased by her sudden arrival, Mr. Wallace performed a deep bow. "Good morning, Miss Honeywell, and may I add Happy Christmas."

Wavering between the manners her mother had painstakingly ingrained into her and the desire to put as much distance between herself and this unpleasant man as possible, she at last forced a stiff smile to her lips.

"Thank you."

"Were you searching for Fox?"

Grace hesitated. She had no desire to confess she had been seeking a spot to brood upon her unpredictable heart. Besides, a fiancée could hardly deny wishing to be with her beloved.

"Yes."

"I believe he is currently involved with Lady Falwell." His hand raised to point out the window.

Barely aware she was moving, Grace crossed the carpet until she could clearly see Alexander and Lady Falwell standing upon the terrace. Her heart gave a painful jerk as she realized that Alexander was gently holding his companion's hands as he gazed into her upturned countenance.

At least she now understood what had drawn Mr. Wallace to the room, she thought with a flare of disgust. She had known it could not have been for any love of literature.

"I will speak with him later," she muttered.

Clearly realizing that she meant to leave, Mr. Wallace boldly reached out to grasp her elbow. "She is very lovely, is she not?"

Grace shuddered at his touch. What could she say? Lady Falwell was without a doubt the most beautiful woman she had ever seen. So beautiful that it would be a miracle if any gentleman did not fall beneath her spell, she thought with a pang.

"Yes, she is. Lord Falwell is a very fortunate gentleman," she said stiffly.

Wallace gave a sly laugh. "Not all would think so."

"Oh?"

"There have been very persistent rumors that she is often seen in the company of Fox."

Grace's heart grew cold as she recalled the numerous occasions that Lady Falwell had managed to intrude into her moments alone with Alexander. And how readily he had dismissed her to be with the married woman.

Then, with an effort, she reminded herself that this gentleman was determined to cause trouble for Alexander. What better method than making his fiancée believe the worse?

"Well, there will always be those anxious to spread scandal, even if it is pure conjecture," she retorted in pointed tones.

"Oh, certainly, and I suppose it is only natural that the two would seek out each other's companionship since they were neighbors in their youth."

"Quite natural."

The evil eyes narrowed. "Still, one cannot completely dismiss the fact that they have been seen together in a posting inn near Surrey."

Grace caught her breath in shock, although she managed to keep her composure intact. "More gossip."

His smile twisted in an ugly fashion. "If you insist."

"I do."

He leaned closer, the cloying scent of his cologne nearly overwhelming. "I suppose you would also insist that Fox included me in this cozy country gathering simply because he takes such great delight in my company?"

Grace shifted back in unease. That was a question that

Alexander had been obviously unwilling to answer. "Why else?" she asked cautiously.

"It occurred to me that he might wish to convince me that all is splendid between Lord and Lady Falwell and of course, reveal his most convenient engagement to you, my dear. What better means of putting a halt to the rumors flooding through London?"

Grace did not want to listen. Wallace was as vicious and poisonous as a snake. And certainly he would love nothing more than to harm Alexander. But made suddenly vulnerable by the pain twisting in her heart, she discovered her normal common sense eluding her.

She needed to be away from this ghastly man. Somewhere where she could think in a rational manner.

Very conscious that Mr. Wallace was regarding her with a growing smile, Grace composed her features in an icy expression of disdain. Whatever her inner thoughts, she would not give this man the satisfaction of knowing how deeply he had disturbed her.

"Are you always so suspicious when you receive an invitation?"

He shrugged. "It all depends upon who has issued the invitation."

"How very lonely you must be." She offered him a regal nod of her head. "Please excuse me."

Not giving him the opportunity to halt her, Grace swept from the room. Then, with swift steps she hurried to the back of the house and through the door that would lead to the parklands. It was bitterly cold, even with the cloak she had gathered during her flight through the house, but it was the one place she could be assured of being alone. Wrapping her arms about her, she blindly walked toward the distant woods.

Blast Mr. Wallace.

She did not want to think Alexander capable of loving another gentleman's wife. Or worse, using her to hide his secret.

But while she told herself that Alexander was an honorable and trustworthy man, those insidious accusations refused to be dismissed.

Alexander and Lady Falwell were indeed very close. Far closer than mere acquaintances. And few gentlemen would not find Lady Falwell desirable.

And, of course, there was his rushed engagement with her. He claimed it had only been to protect her reputation, but could it have been instead a heaven-sent opportunity to continue his liaison with Lady Falwell while pretending to be nicely engaged?

Grace pressed a hand to her throbbing heart. In truth, Alexander's motives were none of her concern, she told herself in an attempt to chide her dark thoughts. Their engagement was no more than a sham, and he had never once encouraged her to believe it would be anything more. What he chose to do with his life was his decision, and his decision alone. She had no right to judge him. But the sharp pain that flooded her body was answer enough to the troubles that had kept her awake long through the night.

She had fallen in love with Alexander. And while her unrequited feelings would be difficult enough to bear, it would be even more difficult to accept that she had been so mistaken in him.

Grace shivered as the sharp wind tossed back the hood of her cloak. Halting to tug it back over her tousled curls she suddenly froze as a tall form appeared beside her. She knew who it was before she lifted her head to meet the impossibly blue eyes.

"There you are." Alexander smiled, although a hint of puzzlement could be detected in his tone.

He no doubt thought she must be a bit daft to be walking in such weather, she told herself.

"Good morning."

"I waited for you at breakfast."

Her stomach quivered at the sight of his smile. How handsome he was. So tall and strong, with a hint of devilish amusement in his eyes.

Did Lady Falwell care so deeply? Or was she just amusing herself?

"Is there something that you need?" she forced herself to ask.

"Merely to give you this."

He held out a small box, and before she could halt the instinctive movement she had reached out to take it from him.

"What is it?"

"A small Christmas token."

Slowly opening the box, Grace gave a sharp gasp. Lying upon the dark satin was a delicate gold chain and on the chain was a tiny charm shaped as a musical note. Tears of pleasure rushed to her eyes at the thoughtful gift.

"Oh."

"Do you like it?" he prodded.

"It is beautiful," she breathed. Beautiful and perfect, she acknowledged even as a voice in the back of her mind told her that she would be a fool to think it was anything more than another ploy to convince others of the supposed engagement. "But this is too much."

"Nonsense." His smile remained, but his raven brows faintly lowered. "It is a simple thank-you for the wretched burden of being my fiancée."

For once his teasing failed to amuse her. "I fear that it has not been enough," she warned.

"What do you mean?"

She forced herself to meet his gaze squarely. "Mr. Wallace believes that our engagement is a ploy to hide your relationship with Lady Falwell."

He visibly stiffened, a guarded expression descending upon his countenance. "I see."

"I denied his accusations, of course."

He studied her pale features for a long, unnerving moment. Then something that might have been disappointment flashed through his eyes. "But you believed them," he said in low tones.

Her hands clenched onto the box until her knuckles turned white. "It is none of my concern."

He stepped back as if she had physically slapped him. "Do you think me capable of inviting my mistress along with her husband to my own home?"

Grace gave a slow shake of her head.

What did she believe?

Standing next to him Grace would have sworn that Alexander was incapable of such treachery. But she could not completely dismiss the image of him holding Lady Falwell's hands as he gazed down at her lovely face.

"As I said, it is none of my concern."

Her words had a startling affect upon Alexander. Suddenly the charming companion she had come to love over the past weeks was replaced by the icily aloof stranger she had encountered in his bedchamber.

Her heart felt as if it were being slowly ripped apart at the sight. She stepped forward, but his unrelenting expression halted her in midstride.

"Do not stay out long; it is quite cold," he said stiffly. Then with a small bow he turned and walked away.

Left on her own, Grace lifted a hand to her lips as tears suddenly fell.

Ten

It was cold.

Her nose had long ago turned red and her toes numb, but still she remained standing in the falling snow.

After Alexander's abrupt departure she had wandered until she had arrived at the lake. Then, uncertain where to go she had simply halted.

She had been a fool, she told herself sternly. The moment she had seen the expression on his face she should have realized the truth. He had not been a man wracked by guilt, but rather a man wounded by her lack of faith in him.

Her first impulse had been to scurry after him and confess that she did not believe he could be so treacherous any more than she could be so treacherous. That it had only been the uncertainty of her tumultuous feelings that had made her trust waver for even a moment.

Then sanity had halted her impetuous desire. She could not confess her feelings. Not unless she wished to become a ridiculous object of his pity. Perhaps it was best that their former companionship had become strained. Already the thought of him leaving Chalfried was enough to make her heart ache. Surely only the worst sort of fool would allow herself to be lured even further into his enchantment?

Feeling sadly out of sorts, Grace gazed down at the necklace clutched in her hands. If only he were not the most eligible bachelor in England, she sadly thought. If only she were not a plain country miss with no prospects. If only . . .

Her futile thoughts were suddenly interrupted by the faint cry of a kitten.

With a frown she turned about only to discover Boswan standing mere steps away. Grace felt her breath falter in shock.

"You. What are you doing here?"

He revealed his blackened teeth as he regarded her startled expression. "I warned you I would be back. I even brought you a present."

An uncontrollable fear inched down her spine as he slowly held up a bag. She could not imagine what he might have brought. Indeed, she had no desire to try to imagine. Then the muffled sound of a kitten's cry could once again be heard.

"Byron," she cried, reaching out for the bag.

It was deftly held out of reach as Boswan gave an evil laugh. "I threatened more than once to drown that filthy cat of yours. This one will do as well."

Her breath caught. Heavens above, the man was demented.

"No."

He laughed at her obvious distress. "Be glad it ain't you in this bag."

Grace watched in horror as Boswan shoved his way past her and with all his might hurled the bag toward the center of the lake. Her scream echoed through the air as she scrambled toward the water, knowing the poor kitten would drown within moments.

"No . . . Byron."

Ignoring Boswan's grating laugh Grace prepared to wade into the lake, indifferent to the sharp cold of the water. Then, seemingly from nowhere, Alexander was plunging into the lake before her.

Frozen in horror, Grace watched as he dived beneath the surface.

"Lord, please, please . . ." she silently prayed. She could not bear it if Alexander were harmed. She would rather have her own life ended than to lose the man she loved.

Indifferent to the cowardly servant who was hastily beating a path toward the woods, Grace continued her prayers. A century seemed to pass before he appeared with a loud splash. With slow determination he struggled back to shore. Grace gave a sob of relief as she reached out to grasp his arm.

"Here." Despite his shivering, Alexander fumbled to open the bag and hand the indignant kitten to Grace. She hastily tucked Byron into the pocket of her cloak, her concern momentarily centered on the man trembling with cold.

"You must get inside," she urged, then realizing they were a considerable distance from the house she whipped off her cloak and put it about his wet form.

"You will freeze," he protested as she pulled him away from the lake.

"Nonsense." She clenched her teeth, refusing to shiver. She did not care if she froze to the bone as long as he was safe. "I could throttle that horrid Boswan for putting you in such danger."

"I fear you will not get the opportunity. I discovered the missing sheets from the ledger that prove he was indeed stealing from my cousin. I intend to turn them over to the magistrate who I have no doubt will soon apprehend the thief and ensure that justice is carried out."

She breathed a sigh of relief. "Thank God. You might have drowned because of him. He belongs in Newgate."

Ignoring his speculative glance at her fierce desire to see Boswan punished, she marched them both to the house. They entered through a side door, startling a maid who halted to regard them with wide eyes.

"Oh, Maggie, will you have a hot bath drawn for Mr. Dalford?"

"At once, Miss Honeywell," the servant stuttered.

"And have a bottle of Mr. Crosswald's private brandy sent to his room."

"Of course."

With a hasty dip the maid scurried away, no doubt anxious to spread the word that Grace was towing about a soggy Mr. Dalford.

Turning she met his oddly glittering gaze. "You must change from those clothes at once."

He ignored her anxious command. "I came back to speak with you about Lady Falwell."

"That can wait," she insisted.

"No, it cannot."

"Alexander . . ." She found herself lost in the tender blue of his eyes. Right or wrong she had to assure him that she could not believe he would be anything less than honorable. "I do not think that Lady Falwell is your mistress."

His breath rasped between chattering teeth. "You do not?"

"No." She gave a slow shake of her head. "You are a kind and generous man, with more honor than anyone I have ever known."

"Grace . . ." His arms reached upward and the cloak fell away. With an offended cry Byron untangled himself from the heavy wool and pranced toward an open door.

With a rueful smile Grace pressed her hand to his wide chest. "Please, you must go upstairs and change before you become ill."

He paused as if determined to have his say; then a violent sneeze wracked his large form and he conceded defeat. "Very well, but we will speak as soon as I am dry."

"Yes."

Loving him more than she ever thought possible, Grace watched him slowly climb the stairs to his chambers. How swiftly he had rushed to the rescue of Byron, she thought with a flare of pride. He had not even paused to consider his own welfare.

"Miss Honeywell."

Startled by the soft sound of her name, Grace shifted to view Lady Falwell standing in the doorway of the back salon. Grace felt a hint of embarrassment as she realized the older woman was bound to have overheard her conversation with Alexander.

"Yes, Lady Falwell?"

"May I have a moment?"

Grace hesitated. She had no desire to leave her post beside the stairs, but telling herself it would be some time for Alexander to bathe and change she gave a small nod of her head. She couldn't deny she was a bit curious at what would possess Lady Falwell to seek her out.

"Of course." She moved to join Lady Falwell in the salon.

Waiting until Grace had perched on the edge of a sofa, Lady Falwell restlessly paced to the center of the room.

"I heard you speaking with Alexander and I wished you to know the truth between us," she abruptly burst out.

Grace widened her eyes in astonishment. "Very well."

"I have known Alexander all my life. He has always been a good friend to me and the one person I could depend upon."

A small smile curved Grace's lips. "He is that kind of gentleman."

"Yes." The beautiful features seemed inordinately pale as Lady Falwell nervously twisted the large diamond ring upon her finger. "Now, what I tell you must be kept in the strictest confidence."

Grace's curiosity deepened at the raw tone. "Of course."

Lady Falwell still wavered at revealing her secret. "Six years ago I was very young and foolish and imagined myself in love with an actor," she at last confessed, her eyes dark with remembered pain. "We ran off together, and I naively believed that we were on our way to be married. Of course, it was no more than a ploy, and my companion promptly disappeared. The result was that I discovered myself with child. Alexander arranged for me to travel to Paris, where I had the baby. He then had the baby placed with a family on his estate." A heart-wrenchingly sad smile curved her lips. "On occasion he brings me letters from my daughter and even arranges for me to visit her at a secluded inn."

Grace gave a slow shake of her head. "So that is why you were seen at an inn together."

Lady Falwell gave a startled frown. "Yes."

How dreadful, Grace silently acknowledged. To have been seduced by a common scoundrel and abandoned. Then to have the torture of giving your child to another. It was little wonder she had turned to Alexander.

"Does Lord Falwell know?" she asked softly.

Lady Falwell's lovely features twisted into a grimace. "Not yet, but Alexander has convinced me I must tell him the truth. I only hope his love is strong enough to bear the shock."

Grace had seen the manner in which Lord Falwell gazed at his beautiful wife. It would take more than this to shatter such devotion.

"You have nothing to fear," she assured her.

"I hope you are right. Love is a very special emotion." She regarded Grace with a shrewd gaze. "You should tell Alexander how you feel."

Grace awkwardly rose to her feet, too startled by the sudden remark to even deny the truth.

"I do not wish to burden him with my foolishness," she muttered in embarrassment.

The older woman smiled with kind sympathy. "It will be a most welcome burden, I assure you. Alexander lost his heart to you long ago."

Stunned, Grace watched in silence as Lady Falwell swept from the room. Alexander had lost his heart to her? But it wasn't possible, was it? After all, there were any number of suitable reasons that such a thing was not possible. Hadn't she painfully gone over them enough times during the past few hours?

She was still pondering the unbelievable accusation when Alexander hesitantly entered the room. Her heart gave a painful kick at the sight of him. Every bit about him was dear to her, from his damp raven hair to the tips of his glossy boots.

"How do you feel?" she asked softly.

"Like a schoolboy facing his first maiden."

She gave a blink at his odd words. "What?"

With a rueful smile he moved to stand mere inches away from her. "I do not know whether to flee or give in to my desire to pull you into my arms."

Her breath became annoyingly elusive as she tilted back her head to meet his brilliant gaze.

"What do you wish to do?"

With a groan he roughly pulled her into his arms, the scent and heat of him clouding her mind with a dizzying pleasure. "Marry me, Grace. Make this engagement real."

Grace did not even mind the lack of flowery poetry in his proposal. There was something sharply poignant about his blunt urgency.

"Are you certain? I have nothing to offer," she said in hesitant tones.

"You have everything," he argued in husky tones. "Courage, a gracious heart, and a sense of humor that matches my own. And, of course, you will fill my life with the music that my grandmother foretold all those years ago."

Batting back tears of happiness Grace lifted a tentative hand to his cheek. "I do love you, Alexander."

A fierce flare of happiness seared through his eyes as he slowly lowered his head toward her waiting lips.

"Happy Christmas, my beloved."

Poised on the mantel Byron carefully awaited the best moment to pounce. He had discovered it was wonderful fun to leap on his victims when they were fully distracted. Then, with a great deal of reluctance he slowly relaxed his muscles and gave a wide yawn.

The two were far too engrossed to be properly appreciative of his fine pouncing skills.

He would leap on them tomorrow, he decided, as he made himself comfortable on the mantel. In the manner they were so enthusiastically kissing, he was quite certain there would be plenty of tomorrows.

More Zebra Regency Romances